The Islanders

Mary Alice Monroe

The Islanders

with Angela May

ALADDIN

NEW YORK LONDON TORONTO SYDNEY NEW DELHI

ALADDIN
An imprint of Simon & Schuster Children's Publishing Division
1230 Avenue of the Americas, New York, New York 10020
First Aladdin hardcover edition June 2021
Text copyright © 2021 by Mary Alice Monroe
Illustrations copyright © 2021 by Jennifer Bricking
All rights reserved, including the right of reproduction in whole or in part in any form.
ALADDIN and related logo are registered trademarks of Simon & Schuster, Inc.
For information about special discounts for bulk purchases, please contact Simon & Schuster Special Sales at 1-866-506-1949 or business@simonandschuster.com.
The Simon & Schuster Speakers Bureau can bring authors to your live event. For more information or to book an event contact the Simon & Schuster Speakers Bureau at 1-866-248-3049 or visit our website at www.simonspeakers.com.
Designed by Tiara Iandiorio
The text of this book was set in Adobe Caslon Pro.
Manufactured in the United States of America 0521 FFG
10 9 8 7 6 5 4 3 2 1
This book has been cataloged with the Library of Congress.
ISBN 978-1-5344-2727-3 (hc)
ISBN 978-15344-2729-7 (eBook)

~~~

This book is dedicated to my grandchildren:
Jack, Teddy, Delancey, Wesley, Penelope, and Henry.
—M. A. M.

This book is dedicated to my children:
Maeson and Aeden.
—A. M.

~~~

CHAPTER 1

The Ferry to Nowhere

We each have to do our part.

THIS WAS GOING TO BE THE WORST SUMMER ever! Here I was, waiting for a ferry, forced to spend my entire summer vacation living with my grandma in the middle of nowhere.

Baaaaamp! Loud horn blasts from the ferryboat vibrated the long wooden dock. My stomach twisted at the sound.

"It's time to board, Jake," Mom said.

I could tell her smile was fake. I hadn't seen a real smile on her face for weeks. But neither of us felt like smiling after the phone call about what happened to Dad.

A big sign over the dock read DEWEES ISLAND FERRY. A lot of

people were waiting for the white double-decker, standing near their metal carts filled with groceries, suitcases, fishing poles, tackle boxes, even beach chairs. Two small dogs barked in excitement as they trotted past me on leash.

"Do I have to go?" I asked my mom in a last-ditch effort. "I want to stay with you. *Please!* I'll be good. I promise."

Mom's shoulders slumped. "Jake, we've been over and over this. I don't know how long I'll be there, and I can't leave you alone in a rental all day."

I was trying to be strong. But her words made me explode.

"It's not fair! You're dumping me on that island! What kind of summer vacation is this?"

I knew I had crossed the line. Mom was a lieutenant colonel in the Air Force and flew those giant C-17 transport planes. She was all about duty and following orders. She stepped closer to me, lowering her voice.

"I know you don't want to go," she said. I saw a flash of sadness in her eyes. Then she straightened her shoulders and I heard the commander in her voice. "We have to do what's best for your father now and put our personal wants aside. We don't know how bad he's been hurt or how long his recovery will be. This isn't a vacation, Jake. We each have to do our part. For Dad."

I lowered my head, ashamed. Still, it was hard hearing that my dad was hurt but not knowing how bad or what happened to him.

"It isn't good for you to sit around in hospitals all summer. And," she said, reaching out to lift my chin so I looked into her eyes, "your grandmother needs you. *She's* worried about your dad too."

"I know, but . . ." I paused to take a shaky breath in. "I want to see him."

"I know you do. But remember, you're helping your dad by helping Honey. He'll feel better knowing you're with her."

I scrunched my face and nodded in understanding.

I met her eyes and she flashed a soft smile.

"You're in charge now, Private."

She got me there. My dad was an officer in the Army, and he always called me Private. I tugged at my Army ball cap to hide my eyes.

"Yeah," was all I could muster through the lump in my throat.

"All aboard!" called out the ferry captain.

"Let's go!" said Mom, trying to be cheerful. I felt her gently nudge my back.

We walked down a metal ramp to the waiting ferry. The mate greeted us and wheeled my cart of stuff on board with everyone else's belongings.

"I'll call you as soon as I know anything," Mom said, and then leaned in to kiss my cheek. "You'll love Dewees Island. There's so much to do—the beach, the woods. You had the best time when you were there before."

"I was six, Mom."

"Well, you're almost twelve now, so that means you'll have twice as much fun."

"Right. It's going to be great stuck on an island with no cars allowed, or stores, or restaurants. Are there even people there, other than Honey?"

"Of course there are."

"At least I can game online with Carlos and Nick."

Mom's face cringed. "Well . . ." She hesitated. "There isn't any Wi-Fi."

"*What!*" I couldn't believe there was a place on earth without Wi-Fi.

"You mean I not only have to spend my summer away from my friends, I'm stuck alone on some faraway island with my grandma? *And* I have no internet?" My jaw hung wide open in disbelief. "Tell me you're joking."

Mom laughed. I hadn't heard her laugh since the first phone call about Dad.

"Come on, Jake. You've endured far worse. There's Wi-Fi on the island, just not at Honey's house. She doesn't think she needs the internet." Her voice lowered. "Your grandmother can have strong opinions about things."

"Or she's just weird," I muttered. I had thought things couldn't get any worse, but they just did.

"Ready!" called out the captain, opening wide the passenger door. He was urging us to go.

"Time to move," Mom said, trying to sound cheery.

I puffed out my breath. Being a military family, we moved around a lot. I was always the new kid and making friends. I was used to saying goodbye to my parents.

But it never got easier.

"Bye," I said, looking down.

Mom gave me a quick final hug. I didn't want to return it. My arms hung limp at my sides.

She stepped off the ferry back onto the deck. I looked over my shoulder to see her walking down the dock, shoulders slumped.

"Mom!" I called out.

She stopped and turned as I ran toward her. She opened her arms, and I ran into them and hugged her with all my might.

"I'll miss you, Mom," I said, my face muffled in her chest.

I felt her arms tighten around me. "I'll miss you too." She kissed my cheek and I could see the tears in her eyes, just like mine.

"I'll call you!" she said.

"I love you, Mom," I called out as I ran back to the boat. The captain waved me inside and shut the door behind me.

Inside, the benches were filling up. I raced up the stairs to the top deck of the ferry. The sun glared hot in the sky, making the metal railing warm to the touch as I leaned over to wave goodbye to Mom.

But she was already gone.

CHAPTER 2

Welcome to the Island

It's a Huck Finn life.

I N A BLAST OF BUBBLY GROWLS, THE FERRY'S big engines fired up. The boat moved as slow as a turtle through the Intracoastal Waterway, past Isle of Palms where big white motorboats and Jet Skis waited at docks in front of enormous mansions.

The farther we got from all the docks, the farther away I felt from the world I knew. I wondered what my friends in New Jersey were doing right now on their first day of summer break. I pulled out my phone and texted: Hey guys, what's up? Check out this selfie of me heading out to no-man's-land.

I backed out of the text screen and looked at the surrounding landscape. I sure wasn't in New Jersey anymore. All around me, the blue water spread out as far as I could see. Acres of bright green marsh grass waved in the breeze along the shore. I spied a long line of brown pelicans flying low over the marsh in tight formation, their six-foot wingspans almost touching the water. My dad called them "bombardiers on patrol."

The clanging of footsteps on the metal stairs caught my attention. Turning my head, I saw a boy standing at the top of the stairs. He looked like he was my age, with short cropped hair and brown skin. I felt a shot of hope that there were other kids on the island. The boy was wearing gold-colored wireless headphones and blue Nikes. My parents would *never* buy me shoes that expensive. I wiggled my toes inside my sneakers, an old gray pair I'd had since Christmas.

I caught his eye and nodded at him, but the boy acted like he didn't see me as he walked to the bench farthest away from me, gripping the boat railing.

Suddenly the captain went full throttle. The big engine churned and the boat took off so fast, my ball cap lifted off my head. I lurched after it. My phone slipped from my hand to the floor. I watched, frozen in horror, as it slid across the deck and disappeared over the edge into the white-capped waves that churned below.

"Noooooo!" I yelled.

I gripped the railing and leaned over, staring in shock and disbelief as sprinkles of salty water splashed my face. A white, foamy boat trail faded away into the deep blue. My last connection to home was gone. I swallowed hard and glanced over at the other kid. His hands were locked on the railing like his life depended on it. He cast me a quick glance and shrugged in commiseration.

I plopped down on the bench, my elbows on my knees, my hands feeling empty. The next fifteen minutes were a blur as we raced across the waterway.

When the ferry engines slowed to a gurgle, I looked up. We were approaching the island. I saw a dome of dense green trees and shrubs, like the island was a lost world, shrouded in mystery. I almost expected to see a dinosaur rush out. I stood and returned to the railing and watched as the ferry approached a long wooden dock.

I squinted in the glare of the sunlight and spotted my grandmother standing beneath a wooden sign that said DEWEES ISLAND, SC. WELCOME. Honey was smiling and waving both hands above her head like she'd been shipwrecked and I was coming to save her.

At last the boat stopped. In a whir, the boy in the Nike shoes raced past me down the stairs. I hoisted my backpack and followed him off the ferry and up the dock, our footsteps pounding the wood.

"Jake! My boy!" Honey cried as she wrapped her arms around me in a tight embrace. "Child, look at how you've grown. You might be taller than me now."

"That's not hard to do. Everyone's taller than you, Honey," I said.

It had been almost a year since I last saw Honey. She came

to stay with me when both of my parents were away on missions. But she looked much older. Her usually tan skin was pale, with a lot more wrinkles on her face than I remembered.

"Let's get you to the house. You must be starving after that long trip. My cart is parked just over there," she said, pointing to the long line of golf carts parked near the dock. There were no cars on the island, so everyone drove a golf cart.

The boat captain pushed a cart with my duffel bag to our side and greeted my grandmother.

"Ms. Helen, aren't you a sight to see! Sure is nice to see your bright smile out and about again."

"I have the best reason to be out today. My grandson arrived. He'll be staying all summer," she said. "Come along, Jake. Let's get you to the house."

I followed Honey down the walkway to her golf cart. There were some nice ones all decked out. There were plain ones, mostly tan or gray. Then there was Honey's cart. It looked like it was the oldest one in the lot, and worse, it was covered in sand and dirt. A small green flag with the words TURTLE TEAM was duct-taped to the back corner of the cart's roof.

"Hop on." Honey slipped on sunglasses.

I tossed my duffel bag and backpack onto the back seat of the cart and climbed in next to Honey. The sound of an approaching boat caught my attention. I swung my head around and did a double take. The driver of the single-engine motorboat was a girl. She was about my age—and she was alone.

"Honey, there's a kid driving a boat. By herself!"

Honey looked over her shoulder. "Oh, that's Lovie Legare." She didn't seem the least bit surprised.

"But . . . how can she drive a boat . . . by herself? I can't even drive a golf cart."

Honey chuckled. "Actually, I can get you permission to drive a golf cart on the island. You just got to pass my driving test. As for the boat, you can learn to do that, too."

My mouth slipped open. I turned to watch in awe as Lovie tied up her boat and leaped onto the dock with the ease of a sailor. She had a long blond braid that hung down her back like the rope in her hands. When she lifted her gaze toward us, I quickly looked away.

The cart made a high beeping sound as Honey backed out of her parking spot. She stopped and turned the wheel.

"Lovie comes to Dewees from the Isle of Palms almost every day during the summer to stay with her Aunt Sissy while her mama's at work." She flipped a switch from reverse to forward. Before she turned her gaze back to the road, she told me, "Close your mouth, son. You'll catch flies."

As Honey sent the cart lurching forward, I shut my mouth in a big grin. "Can I really learn to drive a cart this summer? Even a boat?"

"Why not?" she asked as she drove out of the parking lot. We headed into the deep shade of the trees. Honey glanced at me appraisingly. "You're not a little tyke any longer. You're old enough to operate a cart. Even a boat. Course, you'll need to pass a boater safety class."

"I could do that," I said, and imagined myself driving a boat on the water—fast.

Honey turned right onto a dirt road and took off in the golf cart. As we bumped along the shady path, the breeze ruffled my hair and cooled the sweat from my brow. The air smelled sweet, like flowers.

"Child, look around you," Honey said, extending her arm. "Dewees is a very special place. There aren't too many folks who live here. Mostly animals and birds and trees and all kind of wild." She smiled. "The whole island is yours to explore."

"Really?"

"Yep," Honey said, and turned her head to wink at me. "It's a Huck Finn life on the island."

Suddenly I felt the first spark of happiness breaking through the gray of this terrible, dreadful day. Maybe it wouldn't be the worst summer ever after all.

There were no paved roads on the island, only dirt paths with shells, pebbles, and ruts that we bounced across. Tall trees loomed over us, shading the road like a tunnel. I felt like I was in a jungle. To my right was a dense thicket of trees and shrubs and maybe a peek at a house far back, hidden from the road. To the left I saw a shimmering lagoon surrounded by tall marsh grass and more trees arching over the water like bony, long fingers.

Everywhere I looked were birds. Little ones flitting about in the trees, big white ones standing in the mudflats, and wading in the shallows of a lagoon were several bright pink birds. They looked like flamingos. I sure wasn't in New Jersey anymore.

"What kind of birds are those?"

Honey turned her head, but she'd already zoomed past the lagoon. She pointed to a circular wooden building up high on stilts.

"That's the Nature Center," said Honey. "Remember it?"

"No."

"I guess it was a few years back. That's where you can learn all about what birds you spot here. Animals, too. They've got all sorts of information in there. You used to like to go there."

"That was a long time ago," I said.

Honey was silent as she drove. "True enough," she said. "You know, Jake, I wanted you to come visit here every year. I asked over and over. But with your mama and daddy's work schedules, and your school and sports schedule, it was hard to find a time that y'all could come visit me. Such a shame, because you used to love it here." She sighed heavily. "Just like your daddy."

I swallowed hard. "Yeah."

"Well, you're here now. Right?" She tried to sound cheerful and turned her head to smile at me.

Honey's driving had me clinging for my life to the cart. I gripped the windshield frame with one hand and the back of our seat with the other as she plowed through a deep puddle.

"Oops, I didn't see that one," she said with a giggle. Honey's short, gray, curly hair was puffed up from the breeze. I saw lots more gray in it than I remembered.

I couldn't figure out if Honey could or could not see the puddles, because she seemed to splash through more than she dodged. And I wasn't sure whether to laugh or be scared.

"What happens if a golf cart flips over?" I asked.

"Good question. What do you think you should do?" Honey asked.

"Uh ... pray?"

"Nope. Island rule number one: If you start to fall off a golf cart, just let go."

"You mean, fall off?"

"Yep."

"Are *we* going to flip?"

"Well, I don't plan on it. But whoever does?"

I gripped the cart tighter as we drove a little farther down the road. Honey suddenly brought the cart to a stop. I jerked forward in the seat.

Honey pointed to a lagoon in the distance. "This lagoon here's where Big Al likes to hang out. Here's island rule number two: We all leave Big Al alone."

"Who's Big Al?"

"Just the biggest, baddest alligator on the island. We have several alligators on Dewees, but Al is the biggest bull of them all. You won't mistake him." She pointed to the platform floating in the middle of the lagoon. "That's his favorite spot. Did you know when a gator is sunning, it's actually digesting its food?"

I shook my head, feeling a little scared that I was on an island with a bunch of gators.

"If you're driving the golf cart and come across Big Al sunning himself on the road, put the golf cart in reverse and go the other way. No one messes with Big Al."

Before I could respond, she tapped the steering wheel and said, "So, want to take a lesson?"

I was still imagining just how big Big Al really was—and where he was hiding—but her question quickly pushed that out of my mind.

"A driving lesson?" I asked. "Now?"

"Of course. You must learn to drive the golf cart. Else how are you going to get your chores done? You ready?"

"Uh, sure." I couldn't believe my luck.

Honey slid from the driver's seat and patted the cushion. "Well, come on."

I was getting the sense that Honey didn't fool around. When she said something, she meant it. I scooted over on the front seat and took hold of the wheel. I was excited she was going to let me drive.

"First thing to learn is that this isn't a toy," Honey began in a teacher voice. "It's a powerful machine and deserves respect. Follow the rules and you shouldn't get hurt. But start acting like some fool race car driver and you'll not only get hurt"— she paused to give me the stink eye—"I'd find out before you could park the cart back at my house. That would mean the end of your driving privileges. Got it?"

"Yes, ma'am."

"Okay then." She pointed out the accelerator, the brake, the switch for reverse and forward.

"Seems easy enough."

She chuckled. "Well then, let's go."

"Now?"

"I sure don't mean tomorrow."

I scooted forward on the seat and put my foot on the accelerator. I imagined it was like driving a go-kart. I had done that bunches of times back home with Carlos and Nick. So I pressed hard on the pedal. The cart lurched forward. Shocked, I lifted my foot off the accelerator. We jerked to a stop.

Not too smooth. I was embarrassed, but Honey only laughed.

"That's normal for the first time. But Jake, don't rush it. You've got to remember to take it slow and easy. Kind of like life, eh?"

I took a deep breath. *Slow and easy*, I told myself. I carefully pressed the accelerator. This time, we took off without a jerk. I clutched the wheel tight. I was driving!

"Driving a cart is like riding a bicycle," Honey said. "You have to find the right pace and balance for you."

Honey guided me along the bumpy road. I drove really slowly, but Honey didn't mind. Another cart zoomed by us, kicking up a dust cloud. I glanced over to see a woman wave. She was wearing a flowing dress with all the colors of the rainbow and big jewelry to match. She looked like she could be the queen of the island.

As they passed, I spotted the boy from the ferry riding in the back seat. He didn't wave or smile, but his eyes widened and his jaw fell open when he spied *me* driving the golf cart.

I sat up a little straighter, pretending I didn't see him. We caught up with their cart when they slowed to turn right onto a narrow driveway.

Honey waved cheerfully. "That must be the Simmons family. Moved in across the way from us. I'll have to bring a pie to welcome them."

In front of their driveway I saw a wooden sign that read TESSA & REGINALD SIMMONS, ATLANTA, GA.

"All the property owners out here mark their place with a sign that says where they are from," Honey said. "Most folks here split their time between the island and elsewhere. Not many of us live here year-round."

"Like you."

"Like me," Honey replied.

We drove a little farther when Honey told me to slow down and turn right onto a narrow path marked with a sign that read THE POTTERS, DEWEES ISLAND, SC. Weeds were starting to grow in front of it.

The dirt lane to Honey's house was even more marked with ruts and overgrown vines and branches that smacked the sides of the cart. Tall, thick grasses scraped the bottom.

"I feel like we're going through a car wash," I said, ducking my head to avoid getting smacked by a thin, leafy branch.

"Oh dear. I'm afraid I've let this place get a bit out of

control," Honey said. The tone in her voice changed. "I've been meaning to get out here with clippers."

A machete, more likely, I thought to myself.

But I couldn't really think about that. I was too worried about getting through the tangles of vines and weeds. At the end of the winding path, looming high in the treetops, stood what looked like a gigantic tree house.

"Welcome home," Honey told me.

I stopped the golf cart with relief. Taking a breath. *Home?* This wasn't my home. Not really, I thought. But . . . where was home now?

Suddenly my dad and mom felt a million miles away.

CHAPTER 3

The House in the Trees

Books take you on an adventure.

I PARKED THE GOLF CART IN AN OPEN AREA under the house that looked like a garage without any walls. A mixture of dirt, sand, and dead leaves covered the concrete floor. Cobwebs dangled from the ceiling. Yard tools and beach chairs hung from the walls.

All the houses on the island were built high off the ground on pilings of wood or cement, in case of flooding. This made the entrance to the house a long walk up. Honey led the way up the two flights of stairs, but so slowly I had to stop and wait as I followed behind, carrying my duffel bag and backpack, which were getting heavier by the second. She stopped one time to "look at the view," she said, winded.

We finally reached the top. Her front door was painted a bright ocean blue with a metal turtle door knocker. On either side of the door were flowerpots filled with dead brown plants and sprigs of green weeds.

"Home sweet home," Honey said, and pushed open the door.

I followed my grandmother inside the shadowed house. I caught the dank scent of dust and something old, maybe old fruit. I'd last been here when I was six but didn't remember anything. From what I could tell, everything was made of wood, from floor to ceiling. Big windows opened to all the trees surrounding us.

"I call this place my Bird's Nest. Don't you remember?" Honey asked.

"Yeah," I said, and thought it was a good name. That's what it felt like up here in the trees. I dropped my backpack to the floor and craned my neck as I turned from left to right. Honey flicked on the lights.

Books were everywhere. On tabletops, the fireplace mantel, stacked on every surface and tilting in towers on the floors. I have to say, I love books. I won my school's award for the most books read over the summer. But this many books lying around was kind of crazy. And not just books. Magazines were stacked twenty high under tables.

I scrunched my nose, holding off a sneeze. The books, the magazines—everything was coated with dust. Dirty coffee mugs and crumpled tissues were scattered on the table. This house looked more like a forgotten library than a home. Where would I sit down? Or eat?

Honey must have seen my expression. She hurried to the windows.

"I have to tidy up a bit. Your coming was a surprise. A happy surprise," she hurried to add. I could tell she was a bit embarrassed. "I'll throw open a few windows," she said, and began pushing a few open. The air from the ocean gushed in, summer warm and smelling of the ocean not far away.

"Well now," Honey said, wringing her hands. Her face wrinkled with worry and she glanced around the house with uncertainty. "I suppose you want to see where you'll be sleeping?"

"Yes, ma'am," I said.

Her pale blue eyes glanced up toward the ceiling as she pointed. "It's right up there."

I looked up. The ceiling vaulted two stories high. I spied a wide wooden ladder against a wall that led up to a spindled railing.

"Up there?" I asked with doubt.

"It's a loft!" she exclaimed. "Don't you remember? Come along, child. You'll love it." She led me to the ladder. "Well, what are you waiting for?"

I gripped the sides of the ladder and, curious, scampered up. From the top I could look over the wooden railing down below to the entire first floor of the house. The area itself was small and compact, but cozy like a fort. It was private even though the space was missing a wall. But it was cool!

"This is better than a room," I said as I walked toward the enormous round window perched over the bed like a window to the world. It dominated the wall and made me think of the window I'd imagined in a book my dad had read to me called *Heidi*. Only in that book, Heidi went to the mountains to live with her grandfather. I was sent to an island to live with my grandmother.

As I looked out, everything was so different from the small, square, treeless backyard I had in New Jersey. Here, I couldn't see another house. Only the high branches of trees, tangled vines, and far beyond, a small glimpse of the blue ocean.

I heard Honey climbing into the loft.

"Lord help me, I'm too old to climb up here any longer." She put her hand to her chest. "I need a moment to catch my breath." Her face softened to a slight smile. "Do you know whose room this was?"

My gaze traveled to the wooden twin-size bed covered with a blue and gold star-patterned quilt. Beside it was a wooden nightstand, and on it a lamp carved in the shape of an anchor. Across the room stood a painted blue dresser. A wall of shelves stretched from floor to ceiling. I walked to it, curious. They were jammed full. Lots of kids' books filled two shelves. They looked like they'd been read many times. There were some shark teeth, a small animal skull, and a small collection of stones. A tortoise shell sat next to a few faded green military action figures. I reached out to touch a pair of antlers, but my hand paused when I spotted a few framed photos. I picked one up.

21

A boy, about my age, with brown wavy hair dangled by his arms from an enormous tree branch. Standing beside him was a redheaded boy of about the same age. I reached for the second photograph. In this one, the brown-haired boy was at the beach, holding a dripping ice cream bar. His arms were wrapped over Honey's shoulders—a younger Honey. I knew who the boy was.

I looked up to see my grandma watching me. "Is this my dad's room?"

Honey's lips curved into a grin and she nodded. But her eyes were teary. "Seeing you standing in this room . . . I swear, you're the spitting image of your daddy when he was your age. Same brown eyes. Shaggy brown hair. Same posture even."

My chest swelled—I was happy at the comparison.

"Eric spent a lot of time up here." She pointed to the bookshelf. "He read every one of those books. Books take you on an adventure, you know. And your dad loved adventures." She smiled at the memory. "Those were his favorites."

Honey walked to the bed and smoothed out the wrinkles in the quilt. I noticed that this room was spotlessly clean. That made me feel she was happy I'd come to visit.

"I don't come up to this room much," she told me. "I can barely make the climb. Being up here sends my heart worrying all over again about your daddy." She turned toward me, her eyes searching my face. "How are *you* doing since the news?"

I wanted to confess, *I'm horrible. I have nightmares every night. I hate to see Mom so sad.* But I was spared by the ringing of the doorbell.

"Jake, be a good boy and get the door. I'm slower than a slug getting down that ladder. It's probably just a neighbor checking on me again."

I flew down the ladder to the door, pulled it open, then stood stock-still. I was face-to-face with the girl who drove the boat. I recognized her long blond braid.

She shot out her right hand and said, "Hey! I'm Lovie Legare. You must be Jake. Honey talks about you a lot. Except when she's talking about animals, and . . . oh!" Her smile fell. "I'm sorry to hear about your daddy. We all hope he's going to be okay."

Lovie was talking so fast I couldn't even speak—which was good because I didn't know what to say. I just extended my hand to shake hers.

Honey came up behind me. "Jake, where are your manners? Invite her inside and shut that door before all the mosquitoes swarm in."

"Oh. Sorry," I said, and quickly dropped Lovie's hand.

Lovie stepped inside and held up a woven basket with her left hand. "Mama and I picked these out at the farmers market just for you, Honey."

I was surprised to hear Lovie call my grandma "Honey." Lovie showed us everything in the basket. "We got you fresh-baked bread, jam, tomatoes, and farm eggs. And I picked these wildflowers myself on my way to your house."

"Mercy, what a treasure. Thank you, dear. And thank your mama. This is the second-best gift I've received today." She smiled at me.

"You're welcome," said Lovie. "Mama told me I must bring the sweetgrass basket back, though. She'd kill me if I forgot it."

"I know those baskets are treasured local art. You tell her I'm honored she used it for me." Honey turned toward me. "I see you've met my grandson, Jake. I think y'all are the same age. He's eleven, going into sixth grade. Isn't that right?"

"Yes," I said a bit shyly.

"I'm going to middle school this year too," Lovie said to me.

I smiled. She seemed to be trying to be friendly.

"Isn't that a nice coincidence? I have a feeling you two will be fast friends." Having emptied the basket, Honey returned it to Lovie. "You wouldn't mind showing Jake around the island, would you? He doesn't know anyone from here."

"Sure, I will. But first I've got to go check in with my Aunt Sissy." She turned and flashed me a smile. Her eyes were bright blue, and her nose was lightly freckled. "See ya, Jake."

I waved. With her, I could barely get a word in.

"Such a sweet girl," Honey said, turning to begin putting away the food.

I turned to my grandmother. "What kind of name is Lovie?"

"Why, it's her nickname. Her real name's Olivia. She was named after a dear woman who passed a while back. She's been Little Lovie since she was born. But now, seems everyone just calls her Lovie."

Olivia . . . Lovie. No matter what her name was, I wanted her to show me her boat.

CHAPTER 4

The Tropical Depression

A naturalist observes and listens.

MY SUNNY ARRIVAL TO THE ISLAND WAS quickly dashed by two straight days of rain. The sky opened up and dumped bucketloads. Outside, the wind whistled and rattled the windows. Honey's dirt driveway turned into a muddy creek. It was as if the house had become its own island.

Honey said the summer storm was called a tropical depression. It was depressing, all right, being cooped up in the house without a computer or video games or my phone. After breakfast of a piece of Lovie's bread and jam, I walked around the house, browsing through the books, looking at photographs in frames on the tables and paintings of sea turtles on the walls. I even tried to make the TV work.

It looked older than I was and had skinny metal antennas that she called "rabbit ears." After a lot of wiggling around I managed to get the local news station and one other that came in fuzzy because of the rain. It was so lame, I didn't care and turned it off.

Honey seemed down in the dumps too. She cleared the table and washed the dirty dishes, then swept the floor. It made a dent in the cleaning. But I could see her heart wasn't in it.

"Honey, want to play a game of cards with me?"

She offered a tired smile. "Not today, Jake. Maybe tomorrow, okay?"

She picked up a book from the table and walked over to a faded blue recliner in the corner of the living room. There was a table next to it with a lamp made to look like the shell of a turtle. As the rain pattered the roof, Honey sat in her recliner reading, or sometimes took a nap in her room. Her mood seemed to change just like the weather. One minute she was cheery, the next she seemed sad.

The worst part about sitting around with nothing to do was that I worried about my dad . . . a lot. It was not knowing about Dad's condition that made the waiting so hard.

I wondered if a person could die of boredom. To pass the time, I hung out in the loft. I felt closer to my dad being with all his stuff. I studied the different shells my dad had collected.

He carefully labeled each one in a shadow box: moon shell, whelk, angel wing, pen shell, lettered olive. He had a mason jar filled with sea glass and another with shark's teeth. He even had a big horseshoe crab shell. Its rounded shape looked like an old Army helmet. I checked out his collection of rocks, too, careful not to peel away the layers of mica. I even played with the Army soldiers, but that didn't last long.

As the afternoon passed, I turned to the bookshelf. It was jammed full of books. My dad was always reading something—a newspaper, a book, a magazine, even a cereal box. He had books by his bed, in his truck, downloaded on his phone. He even packed a book on our camping trips. I guess he was a lot like his mom.

I liked books too, but I liked playing video games more. When I squatted down to scan the book titles, I remembered all the times Dad read to me at bedtime when I was little. It was our ritual any night he was home from duty. He read to me even after I could read chapter books on my own. We would sit side by side in my bed, our legs outstretched and our backs against pillows. Sometimes his voice would lull me to sleep. I closed my eyes at the memory, wishing I could transport myself back to that time, when we were together . . . and safe.

I looked at all the books and magazines on the shelf and thought, *Did Dad really read all of them?* My finger slid past the titles: *Hatchet*, *The Call of the Wild*, *Where the Red Fern Grows*, *The Swiss Family Robinson*, *A Wrinkle in Time*. He must've liked Roald Dahl because there were a lot of titles of his. There were also nonfiction books, mostly about animals and living in the wild. The *U.S. Army Survival Manual* stood out to me. It was tucked among several guidebooks about Carolina beaches, identifying fossils, and night sky constellations.

I pulled *My Side of the Mountain* off the shelf and read the back cover. It was about a boy who taught himself to survive in the wild. I figured I had a lot in common with this kid and decided to read this book first.

Outside my window the storm moaned, and the trees shook like wild things. I clicked on a table lamp, lay down on the bed beneath the portal window, settled the pillows, and opened the book.

I don't know how much time had passed, but when I suddenly looked up, it was dark outside. It wasn't the noise of the storm, but the lack of it that distracted me. I looked outside the big, circular window to see that the storm had passed. In the foggy night, a sliver of moon was rising.

What time was it? My stomach rumbled. I climbed from my bed and went to lean over the railing. I could see the living room, kitchen, and the hall leading to Honey's bedroom, but she was nowhere. I was shocked that Honey had not made dinner, or even hollered to tell me she was going to bed. In just my short time here, I'd learned that Honey wasn't into cooking or cleaning or grocery shopping. But still, I was just a kid. And I was hungry.

I climbed down the ladder and began snooping around the

kitchen. I didn't see much to eat in her cabinets. Next, I opened the fridge. It was packed full! I had hope as I pulled out a small Pyrex bowl and peeled back the plastic wrap. Yuck! My stomach turned at seeing mold on whatever tomato sauce it was. I put that back and grabbed another plastic container. This time I was wary as I pried off the top. It looked like pasta salad, but giving it a whiff, I almost hurled.

Package after package I opened and gave it the sniff test. By the time I was through, I felt sick to my stomach. There wasn't anything I could recognize or want to eat. Not even a frozen pizza.

My stomach rumbled again. *Okay, so maybe I won't die of boredom here. It'll be starvation!*

Then I remembered the bread that Lovie brought over. There was still half a loaf left. I sliced off a big piece and wrapped it in a paper napkin. Not trusting the milk, I poured water from the filter into a tall glass. Then I climbed back up to the loft with my loot. I lay back in bed, clicked off the lamp, and nibbled my bread while staring out the window, watching low clouds drift by in the moonlit sky.

My thoughts shifted to my dad lying in a hospital bed. Even though we were hundreds of miles apart, we were both lying under the same moon, the same stars. I wondered if he could see the night sky. If he was hungry. If he was hurting. Or if he was even thinking of me.

I'm not ashamed to admit I prayed that night too.

≈

"Breakfast," Honey hollered from downstairs.

"Oh boy," I muttered under my breath. The only thing worse than the tropical depression was Honey's food supply.

I rolled out of bed, made my way down the ladder, and plopped down on a wooden stool in front of the kitchen island, brushing away old food crumbs where I rested my arms.

"Morning, Jake," Honey said.

She was still in her pajamas and slippers, like I was. My mom and dad always had me rise, wash, and dress before I showed up for breakfast. "Shipshape," my mom liked to say. Being in the military, they didn't lounge around much in their pj's.

Honey stood peering into the fridge, though I couldn't imagine how she knew what was inside all those foil-wrapped containers.

"I guess I fell asleep early last night and plumb missed dinner. I'm sorry," Honey said. "I could do that when I lived alone, but now I have to think of you, isn't that right? A growing boy has to eat." She handed me a container of orange juice. "I reckon I wasn't feeling myself."

"Were you sick?" I asked, pouring juice into a glass.

"Oh, the rainy weather just got me down. But the sun's out now, right?" she said more cheerfully. "I'm making scrambled eggs. Want some?"

I glanced past her to see that she was using the fresh eggs Lovie dropped off the other day.

"Yes, please. And may I have a slice of that bread Lovie brought over too?"

"Help yourself," she said, pouring the whisked eggs into the hot pan. "That loaf of bread is disappearing fast."

I didn't reply as I cut two slices of bread and popped them in the toaster. I watched Honey as she opened a small plastic container from the fridge and sniffed it. "This one smells like ham. I think." She held it out. "Want some?" she asked.

"No thanks," I replied quickly. *Not eating that.*

That fridge was a time machine. As far as I could tell, almost everything in the kitchen was expired, smelled bad, or was as withered as an unwrapped mummy.

"Want some milk?" Honey asked, pulling out a carton.

"Uh, Honey, the milk is past the sell-by date."

Honey waved her hand and said, "Oh, don't you know those dates are just a suggestion? This milk has got a lot of life still in it."

Like bacteria, I thought with a grimace. "No thanks. I'm good with orange juice."

"Eggs are ready," Honey said, sliding the plate across the countertop. "Want some shredded cheese on it?"

I remembered watching her slice green fuzz off the cheese block.

"Just plain, please."

She handed me the plate and I dove into the eggs. When I was done, I spotted a sheet of paper on the counter that had my name on it. I pulled it close.

"What's this?"

"That's your list of chores," Honey said. "You have to help out while you're here."

Chores? Wasn't going to your grandma's house supposed to be a treat?

"First and most important, I need you to fetch our drinking water," she said.

"From a well?" I asked.

"Not quite," she answered with a chuckle. Honey grabbed her coffee mug and leaned against the kitchen counter.

"Jake," she began in that voice that told me she was going to explain a lot. "Here on the island, we're very green." She saw me smirk and shook her head. "You know what that means. We care for the nature around us and try to live *with* it instead of ruling over it. What's good for the island comes first. Not people. We do what we can to protect the island. That's why you won't see cars here, or golf courses. That's why we never use pesticides. When we fish, we only catch what we can eat in one meal. We let nature show itself off, the way the good Lord intended. We recycle, of course. Try not to use single-use plastic. You know those plastic water bottles everyone buys by the case? They're littering our world. We don't allow them on the island."

Honey took a gulp from her coffee mug and continued. "Now to your chores. You'll be in charge of taking out the trash and recycling. And you'll be the one to fetch the water for drinking. The water from my faucet is perfectly fine," she told me. "But we also have a fancy filtration system here. The drinking water from it tastes so good!" She pointed at a large, empty water jug on the floor. "That there is the water container. Your job is to fill it up over at the Nature Center building whenever it gets low. And while you're out, you can check my mailbox and pick up my newspaper from the ferry dock. It's all right in the same neck of the woods."

I made a face staring at the chores list but didn't say anything.

"You'll have to take the golf cart, of course."

My head shot up. "The golf cart?"

Honey smiled. "I left the keys in the ignition."

"Can I go after breakfast?" I was so ready to get out of the house.

"There's a map of the island in the cart. Basically, the road is one big circle. It's tough to get lost. That should make getting around a breeze."

I slid off from the stool, eager to get dressed for my day.

"One more thing," she called out, waving me closer. "It's an assignment. Kind of like summer homework."

Just when things were looking up. "What kind of homework?" I asked cautiously.

"The fun kind. When your daddy was a kid, he'd be out the door after his chores lickety-split and stay outside all day. He only came home to eat. And everywhere he went, he had this with him."

Honey let her hand slide across the cover of a small brown book, then placed it on the counter. I leaned closer for a better look. It looked like it was made of leather, worn and soft with age. On the cover, painted in a kid's handwriting beside a yellow flower, were the words ERIC POTTER.

I ran my finger across my father's name with awe. "What is it?"

"His childhood diary. Oops! I mean journal," Honey chuckled. "Your daddy would get madder than a hornet when I called it his diary." She gently tapped it with her fingers. "It's yours now." She turned and began putting our breakfast plates in the sink.

I reached out to pick up the journal. The leather was so worn it felt buttery in my hands.

"Your daddy explored every square inch of this island. He wrote down things he did and drew pictures of things he saw. He was quite the young naturalist. I think that helped prepare him for the Special Forces." Honey opened a kitchen drawer and pulled out a black-and-white composition notebook. It was the kind I used in school.

"This is for you. It's not as fancy as your dad's, but it'll do. Fill in the pages with notes all about your time here on the island."

I took it in my hands, feeling uncertain. "Like what?"

She shrugged. "A naturalist observes and listens. See, if you go outside and make a lot of noise, all the critters will run from you. But if you walk out quiet and respectful, maybe sit down a spell, if you're lucky, maybe an animal will come out of hiding near you. A butterfly might flutter by. A bird will land. Write down what you see and hear. It doesn't have to be good. No one even has to look at it. Not if you don't want. This is for *you*."

"Can I draw?"

"Of course! It's yours to do with what you will. I want you to explore the great outdoors. Drives me batty how kids these days stay cooped up, rotting their brains on those cell phones and playing video games all the time. Oh Jake, there are adventures to be had, mysteries to be uncovered." She jabbed her index finger to indicate the door. "Now go on. You're wasting daylight!"

CHAPTER 5

Cat and Mouse

Courage is taking action in the face of fear.

MAP OF THE ISLAND? CHECK.

Key in ignition? On.

Reverse switch. Ready!

I squeezed the steering wheel, took a deep breath, and slowly backed out of the open area beneath Honey's house. Looking way up at the house, I could see how she came up with that nickname, the Bird's Nest. I spotted the big round window of my room.

The island was so different from base life. On the base, there were small fenced yards and no big trees. Nothing like the jungle of tall, swaying pines, palmettos, and ancient oak trees here.

Honey's driveway was littered with broken limbs and piles of pine needles, cones, and leaves blown off from the storm. There was no way I'd get the cart out. "This is some vacation," I muttered as I found the rake. I spent a good half hour sweeping the dirt driveway clear of the minefield of debris. Once I was done, the cart easily made it out to the main dirt road. I did a lot of stopping and starting until I got used to the accelerator and brake pedals.

Being alone on the narrow, muddy road was both exciting and scary. Both sides were lined with deep thickets of trees, dark and mysterious. If anything happened to me out here, would anyone even notice? Suddenly a blur of movement caught my eye from the woods. I slowed to a stop. Just steps away from the road I spotted a deer and her white-spotted baby fawn almost hidden behind the leaves. The mother deer locked eyes with me. I held my breath. She was so close, I could see the muscles in her chest flex. Then with a single leap, she disappeared into the safety of the forest, her fawn following her on spindly legs. The last I saw of them were their white tails flashing.

Mental note: *Write that down in the notebook.*

Time to be on my way. I pushed the accelerator down, but strangely, the cart only sputtered at half speed. It began slowing down by the minute, even though I had the pedal pressed all the way to the floorboard. Then it just stopped.

My heart hammered fast. *Now what?* Honey didn't go over the part about what to do if a golf cart breaks down. Could I push it back to the house? I shook my head. I wasn't that strong. There wasn't a person or a house in sight on the path. I sighed. I had no choice but to walk.

On foot, the island seemed even larger and more looming. Trees towered over me, making me feel so small . . . so alone. I didn't have to imagine being on a jungle expedition anymore. I was doing it! All my senses were on high alert. My eyes searched the trees. My ears heard every *crunch*, *squish*, and *snap*.

The forest awakened with sounds. Camouflaged frogs croaked throaty songs in the pine-needle-covered floor. Birds hidden high in the branches called out to one another. I recognized the sharp whistles of the red cardinal and the long songs of a mockingbird.

Around a bend, a lone wooden swing bench overlooked a small pond. Curious, I walked through the tall grasses to check it out. Gnats buzzed by my ears and mosquitoes attacked everywhere. I swatted them, but they kept biting.

Mental note: *Use bug spray.*

The trees opened to reveal a small pond. The water was the color of iced tea. Sunlight danced on the water and I saw the puffy white clouds reflected. A big limb of an old, twisted tree leaned far over the water's edge. Its slender branches looked like long fingers dipping beneath the dark water. And all over the tree sat at least a dozen of the biggest white birds I'd ever seen.

Some of the birds were as tall as little kids! And they were weird-looking. Their heads had no feathers, just wrinkly, leathery skin that made them look prehistoric. My fingers itched to draw them, like my dad did in his journal. While I watched, a few more glided in for a landing. Their long white wings fanned out like an airplane. It made me think of Mom and how she piloted massive cargo planes, smooth and easy, like these birds.

Sweat stung my eyes and mosquitoes buzzed. I retreated to the main path, swatting bugs away like a helicopter. I spied one long white feather on the ground and, surprised, picked it up. There was the faint black tip. I carried it back to draw later.

I hadn't gone far when the sound of sticks snapping in the woods just behind me stopped me dead in my tracks. I held my breath to listen, ready to run. The noises were so loud, they had to come from a big animal. I waited, but didn't hear them again, so I started walking again. A little faster. My senses were now on high alert.

Then I heard it again! The hairs on my arms prickled. *Something is following me!*

I racked my brain. What did Honey say about the animals on the island? Some were not so friendly—alligators, foxes, bears. I imagined being chased by gnashing teeth. *What if something attacks me? How can I defend myself?* I felt defenseless and alone, like a mouse being hunted by a cat.

My heart beat faster as I looked for a big stick to defend myself. Nothing. I grabbed a big pinecone. I could throw it as a distraction if I needed to make a run for it.

I began walking again, faster this time. Once again, the

crackling of twigs and rustling of leaves sounded. *What if it's Big Al?* I wondered. Honey said gators could run fast. *If I got attacked, or eaten alive . . . who was going to even know?*

I remembered being scared in the woods once during a camping trip with my dad. We were asleep in the tent when loud hoots and shrieks woke me up. Dad told me, "When you feel scared, remember that courage is not the absence of fear. Courage is taking action in the face of fear."

Together we peeked out the tent flap. A fat raccoon was sniffing around our campfire. "So ferocious," Dad said. We had a good laugh that night.

I knew what I had to do. My muscles pulsed with adrenaline. I stopped and spun around, lifting my arms wide.

"Raaaaawr!" I growled as loud as I could, like a wild animal. "Get outta here!" I hurled my pinecone toward the sound.

A voice yelled back from the woods. "Ow! Stop!"

I froze, shocked.

It was another kid. And he was wearing very familiar bold blue Nike sneakers. The boy from the ferry. He stepped out from the tree line onto the path, rubbing his shoulder. "Hey, stop with the pinecones. Those things hurt," he complained. Then with a laugh he added, "You've got a good arm."

"Were you following me?" I demanded.

He glanced downward and shrugged.

"Well, it wasn't cool. I thought you were Big Al or something."

His eyes shot up at me. "Who's Big Al?"

"A gator. Only the biggest one on the island."

His eyebrows raised. "Did you know that the American alligator is one of only two alligator species in the world?"

"No. I didn't think about that when I was worried he'd eat me."

"Yeah," the boy replied with a laugh, stepping closer. It broke the tension. "When they're young, alligators eat mostly insects and small fish. Adult alligators go after fish, snakes, turtles, birds, and small mammals."

"You know, *we* are small mammals. . . ."

He shrugged and grinned. "So yeah, maybe he would eat you."

I couldn't help but laugh at that. "You sure know a lot about gators. Are they your favorite animal or something?"

"No, I just like cool facts."

"Here's a fact: It wasn't *cool* that you followed me like that."

He kicked a pebble in the road, then looked back at me. "Yeah. Sorry."

"*Why* were you following me?"

"I don't know. I was trying to follow some animal tracks. I think they were fox tracks. Or maybe a coyote. Anyway, when I saw you walking, I got curious and decided to track you instead. Why'd you ditch your golf cart?"

This time I shrugged. "It broke down. I don't know why."

"Was it plugged in before you left your house?"

"Plugged in?"

"Yeah. You've got to recharge the cart after every time you use it."

41

Honey didn't tell me that part. "It's probably a dead battery, then," I said. "I've got to walk for help."

"Want some company?"

He looked like he was as lonely on this island as I was. "Sure. My name's Jake Potter." I stuck out my hand. "Jake."

He took my hand. "I'm Macon Allen Simmons. But you can call me Macon."

We took off together along the dirt road, jumping over puddles, throwing sticks and pinecones into the woods. It didn't feel so lonely out here with someone by my side.

"Where are you from?" I asked.

"I'm from Atlanta."

"I'm from New Jersey. I'm staying with my grandma this summer."

"*All* summer? Cool. Me too."

We both smiled. Finally, my summer was looking up.

"How'd you get stuck here?" I asked him.

"My mom's having a baby and the doctor said she needed to rest. So we came out here. My mom grew up not far from here. They bought a house for vacations. My dad's going back and forth to Atlanta because of his job. He's a lawyer. He told me I had to help out around the house a lot more."

I smirked. "Yeah, I got that line too."

"Is your dad gone too?"

My smile fell as I nodded. "Yeah. He's a captain in the Army. He was in Afghanistan and his caravan hit an IED."

"Like a land mine?" Macon asked.

I nodded.

"Oh man. I'm sorry."

"Yeah. He's injured. I just don't know how bad yet."

We walked awhile in silence, neither of us knowing what to say next.

Finally, Macon asked, "Hey, do you play video games?"

"Of course!"

"You should come over to my house. We'll hang out and play."

I stopped walking and just stared at Macon.

"What?" Macon asked.

"You've got Wi-Fi?"

"Doesn't everyone?"

"Uh, *no*," I said.

"You're kidding!" His eyes were wide with disbelief. "I'd go nuts."

"Tell me about it. Honey . . . that's my grandma . . . doesn't believe in it or something. She won't have it in the house. She doesn't even have a satellite for TV."

"Whoa," Macon said, shaking his head. "That sounds like a time warp."

We came to a fork in the road. A small wooden sign read PELICAN FLIGHT DRIVE.

"Left or right?" I asked.

Macon shrugged. "I don't know. It's my first day out. The rain . . ."

"Got a coin?"

Macon pulled a quarter out of his pocket.

"Heads we go right. Tails we go left."

Macon flipped the coin, caught it, and flipped it onto his arm.

"We go right!"

CHAPTER 6

New Friends

It was like we were on our very own island.

WE STARTED DOWN THE RIGHT PATH when we heard the steady buzz of a golf cart. We both spun around to see a silver cart coming our way. All I could think was *rescue!* The driver slowed down and stopped next to us—a girl with a long blond braid. It was Lovie.

"Hey, Jake! Y'all lost or something?"

My cheeks got warm. "No, we're headed to the Nature Center."

"Was that your golf cart I passed way back there?"

"Yeah. Dead battery."

"Well, it's going to take you forever to walk there. You're headed in the wrong direction. Hop on. I'll give y'all a ride."

I hopped onto the back of the cart. Macon slid onto the front seat next to Lovie.

"I'm Macon."

She smiled. "Hey, I'm Lovie. You new here too?"

"Yep."

"I'll show you guys around." She giggled. "So you won't get lost."

Lovie turned the cart around and we headed left. She was another know-it-all like Macon, but this time I was glad for the information. Lovie was like a tour guide. She pointed out the paths that led to the beach and took us by the community swimming pool. I held on tight to the golf cart because Lovie would stop without warning to jump off and snap photos of things with her cell phone.

"Nice phone," I told her, missing mine.

"Thanks. My mama wants to keep tabs on me while she's at work. I like to take pictures of the insects and birds and . . . look, there!" Lovie squealed, pointing to a dead, topless tree trunk.

"Where?"

"Straight ahead. In that hole in the tree trunk."

I squinted and spotted a small owl peeking out of a dark hole. Its round yellow eyes were watching us intently.

"Aw, it's a baby owl," Macon said.

"Nope. Not a baby. It's a screech owl! They're just real small.

And don't let the small size fool you. They're fast and furious."

"I've read about them," Macon said as he was getting off the golf cart for a closer look. "They like to nest in old woodpecker holes."

"That's right." Lovie pointed at the cart. "See those binoculars on the seat? Grab them so you can see better."

Macon carried the binoculars and drew closer.

"Are you new here?" asked Lovie.

"For the summer. We're from Atlanta."

"See a lot of screech owls in Atlanta?" she asked in a gentle tease.

Macon smirked. "I'm a Boy Scout and we study wildlife and go on camping trips. I don't see stuff like this in the city," he said, gazing through the binoculars. "Did you know that owls have feathers on their legs and toes?"

I rolled my eyes. Macon was like a human Google.

"That's right," Lovie said, glancing at Macon as though sizing him up. "And the feathers on their wings are different from other birds. They can fly super quiet to snatch their prey."

"Silent but deadly," Macon added.

I watched them smile at each other and wished I knew some cool facts too.

"Maybe we should get going," I said. "My golf cart's still sitting in the middle of the road."

"Okay, hop in, guys," Lovie said, climbing behind the wheel. "But first, I've got one more spot to show you. It's an epic find!"

"Cool," Macon said again. That was obviously his favorite word.

Lovie drove us to what she claimed was her favorite beach spot on the island. She veered off the main path and we bumped along a wide wooden boardwalk that cut between tall trees, rolled over a marsh area, and past two big houses hidden in the trees. We came to a stop so hard I almost tumbled off.

"This is as far as the cart can go," she announced.

"How did she ever get to drive?" I mumbled to Macon as I climbed out.

Macon shrugged. "Beats me. She only has one speed: fast."

Lovie pointed toward the narrow path. "We walk the rest of the way."

"She's kinda bossy, too," I whispered.

Chuckling, we followed Lovie across the soft, sandy path toward the sea. Lots of tiny black ants scrambled by our feet.

"Don't worry," Lovie said when she heard me grunt and lift my feet. "The black ants don't bite like the red ones. We call those fire ants, and let me tell you, their bites sting."

"Look, there's Indian paintbrush," Lovie called out, pointing to the yellow and purple wildflowers that blanketed the sand dunes. She stopped to take a photo with her phone. Macon pulled out his phone and also took photos.

My hands felt empty. I didn't have my phone. Then I thought about my notebook sitting in the golf cart. Note to self: *Carry the notebook with me wherever I go.*

I heard the ocean before I saw it.

We reached the top of a dune and with one step everything changed. Suddenly the blue of sky and ocean loomed before me, stretching out as far as I could see. I stood still, breathing in a breeze in which I could almost taste the salt from the sea. The beach was long and no one else was on it. White crested waves lapped the shoreline.

"Wow," was all I could say.

"What he said," echoed Macon.

"Follow me!" Lovie yelled, and took off running through the loose sand.

Macon and I looked at each other, then took off after her. Our heels dug deep half-moons in the dry sand. She stopped in front of a bright orange, diamond-shaped sign nailed to a wooden stake. It said LOGGERHEAD TURTLE NESTING AREA. Neon orange caution tape was wrapped around two more wooden stakes to make a triangle protecting a small patch of sand.

"What is it?" I asked, panting from the run.

"It's a turtle nest," she replied. "*My* turtle nest," she added, looking very pleased. "I found it my first day of summer break. See here." She pointed to the head stake. "The Turtle Team even wrote my name on the stake. And the date the nest was found."

I bent to study the writing on the wooden stake: LOVIE LEGARE 6/15.

"Hey! That's the day I arrived."

"Me too," chimed in Macon.

"So, what's inside the nest?" I asked.

"Turtle eggs, of course!" Lovie exclaimed with a light laugh.

I felt my cheeks flare. "I mean, I didn't know if there were eggs or baby turtles in there." I shrugged. "There aren't a lot of sea turtles in New Jersey."

"Or Atlanta," said Macon. "But I know turtles are reptiles."

"Right. And just like alligators, they lay lots of eggs," said Lovie.

I could tell she was warming up to the topic.

"This mama turtle laid her nest in a good spot," Lovie continued in a teacherlike manner. "The Turtle Team didn't have to move it, so we don't know how many are in there." She shrugged.

"So, how many do you think?" I asked, thinking two or three.

"Oh, sixty, or a hundred . . . or more."

"Wow, that's a lot of eggs," I said.

"Move it? Why would you do that?" Macon asked. Unlike me, he was eager to learn new facts about the turtles.

"Well, *I* couldn't move it," she explained. "It's against the law to touch the nest. You have to have a permit. The Turtle Team decides if the nest is in a safe place. If the ocean waves can go over it, or if it's near a walkway or something like that, they move it up higher on the dunes. My Aunt Sissy is on the team. So is your grandma, Ms. Helen," she said to me.

I didn't know that. That explained the Turtle Team flag on Honey's golf cart.

"But she just hasn't been out patrolling the beach this summer. Or last year. Did she quit the team?"

"I don't know," I replied. "But my Grandpa Ed died two

years ago. She's been pretty sad about that." I didn't mention my dad's accident. I just couldn't.

"So how do you find the turtle nest?" asked Macon.

"The team walks the beach early every morning, on the lookout for turtle tracks."

"I like to follow tracks. What do turtle tracks look like?" Macon asked.

Lovie smirked. "Tire tracks."

Macon's brows rose. "That's pretty big."

"Yeah, well, a grown mama turtle weighs over three hundred pounds," Lovie said.

Both my and Macon's eyes widened.

"Cool!" Macon exclaimed. "I've got to see one of those."

"It's really hard to catch a turtle laying eggs. She's pretty wary about coming ashore, and she won't if she sees a human or another animal. And it's always late at night in the dark." She smiled. "But we can try. Who knows, maybe we'll get lucky."

"When will the eggs hatch?" asked Macon.

"When they're ready," she replied.

Macon rolled his eyes in a *come on* kind of way.

Lovie smiled. "It usually takes about two months."

I could see the human Google doing the math in his head.

"That means they'll hatch in August, before we go back to school. We could watch them hatch!"

"You better believe it," she said. "I wouldn't miss it. It's my nest," she said again.

"And, did you know . . . ," Macon continued.

I groaned, bracing for more Macon facts.

". . . the loggerhead is South Carolina's state reptile? And an endangered species?"

"Duh," Lovie replied. "It's only my most favorite animal in the world."

That explained her green turtle T-shirt and her silver turtle necklace. *Oh yeah*, I thought. *She's obsessed.*

"It's hot," I yelled, ready to do something else. "Let's go for a swim."

Lovie took off, yelling over her shoulder, "Race ya!"

Lovie and I hit the ocean at the same time. We laughed as we tore off our shoes, then ran through the shallow water, not caring that our clothes got wet. We pushed through the cool water until the waves knocked us down. The water was much warmer in South Carolina than in New Jersey. We stood up on the soft, sandy bottom, laughing and splashing each other, my soaked clothes dripping and sticking to my skin.

"Come on, Macon!" I yelled. "The water feels great!"

Macon was standing on the beach, watching us. "There's no way I'm going in there with all those sharks!" he called back.

Sharks? My skin pricked with alarm as I scanned the waves. "Lovie, are there sharks in here?"

"Sure, they're everywhere," she called back, and then laughed when shock flashed across my face. "But don't worry. We're not their food. They're not interested in you . . . usually."

She smirked and then dove back into a wave and swam farther out.

I turned and looked back toward the shore. Macon was beachcombing for shells. Behind me, Lovie was backstroking and splashing. No one else was out here. It was like we were on our very own island.

I have friends, I thought with wonder.

For the first time this summer, I didn't feel alone.

CHAPTER 7

The Journal

Find what you're good at and have fun.

THE GOLF CART WAS TOWED BACK TO MY grandmother's house. Honey wasn't mad. After all, she was the one who forgot to charge it. She gave me a lesson on how to plug it in after each use.

The cart was totally filthy. Mud, sand, and leaves were everywhere. I wondered when was the last time Honey cleaned it. I got a bucket of soapy water and some rags and set to work. I swept away the leaves, washed away the dirt and grime, wiped the windshield and the rearview mirror, and even polished the dashboard and headlights. It felt like *my* golf cart now.

"Lunchtime!" Honey hollered from upstairs.

I was starving, but sighed, remembering the contents of her fridge. "Coming!"

Honey was dressed in a green Turtle Team T-shirt like Lovie's, and shorts.

"What kind of sandwich would you like, Jake? Ham and cheese?" She turned from the fridge with a container in hand. "Ooh, look! Some old turkey slices. I had forgotten about those." She sniffed the container. "Yep, still smells all right."

I grimaced. "I'm not hungry."

"Not hungry? Look at you. You're as slender as a sapling! You must eat, or your mama's going to be none too pleased with me. So, what'll it be?"

Secretly I dreamed of a foot-long sub or a hot slice of pizza. No, scratch that . . . an entire pizza! How do people on this island survive without a *single* restaurant, fast-food place, or even a convenience store out here?

I spied the last slices of Lovie's loaf of bread on the counter. "Do you have any peanut butter?"

Honey reached far into the cabinet, rummaged around a moment, then with a satisfied grunt pulled out a jar and handed it to me.

"You're in luck. I forgot I even had this."

I sure was in luck. The jar was unopened. She handed me a plate with the last of the loaf of bread. I sliced it into two pieces, spread the peanut butter thick, and wolfed it down. I looked at my empty plate and wondered, *What will I eat next time?*

After lunch, I tried to get Honey to come outside with me

to see the golf cart. She hadn't left the house since the rain.

"I shined it up and it looks brand-new," I said with excitement. "I'll take you for a ride. Maybe we'll see Big Al."

"No, no," she said, shaking her head. "My hip's acting up. I'll just sit and read a spell. But you go ahead."

I watched her retreat to her bedroom with a book in her hand. Just looking at her made me sad. I looked around the empty house, the unwashed dishes, the tilting piles of books, and remembered my mom telling me that Honey needed help.

So I did. I cleared the table and washed the dishes. While I was at it, I cleaned the counters, too. I opened the fridge and saw the shelves packed with wrapped food.

What would happen if I just tossed out all the bad food? I laughed. That would empty the whole fridge! But what if Honey ate something bad and got sick? There wasn't a hospital on the island. Someone had to clean house.

I figured that someone was me. I stretched out my arms as far as I could, pulled my head back, and opened one container. Yuck! I gagged when I saw the mold in it! I held my nose as I tossed out the mystery food.

Boy, was I done! But it was a start. Then, because I really wanted some milk, I pulled out one more thing. The milk carton. I whiff checked it—oh boy, it was sour—and drained the carton. We definitely needed some fresh milk now!

The rain drummed on the tin roof and streaked the windows. I wouldn't be meeting my friends at the Nature Center today as planned. Feeling hungry and a little drippy myself, I went up to the loft and pulled out my notebook. I tried to remember all the new sights I'd seen earlier that day.

The day slipped by as the rain continued to fall. Dinnertime came and, hungry, I went to the kitchen to rummage around for something to eat. Honey must've heard me. She emerged from her room. She looked like she'd just woken up from a nap.

"Honey, do you want me to make dinner for us?"

She gave me a surprised look. "You can cook?"

"I can boil water," I replied with a grin. "I saw a box of noodles. I can make that."

"That sounds just fine," Honey said. "Might be some butter and cheese."

"Uh, Mom makes it with olive oil," I thought, remembering the yucky butter.

"You're the chef," she said with the first smile I saw of the day.

I couldn't wait to cook something I knew I'd eat. I boiled up the noodles, added garlic salt—which I was surprised to find—and black pepper. There was some parmesan cheese in a plastic container that I was willing to take a chance on since it didn't even need refrigeration. I was so hungry, the cheesy pasta tasted even better than usual. For dessert, Honey surprised me with a box of Girl Scout cookies in the freezer. She was holding out! I ate almost the entire box.

After our meal, Honey hung out in the living room, reading a book in her favorite armchair. The blue fabric was so worn she'd placed crocheted doilies on the arms, those things I saw in old-time pictures. Before she got too settled into her book, I hurried up to the loft to retrieve my notebook. I hesitated, blowing out a breath. I was shy to show my drawings.

I liked to draw, but sometimes the other kids teased me about them. But Honey asked me to show them to her, didn't she? And . . . I'd worked hard on them all day. *Courage*, I said to myself.

"Hey, Honey," I said, approaching her timidly.

She looked up from her book, a slight smile encouraging me. "Yes dear?"

"I, uh, I thought you might like to look at my journal. I mean, you said it was like my homework."

Her smile widened with pleasure. "Of course! Good for you, Jake." She patted the chair beside her. "Okay then," she said, reaching out. "Let's see what you've discovered."

I handed Honey my notebook, then sat beside her, leaning far forward so I could see what page she was looking at. I licked my lips and wiggled my foot.

"Well, lookee here," Honey marveled. "You've done a fine job drawing the dock and the ferry." She turned the page. "And the golf cart!" She flipped through a few more pages. "Here we are at the critters. An owl and a deer. I'm partial to these. Oh, and an ant."

"A black ant," I said.

"Yes, thank heavens. Those big ones are carpenter ants. It's the little red ones that bite something fierce." She pointed to the green lizard. "And an anole."

"Is that what you call it?" I asked.

"The devil is in the details," she said. "This one's green. Likely an anole."

She looked at me with pride. "I'm so pleased you saw fit to include the drawings in your journal. Well done, Jake."

I felt my chest expand, eager to draw some more.

"My dad's drawings in his journal are really good."

"Yes, they are. You inherited his talent."

I loved hearing the comparison to my father but found it hard to believe. I pushed my hair back. "I don't know about that. I mean, he's really good."

"True. He practiced a lot." She tilted her head. "Do you draw often?"

I shrugged. "Sometimes."

"The more you draw, the better your skills will become. Your father never went out without his journal with him. He used to say he never knew what he'd find." She smiled at the memory. Then looked at me again. "Think of all the opportunities you'll have to practice with all the new species you'll find here on the island."

I brightened at the prospect.

"And, if you don't mind me suggesting, you might look up the species and add important details to your journal. That's what a true explorer does. He or she records the details of the discoveries."

I thought of my dad's journal and all his notes he'd written on the pages.

"For example," Honey continued, "when you drew this bird, did you know what kind of bird it was?"

I shook my head. "But I found this nearby. I think it's one of their feathers." I handed her the bird feather.

She examined it thoughtfully. "Yes, that's a good start."

With a sudden burst of energy, Honey set her book down, handed me my notebook, and rose from her chair, gesturing for me to follow. She was like a dog on a hunt as she prowled one bookshelf to another. When she pulled out three books, we went to the wood table. Honey's eyes were gleaming as she sat back down. She motioned me closer.

"Now, Jake, you know there are all kinds of birds, countless sizes, shapes, and colors. It can get confusing to figure out what kind of bird you're looking to identify. But there are tricks to use when you begin your search in your guidebooks. After doing this awhile, you'll have a favorite book." She tapped the one in front of her. "This one's mine. The first thing I ask myself is where I saw the bird. In a tree? On the beach? Or in a marsh or pond?"

"A pond."

"Then it's a water bird. Was it floating or standing around?"

"It was standing. It had long black legs."

"Good detail," she said as she wrote down the information. "Now, what about its size? Big or little."

"Big," I answered, and moved my hand to show her how tall the bird was.

"About three feet," she said as she wrote down the detail.

"Now tell me all the details you can remember about this bird. Its color, eyes, and especially its head. Anything unusual?"

I had to think a minute, recalling the tall white bird. "When I saw it fly up to the tree, I remember it had black on the wings. And," I added with excitement, "it had the weirdest head. There were no feathers on it. It was bald, real scaly. And it had this long beak." I gestured to show how long.

"Good details." She looked again at the notebook. "What color was the beak?"

I scratched my head. "Sorry, I can't remember."

"That's okay. You gave us a lot to work with. Now comes the fun part." She wiggled her eyebrows. "The hunt!"

Honey's fingers paged through the book. I could see she was having a good time.

"Here!" she exclaimed, moving so I could get closer. "Given your fine details, we have a couple of choices to consider."

She pointed to one bird. "This is the ibis. Let's check it against our list." She read out of the book. "It's a white wading bird. Check. It has black tips on the wings. Check. Look at the beak. It's curved and red." She looked up at me. "Could it be an ibis?"

I shook my head. "No. It's too small. And I think the bird I saw had a black beak."

"The color and shape of the beak are important details." Honey flipped through more pages before stopping and pointing at another bird. "How about an egret? It's a white bird. And it's a wader. And it has a black beak."

I shook my head again. "The birds I saw were bigger. And

the head's wrong. The egret has feathers on its head. And that bird doesn't have any black on the wings."

"Right. You have a good eye. This bird is a snowy egret. You say it's bigger. Hmmm. I wonder . . ." She turned a few pages and pointed. "Is this it?"

I immediately recognized the large white bird with the long legs and bald, scaly head and neck. I felt the thrill of discovery. "Yes, that's it!"

Honey grinned. "You saw a wood stork. You can't mistake those. They're easy to tell apart by their size and their bald heads. Though, note how the black beak curves, more like the ibis. You were right about how they roost in flocks in trees by the water." She once again picked up the long feather.

"I'm old enough to remember when the wood storks mostly lived in Florida and were put on the endangered species list. That was back in the 1980s, when your daddy was born. Then they began to show up more and more in South Carolina. Now just in the time your daddy's been alive, wood storks are off the endangered species list. That's something, isn't it? Though they're still considered threatened. We're lucky to have such a good population right here on Dewees Island." She returned the feather and patted my cheek.

"I'm right proud of you, Jake. You're on your way to becoming a naturalist, every bit as good as your dad. And you know what? I don't know when I've had such a good time. I like to say, find what you're good at and have fun with it! You're mighty good at drawing. So have fun, Jake."

I smiled back, pleased for the compliment, but more, because Honey was happy.

We spent the evening together with Honey teaching me how to identify a bird by its size and shape, color and habitat, or where it lived. This was the Honey I remembered, someone who was curious about life, always ready to explore. Someone who knew a lot about nature. Now the books bonded us rather than dividing us.

Later that night I lay on my bed with my hands behind my head. I stared out the big, round window at the night sky. There were no city lights to block the stars. They shone bright in a sky as black as the tip of the wood stork's wing.

I wondered why my mom hadn't called yet. Did that mean good news or bad news? If I had my cell phone, I could flood Mom's phone with text messages. My breath hitched. Mom didn't know I'd lost my phone! Maybe she'd been trying to call me. But she had Honey's phone number too. I sighed. Mom hadn't tried to call Honey, either.

How is my dad? I wondered. I wanted to tell him I was reading his journal. That I was trying to be like him. I wanted to hear his voice.

I started getting teary-eyed, so I sat up and went to the small wooden desk in the corner. I pulled out my journal. I had a long way to go to fill it up with words and drawings like my dad's. But the pages were no longer blank. They were beginning to fill with the drawings and details about the animals *I'd* drawn. I felt the weight of it in my hands. This was *my* life. My observations. A diary of my days. This journal was important to me.

Honey suggested I write about my day too. Not just what I saw, but how the things I did or saw made me feel.

Easier said than done. But I tried. I wrote down a few sentences, then stopped, bored I wasn't so good at writing my thoughts and feelings.

In my dad's journal he wrote when he felt lonely or happy. He described things he did with his pal Red. Reading his words, I felt like he was talking to me. Like I knew him better.

When I looked at what I wrote, it seemed so . . . school-like. *I went to the Nature Center. I got water. The cart broke down.* I was telling facts, not sharing my feelings. I scratched out the words. How could I make my words mean something? How could I write like my dad?

Then the idea hit me. I could write *to* my dad.

I tore a fresh page out of the notebook, smoothed it on my desk, took a deep breath, and imagined my dad's face. The way he smiled. Smiling back, I began to write.

> *Dear Dad,*
>
> *I miss you. Mom too. A lot!*
>
> *Honey gave me summer homework. Can you believe that? At first I was mad, but it turned out to be okay. She gave me a notebook and told me it was my journal. I had to draw and write in it all about the things I saw and did on the island. Just like you did when you were a kid. Honey*

gave me your old journal. I hope that's okay with you. I'm reading it and it's really good. I like hearing what you had to say. It makes me feel like you're here, talking to me.

Today, I tried to draw these huge white birds I saw in the lagoon. They had scaly heads that reminded me of dinosaurs. Or maybe even a dragon. Can you guess the creature? A wood stork!

But Dad, it's weird here with no Wi-Fi. Or a cell phone (don't ask). Not even decent TV. How did you stand it?

I met two kids here. I was worried I'd be the only one on the island. They're both about my age. Macon is from Atlanta. He's real smart and big. I think he's rich, too. Then there's Lovie. She lives on the Isle of Palms. She drives a boat over here all by herself! I gotta learn how to do that too. Honey said all I must do is pass a test. But guess what? I know how to drive a golf cart!

That's about it. Tell Mom to call. Honey's worried about you. She tries to act normal, but I can tell it's fake. I know how she feels. I'm worried too.

I love you, Dad!

Your son,

Jake

CHAPTER 8

The Phone Call

Look on the bright side of things.

I WAS GETTING USED TO MY ROUTINE. EACH morning I rose, dressed, and showed up for breakfast. Honey was doing better with routine too. She didn't appear in her pajamas anymore. She was dressed in time for her first cup of coffee. I hopped on the golf cart by 0800 hours—that's military time for eight a.m.—to get my chores done. By the time I finished, it would already be sunny. And *hot*.

I was getting to know my way around the island pretty well now. Most mornings, Macon, Lovie, and I liked to drive our carts to the Nature Center. It was kind of our hangout. Inside, the walls and furniture were all wood and the ceiling was arched high, with big whirling fans. All over the walls were maps of the island, posters about plants, ocean life, and wildflowers, and photographs of the island's history.

Best of all were the glass cases that displayed all kinds of weird things like snakeskins, real turtle shells, and rare seashells. There was also a glass tank with a real, live diamondback terrapin. We named the turtle Pirate because we learned it lives in salty water. It used its webbed feet to swim up to the glass, revealing grayish white skin with a black speckled patterned.

"Come look at this," Macon called out.

He was standing in front of one of the glass exhibits. Macon was pointing at one that had animal skulls of different sizes.

"Skulls. Cool."

He read from the sign. "Eyes in front, likes to hunt. Eyes on the side, likes to hide." He looked up and grinned. "That's easy to remember."

"Has a ring to it," I teased.

Lovie pointed. "Look at that gator skull. Total predator. Its eye sockets are facing forward." She leaned in to look at another skull. "And this one is a deer. See? Its eyes are on the side. It likes to hide."

"It's the fight-or-flight instinct," Macon said.

I remembered the deer and fawn I saw from the cart and how they jumped away when I was near. I went to my backpack and pulled out my journal, then returned to set it on the glass. I wrote down the phrase and began to sketch the two skulls. Macon and Lovie crowded around me.

"What are you doing?" Macon asked.

"I'm drawing in my journal."

They watched as the two skulls took shape in my notebook. I felt nervous, remembering how I'd been teased about my drawing before. I'd feel bad if my new friends teased me too. But I remembered Honey telling me I was good at drawing. What was I afraid of, anyway?

"Hey, bro," Macon said over my shoulder.

My stomach tightened. "What?"

"You're pretty good."

I tried to hide my smile. "Thanks."

Lovie leaned over, watching. "Looks like you have a lot of drawings in there."

"Yeah. Honey told me to put things I learn about in this notebook. Like my dad used to do. He has this journal with all sorts of cool facts." I glanced at Macon, knowing he would appreciate that. "She's teaching me to be a naturalist."

"Ooh, you're lucky," Lovie sighed. "Your grandmother knows more about nature than most anyone on the island. Least that's what my Aunt Sissy says."

"You mean, she gave you homework . . . during summer break?" Macon asked. He made an exaggerated gagging sound.

"Pretty lame," I replied, finishing my drawing. I looked up at my friends. It was hard to explain what I was feeling.

"It doesn't feel like homework," I began. "I mean, it did

when she told me I had to do it." I snorted. "Of course. But . . . once I started doing it, I got into it. See, when I got here, I didn't know as much about nature as you two. I admit, I was kind of jealous. So every day I go out and explore. I draw and write things I see in my notebook. I'm real careful because Honey said the details are the most telling when we try to identify them later. Honey and I look up what I found in her books. I'm going to learn the names of the birds, plants, trees, critters—all kinds of things here on Dewees. I think it'll make me feel more at home here. And not afraid, because, well, everything isn't strange anymore." I returned to my sketching. "Plus, it makes Honey happy."

Macon shrugged. "Yeah, I guess it's not like homework." He leaned closer. "Can I give it a try? I'm pretty good at drawing too."

I shrugged and handed him my pencil. Macon pulled over a chair and bent over my notebook. Lovie and I watched as Macon began to draw Pirate, the terrapin. He wasn't kidding. Macon could really draw!

"There," Macon said, and handed the pencil back to me. "What do you think?"

"And you did that in, like, what, a minute?" I asked.

"Well, I took classes. In Boy Scouts," Macon explained.

"I can't draw," Lovie said with a shrug of the shoulders.

"But you're great at observing," I told her. "Maybe you can help me identify the names of these things I found today."

She brightened. "Sure!"

I emptied my backpack on the table.

"Nice shells," Lovie said, and immediately began sorting them. "This white long one with a curly edge is called an angel's wing," she said in her know-it-all voice.

"Because it looks like an angel wing," Macon said.

I replied, "I knew that."

Lovie said, "But did you know it's good luck when you find one with the pair of wings still together?"

"Well, my family needs plenty of that right now," I said.

Macon laughed. "Lovie, you totally made that up!"

"Did not!"

We spent the next hour working together on my journal. Macon drew the shells I'd collected while Lovie and I scanned the wall posters and a few books to identify them.

By the time it was time to head home, Macon and Lovie decided that they were going to begin journals too.

When I returned home to the Bird's Nest, I parked the golf cart, plugged it in, then climbed the steps two by two to the front door. With a full water jug in one hand and Honey's mail tucked under my arm, I pushed open the door and hollered, "I'm back!"

Honey wasn't in the living room. Dirty dishes sat on the stove and in the sink.

Uh-oh, I thought.

"Honey?" I called out as I walked through the living room. I heard her voice, but it sounded like she was talking on the phone. Her bedroom door was open a crack. Peeking in, I saw her sitting on her bed. It was no surprise that her room was also a mess. Clothes hung over the chair, and her dresser was covered with stuff. None of that mattered, however. Her face looked very serious.

I quietly walked around her unmade bed to face her. Seeing me, she lifted a finger for me to wait. Her eyes were red and filled with tears.

"Yes, I understand," she said into the phone. "Jake is here now. I'll put him on." Honey looked at me and gave me a watery smile. "It's your mother," she said in a shaky voice.

I took a breath and felt suddenly afraid. Whatever my mom was going to tell me wasn't good news, or why would Honey be crying?

"Mom?"

"Hi, sweet boy."

A rush of emotion filled me at hearing her voice again.

"How are you?" she asked.

"Good." I clutched the phone so tight in my hand, it hurt.

"Jake, I'm going to ask you to be real strong."

"What's wrong? Is Dad okay?"

"Sweetheart . . ." She paused. "Your dad's not doing very well. But he's a fighter. And he's in a fight . . . for his life."

My mouth went dry. "Is he . . ." I swallowed hard. "Is he going to die?"

"We hope not," she replied. "Try to understand. It's like his body is fighting a war. So far, he's won a lot of battles. We're real proud of him. But he's lost some too." She paused and took a shaky breath. "He had surgery this morning."

"Is he okay?"

"Yes. He's out now. But . . . the doctors couldn't save his leg."

I tried to make sense of what this meant. "What happened to it?"

"It was badly damaged in the accident. The doctors couldn't save it." She paused again. "They had to remove it."

My mind went blank. I couldn't picture it. "What do you mean? They cut off his leg?"

"Yes. He lost that battle, but it will help him win the war. Do you understand what I'm saying?"

My throat was closing as I fought off tears.

"Jake? Are you there?"

"Yes," I croaked out.

"You have to remember that your dad is still your dad. Losing a leg doesn't change who he is. And he's going to get better. That's what's most important. So I'm going to stay with him longer. He needs me."

I wanted to say *I need you too.* But I knew she was right. She had to stay with Dad now.

"Okay."

"I'll call you again when I have more news. I know it will be better news. So please try not to worry. Your dad's going to be okay. He loves you. And I love you too. Very much."

I handed Honey the phone and walked out of her room to one of the large windows. I stood staring out, but I didn't see the trees or the sea. I was trying to imagine my dad without a leg.

"Jake?" Honey put her hand on my shoulder. "Want to talk?" I shook my head. I couldn't talk. I just ran from her room and escaped to my loft.

I stayed in my room the rest of the day and into the evening. I didn't come down when Honey asked if I wanted dinner. I tried again to imagine my dad without a leg . . . but I couldn't. . . . I couldn't even imagine him in a wheelchair. Dad was good at sports. He liked to run. *Why did this have to happen to him?*

I looked over at the bookshelf and all the special things he'd collected when he was younger. My dad was a guy who loved adventures. *What must he be feeling right now?* I wondered. He must be really scared. Mom said he was in a fight for his life.

I also couldn't help but wonder what it would be like having a dad without a leg. How would it be different? Would he still play sports with me? Take me on hikes or ride bikes?

Would he still be my dad?

I fell onto the bed and buried my face in my pillow.

Night fell. I ran out of tears. Still feeling dejected, I went to the shelf to pick up my dad's journal. The old leather felt soft in my hands. Inside, on yellowed pages, I traced the letters of his name with my fingers. His handwriting was small and easy to read. His words were as close as I could get to my dad now.

Each entry was dated. I looked for today's date.

June 22, 1989
I broke my arm. Worst pain ever. My summer is
ruined. No pool. No ocean. No fishing. No fun!!!
Mama said to look on the bright side of things.
She said I should make a list of good things. So
here goes.
My friends can write on my cast.
It's not the arm I use for writing and eating.
At least I fell out of the tree after we finished the
best hideout ever.
Maybe I'll get out of chores (doubt it).
I have a lot of time to read.
Okay. Mama was right (maybe). I do feel better
(a little).

I cracked a smile. Dad was always so positive. He never
told me he'd broken his arm. I looked at the date to figure out
my dad's age at the time he wrote this. I knew he was born in
1978, so he would have been eleven years old. My exact age.

I shot up from the bed to grab my journal and pen from
my backpack and took a seat at the small wooden desk. I tore
out another page of my journal.

June 22, 2019
Dear Dad,
Mom just told me the news. I'm sorry you lost
your leg. This must seem like the worst thing ever.
I read in your journal that you broke your arm
when you were my age. You got better! So think:

Even though you lost a leg, you'll get better
again. You always do!
I wish I could be with you at the hospital. I miss
you so much. This might sound strange, but
reading your journal makes me feel close to you,
even though you're hundreds of miles away.
Don't worry about me. Honey and I are fine here.
I love you, Dad. And remember to look on the
bright side of things!
Love, your son,
Jake

CHAPTER 9

The Disappointment

You've got to believe.

THE SONGS OF CHATTY BIRDS AND THE bright sunlight woke me up.

I rubbed my eyes and yawned. And then I remembered the news about my dad. My sunny day turned dark.

I washed, got dressed, and grabbed my backpack. I tossed in my notebook, Dad's journal, my water bottle, and sunglasses. I pulled on my Army ball cap.

Downstairs, the house looked quiet. No lights were on in the kitchen. I sighed, thinking Honey was back to being sad. I walked across the living room to her room. I knocked.

"Come in."

Honey was still in bed and her eyes were puffy. A pile of crumpled tissues sat on her nightstand.

"Good morning, darling," she said in a shaky voice.

I didn't smile back. I was hungry and feeling sad myself.

"I need to mail something." I lifted a white sealed envelope. "What's this?"

"A letter for Dad. All I need is the address. And a stamp."

"Oh. Okay. What a good idea," Honey said with a nod of approval. She reached out for the envelope with one hand, and with the other slid on black-framed glasses. Honey tilted her chin sideways to inspect the envelope. She pulled out an old ratty-looking address book from her bedside drawer and handed it to me. "You'll find the address of your father's hospital in there on that piece of paper on top. And wait a minute . . ." She pulled out two stamps from the drawer.

"Here, take these. Feels a bit heavy. Best to add another stamp. You don't want it returned, do you? Then go to the community mailboxes. You'll see a box for off-island mail."

I turned to go.

"Jake!" she called after me. "Don't you want some breakfast?"

"There's no milk." My voice was flat.

"Yes, I saw that it's gone. I've ordered some from town. It should be here today. With more bread, that peanut butter you like, and a few other supplies too."

"Okay." *Good*, I thought.

"There's cereal. If you can eat it dry."

I grimaced at the memory of the tiny bugs I had found in an old, stale cereal box. I'd have better luck trying to find wild berries in the woods like Sam in *My Side of the Mountain*.

"I'll eat when I get back. I'm going to do my chores and then meet up with Lovie and Macon at the dock." I headed toward the door.

She hollered after me, "Child, how do you survive off the meager amount of food I see you eat?"

I wondered the same about her.

I met up with Lovie and Macon at the Dewees Island main dock. They were talking to a tall man with red hair and a trimmed beard.

He turned toward me when I walked close. "Well, hey there. You're Jake Potter, right?"

"Yes, sir."

"My name's Randall Piper. I'm the fire chief on the island. Everyone calls me Chief Rand."

"Yes, sir . . . I mean, yes, Mr. Chief Rand."

I heard Lovie giggle beside me.

"I knew your dad back when we were kids. We were best friends."

I looked at him carefully. "You're the kid with red hair in his photograph? Hanging on a tree trunk?"

"That'd be me," he replied with a laugh. "Best tree climber this island's ever seen."

When he smiled, I recognized the boy in the picture. "You're Red?"

He tossed back his head and laughed again. "Haven't heard that in a while. Only your dad called me that. How's he doing? Any news?"

His question felt like a sucker punch. I stuck my hands in my pockets and looked at my feet. "My mom says he's got a long recovery. He, uh, he . . ." I sucked in my breath. "He lost his leg."

"No," Chief Rand whispered. "Dang. That's a lot to take in. I'm so sorry, Jake." He closed his eyes and went silent for a moment. Then after a forced exhale, "Here's one thing I know for sure. Your daddy's got a fighter's spirit. He doesn't know the word 'quit.'"

"No, sir."

He gave me a gentle squeeze on the shoulder. "He's alive, and that's what we have to remember. This is tough, but he'll pull through this, Jake. Strong as ever. Nothing ever stops Eric Potter." Rand gave me a slap on the back. "You've got to believe in that. Believe it, for him."

I nodded, then turned my head. I didn't want him to see the tears in my eyes. I slipped off my backpack and reached inside to get the envelope. I held it in my hand, feeling its weight. Inside was my letter and a page of my drawings. *For you, Dad*, I thought. I dropped it into the mailbox.

"A letter to your dad?" Chief Rand asked.

"Yes, Chief Rand, sir."

"I'm sure hearing from you will do him a lot of good."

I tugged my ball cap down over my eyes. "Thanks. I've got

to go." I turned and began walking away from the dock.

Lovie and Macon walked by my side in silence all the way back to my cart.

"Hey, I'm sorry, bro." Macon laid his arm over my shoulder.

"I'm sure he'll be okay," Lovie said, then surprised me with a hug.

My arms froze at my sides when her arms wrapped around me.

Lovie quickly let go and toyed with her silver sea-turtle necklace.

We all stood there in another awkward moment of silence.

"What should we do today?" Macon asked.

I shrugged. "I don't care."

"Want to go to the beach?" asked Lovie. "It's low tide, so we could check out the tide pools. See what kinds of creatures we find in them."

I shook my head and wiped beads of sweat off my brow. "It's too hot." I knew I sounded like a grump, but I felt like one.

"Why don't we go chill at my house?" Macon asked. "Want to play some video games?"

I thought of Honey telling me that video games were not allowed, but that was at her house, not Macon's house. Besides, she didn't seem to care. And today, I didn't care either. I just wanted to get out of the sun and get my mind off my dad.

"Sure," I said with a shrug. "Why not?"

We all hopped into our carts. The black plastic steering wheel felt hot to the touch. Macon led the way to his house.

When we pulled into his driveway, my eyes widened at the sight of his house. It was big—much bigger than Honey's. In fact, it was two houses connected by a covered porch. I parked in the shade and walked over to where Macon and Lovie waited.

"Who lives with you?" I asked Macon.

"What do you mean? My mom and dad and me."

"But you have two houses."

He looked over his shoulder and saw what I was pointing at. He laughed. "Nah, man. That's the guest house. Mom says someday the nanny can sleep in there."

"The nanny?"

"You know, the babysitter. For the new baby."

I shook my head again. "You must be rich."

Macon shrugged. "I guess. I don't know. There's a lot of folks richer."

There's a lot of folks poorer, I thought, but didn't say it out loud. Lovie met my gaze and we both smirked. Yeah, Macon was rich.

Macon knocked his elbow against mine. "I'm starving. I know Mom just went grocery shopping. Let's grab some lunch."

With those words, my stomach growled. I was all in.

Macon's house was a mansion hidden in the forest. Inside, everything was open with white marble countertops and shiny wooden floors. And it was clean. Nothing was out of place. It even smelled good, like warm laundry.

I was instantly jealous of Macon's house. It made me sad to think how dirty Honey's house was. She'd been trying to clean up some, and I was helping. But this morning she went back to her old ways.

Macon opened an enormous stainless steel refrigerator. I could only stare in awe as he opened it. Inside, it was sparkling clean. The shelves were stocked full of fruit I could recognize and not all shriveled, cartons of milk, orange juice, and cups of yogurt with the labels neatly facing outward, just like at the grocery store.

Macon pulled out a big container of lunch meat and cheese slices. I stepped closer and eyed it carefully as he opened it. All the cheese was fresh. Not any mold in sight. I picked up the container of meat and began sniffing.

"What are you doing?" Macon asked, a little offended.

"Sorry. Habit, I guess."

Macon gave me a funny look as he put grapes, carrot sticks, and a carton of chocolate milk on the counter. Then he slid plates and cups to us.

My stomach rumbled so loud Lovie turned her head toward me with raised eyebrows.

"Someone's hungry," she said with a laugh.

If she only knew, I thought. I loaded up my plate with piles of everything. I bit into my sandwich, my eyes closed. Everything tasted so good I thought I'd gone to heaven. I tore into that sandwich.

"Jake, you act like you're never going to eat again!" Lovie said.

I poured a glass full of chocolate milk and only shrugged.

I made a second sandwich, then Lovie and I carried our plates and followed Macon to the family room. Like the rest of the house, this room was big. I could fit three of my lofts into it. Not that I'd trade my loft for any room in the world.

I plopped onto one of his beanbag chairs, and Macon handed me a game controller. He turned to Lovie. "Do you want to play?"

Lovie shook her head no and carried her plate to the sofa.

Macon sat in the second beanbag chair and turned on the TV.

"Where's your mom?" asked Lovie.

"Mom's got to spend a lot time in bed," Macon explained as he set up the game. "She lost two other babies and is being really cautious. That's why we came here for the summer. It's quiet. My dad comes down on the weekends. He's hired a lady to come over and clean and shop and make meals." Macon's brows furrowed. "He expects me to watch out for her. She relies on me."

"I get that. I'm supposed to take care of Honey," I said before biting into my enormous sandwich.

"But," Macon continued with his mouth full, "now that Mom is getting closer to her due date, he wants to find a nurse, too. Just in case."

"My Aunt Sissy is a nurse," Lovie said, popping a grape into her mouth. "Or, she was. She's retired now. But she used to deliver babies in the hospital. Maybe she'd like to help.

It'd be nice to have the nurse on the island. Just in case."

"Sounds good. I'll tell my mom."

Lovie leaped from the sofa, calling over her shoulder, "I'll write down her phone number for your mother."

For the next hour Macon and I chilled playing video games. We asked Lovie to join us, but she said she didn't play video games. Instead, she paced the room, as restless as an animal in a cage at the zoo. She kept looking at the bookshelves, sighing a lot and loudly.

Finally, she slammed a book down on the table. "Seriously, guys, how long are we going to sit around doing nothing?"

Macon and I looked at each other with confusion.

"This isn't nothing," Macon said, holding the game controller in his hand.

"Ooh! You missed it, Macon. Totally scored another point." My eyes stayed glued to the screen.

"I'm so bored, y'all!" Lovie complained.

"We asked you to play the game too. If you would, then you'd be having fun too," I replied.

"Take that!" Macon hollered out at the video game.

Lovie stood right in front of the screen.

"Hey! You're in the way," we both yelled.

"The fun is out there." She pointed toward a window. "The island. Not stuck inside."

"Said no kid *ever*." Macon stood up, trying to get a better view of the television screen. "You're weird sometimes. Now, could you please move?"

Lovie rolled her eyes and plopped onto the sofa and started scrolling through her phone. Her last statement echoed in my head, making me feel uneasy. I was supposed to be outside, *exploring*, as Honey would say. But lounging and playing video games was what I'd been missing.

"I'm going to go back to my Aunt Sissy's house," Lovie announced.

"Fine," Macon fired back.

I shot him a look of disapproval. "Don't go," I said to Lovie. "Look, just give us ten more minutes and then we'll go back out."

"Fifteen minutes," Macon interjected.

Lovie's face brightened at the offer. "Ten minutes and it's a deal."

But just one minute later the doorbell rang.

Macon went to get the door and I grabbed a bag of potato chips. I was putting a handful in my mouth when I froze.

In walked Honey carrying a white baker's box wrapped in red ribbon. She stopped, her eyes as wide as two moons, and stared at me.

CHAPTER 10

The Long Dinner

We have each other.

HONEY STOOD AS STILL AS A STATUE, BUT her gaze moved to the television set with the video game playing, to the table overflowing with food, then back to me.

"Jake," she said in a shocked voice, "what are you doing inside playing video games? I thought you were outdoors with your journal. I haven't seen you for hours."

I swallowed hard. The chips felt like sand going down my throat.

Macon's mother flowed into the room slowly, all smiles, and extended her hand. Her long gown fluttered around her baby belly as she walked.

"Hello! Welcome. I'm Tessa Simmons."

Honey pulled herself upright and smiled back. Standing next to Mrs. Simmons's bright floral dress, my grandmother looked old and faded in her tan pants and Turtle Patrol T-shirt.

"I'm Helen Potter. I live a few houses away from you. In the Bird's Nest. I'm a bit late, but I came to bring you this blueberry pie and formally welcome you to Dewees Island."

"How kind of you. Did you bake it yourself?"

"Oh, heavens no. I can't bake worth a lick. I ordered it from town. The ferry brought it over."

I sighed in relief for Mrs. Simmons. I didn't want her getting sick from Honey's food.

She handed the box to Mrs. Simmons, then turned and gave me the stink eye. She said in that voice that told me I was in big trouble, "I'm sorry, but I didn't know my grandson was here. I thought the children were at the Nature Center."

Mrs. Simmons smiled and accepted the gift. "The children are welcome here anytime. We were worried our Macon would be bored on the island all alone, so we're very happy he's made friends."

Honey turned to Mrs. Simmons. "I'm sorry to be rude. I'm just as pleased as you are that the children found each other. Summer's all the sweeter shared with friends. It's just that I must bring Jake home now. You see, I don't allow video games."

She put up her hand at Mrs. Simmons's surprised expression. "Not that I mean all houses should have the same rules.

But that's mine." She gave me a stern look. "And Jake disrespected it. He's meant to be outdoors." She looked back at me and pointed at the remnants of my sandwich. "I didn't mean for him to eat you out of house and home either."

"It's too hot outside," I said. "And too buggy! It was just this one time. We were getting ready to go back out."

"Excuses!" Honey waved her hand for me to come along.

I didn't budge. "I'm bored!"

Honey's eyes flashed and she stepped closer to me. "Good!" she said. "Boredom is the fuel of your imagination. I will not allow you to sit indoors, rotting your brain away playing video games. Now come along. You can finish lunch at home."

"No!"

Honey's eyes bulged and her mouth slipped open. "Jake, come home," she said. "I'll make you something to eat."

"Your food is bad!"

Honey's face went still. "What did you say?"

A part of me knew I should just stop and apologize, but I felt like a dam of water bursting open.

"The food in your fridge is moldy. Even the cheese. I don't even know what that stuff is in all those containers. And there are bugs in the cereal. It's not that I don't want to eat your food," I cried. "I *can't!*"

I felt my eyes flood but didn't wipe them. I held my hands in fists at my thighs, trying hard not to cry. "I don't want to go back to your house. It's dirty. And it smells. And you're always in your room. I want to stay here."

The room went silent. I stood, stunned that I had just yelled at my grandmother. In front of people! From the corner of my eye I saw Macon's mouth slip open and Lovie shrink into the sofa. When I could look back at my grandmother, I saw that tears had filled her eyes.

Mrs. Simmons cleared her throat and stepped closer to Honey. She spoke in a soft voice. At least, it sounded soft compared to my shouting.

"I think you're absolutely right, Helen. These children should be outdoors. Why don't you and I cut ourselves a nice piece of this pie and discuss it?"

Honey could only offer a watery-eyed smile and nod her head.

Mrs. Simmons gave the three of us a stern look, and though her voice was calm, we all knew she meant business.

"Kids, please turn off the games, clean up this room, and sit outside on the porch while Mrs. Potter and I talk. In private."

Lovie rose from the sofa, her face pale. "Jake, you disappointed me," she said.

I felt crushed. This wouldn't have happened if I had just listened to Lovie earlier.

"Boys, your pie is ready!" Mrs. Simmons called from the kitchen.

Macon and I slunk into the kitchen to collect our plates. I couldn't look at my grandmother. Then we moved out to the porch and nervously shoveled blueberry pie into our mouths. I couldn't taste it.

We didn't talk. Instead we tried to hear the women's voices through the sliding glass door. But the sound of buzzing cicadas in the tall pines drowned out most of the conversation. I could only catch a few words: "internet," "cell phones," "island." When laughter erupted, both Macon and I sighed with relief.

I don't know how long they talked, but when they ushered us back inside, I could tell Honey was feeling better.

"How was the pie?" Mrs. Simmons asked kindly.

I mumbled a polite response as we stood in front of them. I felt like a criminal in court about to find out his sentence.

"Helen and I had a lovely chat," Mrs. Simmons began. "We both agree that being on the island is a special time for you children. A time to play outdoors, be creative. And"—she paused and looked at Macon—"turn off all electronics."

"What!" Macon shrieked. "Why are you punishing me? I didn't do anything."

"It's not a punishment," Mrs. Simmons replied gently. "It's an opportunity."

Macon scowled. "Just because Jake's grandmother doesn't like video games doesn't mean I can't play them. She's not my grandmother."

I saw from Mrs. Simmons's face that Macon had gone too far.

"Well, I'm your mother. And I'm telling you, no video games, TV, or electronics. And no phone."

Macon stiffened and worry replaced his anger. "But what if

you need me for something? I'm supposed to look out for you. Dad said so."

Mrs. Simmons sighed, then nodded in agreement. "You may keep your phone. But only for communication, hear? I forbid videos or games. If I find out you're doing that, you lose the phone. No matter what your father said. Understood?"

"Yes'm."

Macon shot me an angry glance, then walked off to his room without saying a word. I stood there, embarrassed I caused this to happen.

Honey stepped closer to me and put her hand on my shoulder. Her voice was soft and almost contrite.

"Come along, Jake. Let's go home. We have a lot to talk about."

I spent the rest of the afternoon sitting on the porch at the Bird's Nest. I felt I'd just ruined my life. Macon probably hated me. Maybe Lovie, too. I embarrassed myself in front of everyone. And my grandmother was mad, for sure.

Her words, *You disappointed me*, played on a loop in my head. I let her down. And ultimately Mom and Dad, too, because that was my one job. *Take care of Honey*. I put my head in my hands. What could I do to make up for what I did?

An idea flashed to mind.

For the rest of the afternoon I swept the garage area and walkway. Then I cut back the shrubs and branches away from her driveway. The branches scratched my arms and sweat poured down my back, but I didn't stop until the sun started to lower. I'd finished raking up the pinecones, needles, and twigs that littered the front path too. The western sky looked like it was on fire with bright colors of red, orange, and gold as the sun lowered. I was so tired, sweaty, and covered with bug bites. I looked up at the windows, not sure I wanted to go back in. But I couldn't stay outside forever. I had to go up and face Honey. And apologize.

I was putting away the tools when Honey called out from the front porch above me.

"Dinner!"

I sighed. I vowed I would eat whatever Honey put on my plate.

Inside the house the scent of warm garlicky bread filled my nose. And sweet tomato sauce. Honey was at the sink straining a steaming pot of noodles.

"Perfect timing," she crooned. "I made spaghetti and I just pulled bread out of the oven. Wash up! Dinner's ready in just a minute."

"Yes, ma'am." The whole scene had me really confused.

After I washed the dirt off my hands, arms, and face in the bathroom, I took a seat at the wood table. The books were gone and instead there were place mats and tableware. I sat straight in the chair, aware that something important had changed.

Honey carried two plates of hot, delicious-smelling pasta to the table and took a seat beside me. She was dressed in the same pants and T-shirt, but her hair was brushed. I looked at the food with suspicion.

Honey noticed. "I had a delivery today from town. And," she added with a knowing smile, "the garlic bread is from Tessa Simmons."

Relief flooded through me.

Honey held out her hand with a small smile. "Let's give thanks."

I tried to smile back and placed my hand in hers. It felt bony but warm and smooth. She bowed her head in prayer. I did the same.

"For the food before us, the people beside us, and the love between us, we give thanks. And we ask for your blessings for Eric. Amen."

"Amen."

I picked up my fork and took a tiny taste. My eyes widened and I couldn't stop the smile. It was delicious! My plate was empty before either one of us talked.

"This was great," I said, still chewing my last bite.

"I'm glad you liked it, Jake." Honey dabbed her mouth with her napkin and placed it beside her plate before folding her hands together. "We need to talk . . . about today's . . . situation."

"I'm sorry I yelled at you," I said in a rush. It felt good to get the words out.

"Thank you," Honey replied. "And I'm sorry that I haven't taken proper care of you."

"You did . . . ," I interrupted.

Honey held up her hand to silence me. "Tessa and I had a good talk today. Our conversation was . . . eye-opening. I realize I've been neglecting not just you, but a lot of things." She patted my hand. "When I returned home this afternoon, I took a good look around and saw what I've become. A crabby old woman stuck in my shell."

"You're not crabby," I said.

"Sometimes," she replied with a crooked smile.

"More sad," I countered.

Honey's face softened, and then she nodded.

"But why?"

"Oh, Jake . . . it's hard to explain. I haven't felt like myself since your grandfather died. At first, I missed him something fierce. We'd been together for fifty years. When he passed, I felt a part of me died with him. I lost my purpose. I didn't go out much. I didn't see the point of cleaning or cooking just for myself. I stayed home. I reckon I lost myself in books."

I eyed the stacks of books all over the room.

Honey continued, "I stopped taking the ferry most days, which meant I hardly went into town to shop. Plus, in an odd way that's hard to explain, seeing a full fridge made me feel safe. Like I had all I need." She laughed, but it sounded sad. "Even if the food wasn't good."

Suddenly I saw my grandmother differently. She wasn't lazy or forgetful. She was depressed.

"So you've been lonely?" I asked softly.

She nodded. "It's not a good thing for a person to be alone too long. Then, when I got the news about your daddy being hurt, well . . ." Honey sighed and shook her head. "It was all too much. That's when I really let things go."

I thought about my mom's words, *Take care of Honey. She needs you.* I understood a lot more now.

"I let you down." She placed her hand on mine. "I'm sorry."

"I let you down too. I shouldn't have yelled at you. I embarrassed you in front of Mrs. Simmons. I'm sorry, Honey."

She smiled then as her eyes combed my face.

"Jake, dear boy, I know you're having a hard time with the news about your dad and the amputation. We both are. Honestly, I'm still trying to process everything in my own heart too." She took a small sip of water.

"I'm not saying everything will be shipshape in a day. It's going to take some time. And I may need some help. Both for cleaning the house and for my health. I talked to Tessa Simmons about that. I know I've got a lot to do. But if we both remember that Eric's going to be okay, and we both keep trying to be cheerful for him and for each other, I know we'll get through this."

"I'll try, Honey," I said.

"We both will."

"Just tell me what I can do."

Her smile softened her face. "You are already such a help. Just being here. I'm not lonely anymore. You do your chores without fail. I don't thank you enough for that. And I did notice you washed the golf cart all shiny. And today you swept and cleared the driveway. You're doing your part." She straightened in her chair. "Now I'm going to do mine."

"Honey, I have to tell you something."

"What's that, dear?"

"I didn't eat some of that food in the fridge. I threw it away. And the milk."

"Did you, now?" She laughed. "Good decision. Why don't you help me finish the task? We'll clean the fridge and cabinets from port to starboard."

I beamed. "Aye aye, captain."

We rose from the table, each feeling better after our talk. I helped clear the table and dried the dishes she washed. We talked about all sorts of things. I told her what I'd like her to cook for me. She told me what things I might try to do on the island.

"Did you ever see the cannonball in the Nature Center?"

"Nope." Then more politely, "I don't recall it."

"You might want to check it out. Your father and Rand found it, back when they were about your age."

I stopped drying the dish. "A *real* cannonball?"

"Yes, sir."

When I put away the last dish, Honey dried her hands on a towel and stood before me. She was eyeing my face, then reached out to lift my chin.

Honey asked, "Is something else bothering you I should know about?"

If she'd asked me this yesterday, I would have shaken my head and said no. But today, after all that happened, I wanted to ask for her help.

"It's just . . . Honey, is my dad going to be the same now?"

Her brow creased, and when she looked at me, it felt like her eyes were searchlights scoping my heart. "Of course he will. He's still your dad."

"But . . . I can't picture him without a leg," I blurted out.

Honey swiftly reached out to pull me close against her. She smelled of flour and something sweet.

"I know," she said, and her voice was shaky. "I have a hard time trying to picture that myself. Your daddy is still my baby, don't forget." She stepped back and tried to smile and held me by my shoulders.

"Jake, a leg is just a limb. Eric is still the same man he was. He's the same in his mind and in his heart."

I could only nod my head. I didn't know if I could believe her. My throat was too tight to talk.

"It's not going to be easy. But your dad has your mom to help him through this too. And we"—she squeezed my shoulders—"we have each other."

CHAPTER 11

The Explorers

Life can be an adventure.

I WOKE UP TO THE SOUND OF DISHES clattering in the kitchen. I climbed down the loft ladder to discover Honey standing on a step stool clearing out the kitchen cupboards. A big box sat on the counter, half filled with food, boxes, and containers.

"Good morning, Honey!"

"Oh! You startled me." She stepped off the stool. "Good morning, dear boy. I'm just getting started. Time to purge."

"Need help?"

Honey squinted at the side of a can. "Sure, bring your young eyes over here. What's the expiration on this thing?"

I leaned in. "It says 2014. Time for the trash can."

"Goodness, I don't know. They say canned goods keep forever."

"No one says that, Honey."

She laughed and tossed the can into the box. "When I'm done with the cupboards, I'll attack the fridge. Tessa is sending over someone to help me clean today." She paused and looked at the now-full box. She said in a quiet voice, "I'm trying, Jake."

"Me too, Honey. I'm going to see if Macon and Lovie will explore the island today. No video games. Promise!"

Her eyes gleamed. "Good boy. By the way, I'm going to the market today to restock the shelves. Any requests?"

"Frozen pizza?"

"You got it."

"And peanut butter, please. And jelly. And crackers. Some ice cream, too. Chocolate. And—" Honey cut me off.

"I'm not buying all junk! And I do have to be able to carry this home," she said with a chuckle.

"Can I come with you?"

She shook her head. "Next time we'll make a day of it. Who knows what we'll find?"

"Great." I beamed, looking forward to it.

"Oh, child, you're medicine to my soul. You are showing me that even at my age, life can be an adventure."

My first stop was to the island dump. Actually, I had so much trash, it took two trips. When I finished, I drove to

Macon's house, hoping we were still friends. I pulled into his driveway to find him unplugging his cart. I was glad I caught him in time.

"Want to hang out?" I asked.

He cast me a shaded glance, then shrugged. "I guess."

"Hey, man, I'm sorry. I didn't mean for you to lose your phone."

"And my Wi-Fi."

I cringed. "Yeah," I said with a groan.

"Hey, it's okay," he said, giving me a sidelong glance.

"Really?"

"Yeah. I thought I was gonna be stuck on this island alone. Then I'd have nothing to do but play video games."

I smirked. "So you're saying I'm better than video games?"

He guffawed. "Hardly. But yeah. You're okay."

I was relieved. "Let's go get Lovie. If she'll talk to us. Your cart or mine?"

Macon sauntered to my cart. "There's nothing to do around here, so yeah, fine. Let's go."

Lovie's Aunt Sissy's house was smaller, more like Honey's Bird's Nest. It had a great view of the lagoon. Lovie came running out. She was her regular energetic self.

"Where are we going, guys?"

"The Nature Center," Macon and I both answered at the same time. Then laughed.

I drove us down the wide cart path, careful not to hit the big ruts. I told them about the cannonball story. When I parked the cart, we all tumbled out and hurried inside to find it.

Sure enough, we found the cannonball in a display case. It was in a dark corner, closer to the floor. No wonder we'd missed it. A small yellowed card noted the finders—Eric Potter and Rand Piper—and that the cannonball was found in 1985.

"Maybe we can find a cannonball," said Macon.

"Let's try," I agreed, wanting to find one just like my dad did.

"Cool fact," said Macon. "Did you know the first cannon was in China? And that they also invented gunpowder?"

I raised my brows. I didn't know that. "We have to get out and start exploring. What do you say?"

"Y'all, I've got an idea. Follow me!" Lovie said, and darted out the door, right down the stairs.

We ran after her and down the main dirt path.

"Why are we running?" I yelled out. "Let's take the cart."

"No! Keep up!" she yelled back.

"I don't think she knows how to *walk* anywhere," muttered Macon.

Macon and I raced to catch up. Lovie glanced over her shoulder, taunting us, and ran even faster. Her long braid bounced against her back. Macon and I picked up our speed too, zooming right past the crabbing dock where a man and a woman were scurrying around with nets.

Just beyond the dock, the dark blue water teemed with noisy birds of all sorts. We came to another section of the lagoon. There, on a wide, flat dock floating on the water's surface, were several kayaks, life jackets, and paddles. Macon and I were bent over, trying to catch our breath from the run.

We must've had a confused look on our faces, because Lovie called out, "What are you guys waiting for? You said you wanted to explore, didn't you?"

"Yeah . . . ," I replied, straightening.

"Then grab a life jacket. We're going kayaking!" Lovie was already putting on an orange-and-yellow life jacket.

"We can't just take a kayak. They don't belong to us."

"It's okay. They're here for us to borrow."

"I don't know. I haven't been in a kayak since I was six," I admitted. "And I didn't even do the paddling."

"It's easy! I'll teach you." Lovie grabbed a paddle and walked to the edge of the dock. She took hold of the orange kayak.

"First, you have to straddle the kayak on either side, like this," she said, demonstrating. "Then you plop your butt in."

Lovie slipped right into the seat of the kayak. "The secret is to find your center and sit fast. And don't lean too far to either side."

It looked easy enough. I slipped into my life jacket, eager to try. I put my paddle on the edge of the dock and pushed a yellow kayak into the water, careful to do exactly as Lovie had. I was proud of myself when my butt hit the inside of the kayak.

"Good job! Now your turn," she called to Macon.

"No way!" Macon shouted. "I've never kayaked before and I'm not going to start now."

"Oh, come on, party pooper. Aren't you a Boy Scout?" Lovie called back.

Macon tensed up like a mad cat in a corner, ready for a fight. "Well, this Boy Scout prefers keeping his feet on dry land. I've seen all the dark alligator heads and the lumpy ridges of their backs at the water's surface. I'm not gonna be gator food. Y'all ridiculous people go right on ahead."

His words made me feel a little less brave. I quietly scanned the lagoon . . . just in case.

"Oh, come on! Look at Jake. He barely knows what he's doing and he's trying."

"Hey, thanks a lot," I kidded.

"It'll be so much fun. Pleeeeease . . . ," Lovie begged.

Macon crossed his arms. "Fact: Drowning is the fifth leading cause of unintentional death. You think I'm crazy enough to get in that wobbly excuse for a boat? Nope. Nada. Not happening."

Lovie rolled her eyes. "Don't be so dramatic. You won't drown if you're wearing one of these." She pointed both index fingers to her life jacket.

"The facts still stand. One in every five drownings is a kid fourteen or younger. That's my demographic. And that life jacket won't save any of you from a hungry gator."

"Would you stop bringing up the alligators please," I said.

"They're not going to eat us in the kayak. Come on, Macon," Lovie shouted out. "We'll be explorers!"

"I'll tell you what," he called back. "You guys paddle to my boat dock. I'll track you on the land. And we'll see who gets to my dock first."

"Sounds good to me," I said. "We can be Lewis and Clark."

"And I'll be Sacagawea," Lovie said.

"Who's that?" I asked.

Lovie's eyes flashed in annoyance. "If you know who Lewis and Clark were, then you should know her, too. Sacagawea was a Native American woman who helped Lewis and Clark in their expedition. She knew about the wilderness and animals and plants. In fact, they probably wouldn't have made it without her."

"Okay then," I said. "You're Sacagawea."

Lovie smiled, pleased. "High tide's coming in. Let's go!" She pushed off from the dock with the tip of her paddle.

I scrambled to do the same, rocking my kayak.

"I'm off too!" Macon said, and took off running.

Lovie was a good teacher. She was patient as she showed me how to power forward and backward with my paddle. It had a blade on each end, shaped like a bird feather. I took one stroke. Then another. And another. Soon enough I caught the rhythm and was gliding alongside Lovie. It wasn't as wobbly in the kayak as I thought it'd be.

It was just the two of us. Lovie and I stayed in the narrow creeks, close to shore, so I wasn't worried about falling into the water.

Out on the water, the island world appeared so different.

Thick, gooey mud lined the creek banks, and all over them, I could see tiny crabs. They all had one larger claw that they lifted into the air. When they climbed out of the mud, they made soft popping noises that I could hear up close. But when my shadow approached, they scurried away, ducking into their little muddy holes.

"What are those crabs in the mud with the one Hulk-like claw?" I called out to Lovie.

Lovie giggled. The sound of her high laugh made me smile. "Fiddler crabs," she called back from her kayak. "There are a gazillion of them in the pluff mud."

"What's pluff mud?"

"You're kidding. You don't know what pluff mud is?"

"Why do you think I asked?"

"It's that gooey mud that's all around you."

I crinkled my nose. "It stinks."

She laughed again. "You get used to it. My mama calls it 'the Lowcountry perfume.'"

The sun was bright overhead and sparkled on the water. As we made our way along the creek, I *did* feel like an explorer. There was something to discover at every turn. When our kayaks took the next bend in the creek, a lone white egret burst into the sky with its black legs dangling behind. Small silver fish jumped out of the water ahead of us. A big fish with one black spot on its tail skimmed right next to my kayak, so close I could have caught it with my bare hands.

I ran my fingers across the top of the cool, smooth water.

But I kept my eyes peeled for signs of alligators. Sharks too.

Macon whistled at us from the shore, the two-fingers-in-the-mouth kind of way, which made it extra loud. I raised my paddle up in the air to signal back.

"Hey, Lewis!" I called out.

"Hey, Clark!" He waved and then dashed back into the shadows of the towering trees.

"I can't wait to draw all these things in my journal," I called out.

Lovie stopped paddling to get close to me so we wouldn't have to shout. We floated slowly down the creek, the dark water lapping the edges of the kayaks.

"You're becoming a real naturalist, Jake," she said. "Complete with a journal. I started mine. I'm enjoying writing about my day. It's like a diary."

"I'm not so good writing about my day," I confessed. "I mostly draw pictures. But . . . I started writing to my dad instead. Letters. Most every day. I can tell him everything—what I saw and how I'm feeling. It's like, when I'm writing to him, I feel like he's with me." I shook my head, feeling a little embarrassed. "Sounds weird, I guess."

"No, it doesn't," she said to me.

I looked over to see if she was serious. Her eyes were soft with concern.

"It makes sense." She smiled, kind of shyly. "At least to me."

Before I knew it, I was spilling the beans about all my worries about my dad and his lost leg. Beneath the warm sun, tucked in this watery maze, it felt like the power of the tide pulled it all right out of me.

Lovie grew very quiet. I suddenly realized I'd been doing all the talking.

"Sorry," I said awkwardly. "I'm talking a lot. I'm boring you."

"No," Lovie answered quickly. She shook her head. "It's just . . ." She looked away.

"Just what?"

"While I was listening to you talk about your dad and mailing letters to him, I was thinking about my own father and thought . . . well . . . maybe I should write a letter to him."

"But doesn't he, like, live with you?"

She stopped paddling. I stopped too, and the world fell quiet. Our kayaks floated on the surface of the water, side by side.

"I'm going to tell you something, and you have to promise to keep it secret."

"Okay. I promise."

"My daddy, Ethan"—she paused—"he's not my actual dad."

That didn't seem like such a big secret. "Are your parents divorced?"

She shook her head. "No. They were never married. Ethan is the only father I've ever known. He's my *real* dad. But my biological father, Darryl . . ." She looked away, then blurted out, "He's in prison."

My mouth slipped open. *Prison?* I had never known anyone who went to prison.

Lovie shrugged, seeing my expression. "Yeah, that's how everyone acts when they find out, so I don't like to tell people."

"What did he do to go to prison for?"

"Stealing. He's not a thief. I mean, he stole," she tried to explain. "Darryl's a musician, but I don't think he made much money. So, he stole stuff to keep going." She rolled her eyes. "A lot. Mama said the law finally caught up with him."

"I'm sorry, Lovie."

Lovie looked out at the water. "Nothing to be sorry about. But it's not the kind of thing I'm proud of."

"Do you ever see him?"

She shook her head. "He sent me a couple of letters, but my mama made him stop. She doesn't want anything to do with him. I love my real dad. He adopted me and all. But sometimes, I can't help but wonder about Darryl. I'm curious, you know? Especially when I hear you talk about your dad. Him being so far away, I mean."

"Why don't you write him a letter?" The answer seemed easy to me.

"I don't know," Lovie said with a frown of worry. "What would I even say?"

"How about you ask him how he is? And the things you're curious to know?"

She shook her head again. "Oh boy. Mama would flip her lid if I did that. She doesn't like me to even mention his name."

"I felt better when I started mailing my letters to my dad. I haven't heard back from him. But still, it makes me feel"—I shrugged—"like he's not so far away."

Lovie picked up her paddle. "Let's stop talking about this," she said in that way she had when she was annoyed. "I just wanted you to know why I was acting weird when you were talking about your daddy." She pointed at me and narrowed her eyes. "And promise you won't tell anyone. Not ever!"

I didn't know why she got mad all of a sudden, but I wanted her to feel better. "I promise."

I felt bad, though. I'd been spending all my summer thinking about my father, and not once did I think to ask about her own family. Or even Macon's mom.

"Come on, let's go," she said, digging one end of her paddle into the water to get the kayak moving faster. "Macon's probably already at the dock."

Lovie started paddling. Hard and fast. That was the Lovie I knew. By the time I got my rhythm back, my arms were burning and she'd already disappeared around the next bend.

CHAPTER 12

The Abandoned Boat

Nature is full of surprises.

"**J**AKE! JAKE! HURRY!"

My heart pounded in my ears. *Is Lovie in trouble?* I dug my paddle blades into the water harder and faster than before. Sweat beaded on my brow and my tired muscles burned, but I didn't stop.

At last I rounded the bend. I stopped paddling and stared, panting. I swiped the sweat from my brow. Ahead was a filthy-looking small white boat. And standing on this vessel was Lovie.

"Look what I found!" she yelled, waving me near. She was almost jumping up and down.

I paddled closer and saw that she was standing on a flat-bottomed boat with low sides. It was covered from stem to stern in rust and mud and crusty splatters of bird poo. It was a mess. But I could tell Lovie thought it was great.

"Climb aboard, mate," she said.

"We can't just climb onto someone's boat."

She laughed, her eyes bright with discovery. "It's abandoned. Don't you get it? Finders keepers. Jake, this is now *our* boat!"

What? I brightened and a grin spread across my face. At last, I had a boat!

I had fresh energy as I paddled closer to the edge of the boat. My thrill at owning a boat dimmed when I saw its condition. Up close, it looked even worse. "Are you sure this thing will hold us? It looks ready to sink."

Lovie gave a mischievous smile. "We'll find out soon enough. Now, come on, don't be scared. What's the worst that can happen?"

"It'll sink and we'd get wet," I called back. Then added sourly, "And I'm not scared."

I gripped the rim of the boat. The pluff mud stank and it made the boat's rim slippery. I pulled myself up, careful not to flip out of the kayak. The bottom of my pants was covered with slime, and the bottom of the small boat had a film of mud that covered my shoes. I almost slipped.

"Careful!" Lovie called out. Then muttered with a tease, "Landlubber."

My cheeks flamed as we pulled our kayaks and paddles onto the boat. That left very little room for us.

Lovie went to stand near the motor.

I squeezed in beside her. "What kind of a boat is it?" I smirked. "Besides funny-looking."

"It's a flat-bottomed skiff. Perfect for these shallow creeks. It's not supposed to get stuck in the mud."

"Who would just leave a boat in the creek?"

"Lots of people do. My mama said that people can't afford to tow them when they get stuck or fix them, so they just leave them." Lovie ran her hand across a layer of muck. "Gross!" She immediately wiped her hands on her blue jean shorts, now streaked with brown. "This hunk of junk has been out here awhile. I've seen this kind of thing a few times before when I've been puttering around on my boat."

"Well, if this boat is abandoned, it probably doesn't work anyway." I pulled my backpack off and got out my thermos and two snack bags of chips. "Let's take a break." I poured her a cup of water. She took it gratefully.

"Thanks." Lovie chugged her water.

I chewed my chips while checking out the boat. "Is it hard learning to drive a boat?"

"There's a lot to learn. You have to study. But it's fun kind of learning." Lovie handed me back the thermos and accepted some chips.

I took a long swallow of water, looking out at the acres of waving grass.

"A guy could get lost out here."

"Sure. Some do. But there are a lot of signs and markers you'll learn too," Lovie said. "And of course, rules and safety tips. Like what HELP stands for." She cocked her head. "Do you know that one?"

"I didn't know it stood for anything but . . ." I pretended I was falling out of the boat. "Heeeeellllllp me!"

She laughed. "Close. In boating, HELP means Heat Escape Lessening Posture. It's what you do if you fall overboard and must wait for rescue. Like this," she said, and pulled her knees up to her chest and wrapped her arms around her legs. "See? When you're balled up like this, it keeps you warm."

"Okay."

"Yeah," she said, straightening. "You learn some important stuff in the course. Some of it will save your life. Then you have to take a test. If you pass, *ta-da*!" She spread out her hands. "You're certified. You can drive a boat."

I couldn't wait, but tried to sound cocky. "Sounds easy enough." I crumpled up my chip bag and looked for somewhere to toss it.

Lovie pointed to my backpack. "What you bring to the river, you carry back."

"I was looking for the trash," I said defensively.

"Your backpack," she said, pointing again.

I put the paper bag into my backpack to carry home. Then took a final swig of water from my thermos and put that back in too. I zipped up the backpack; snack time was over.

"I want to get my license before summer's end," I told her. "Will you help me?"

"Absolutely." Lovie gave me one of her firm handshakes. "We can start now." She wiped her hands on her shorts and turned her attention to the boat's motor. "Let's see if I can get this baby to turn on."

"You think you can do that?" I asked in awe.

She gave me a smug smile. "I can try."

I doubted the dirty old motor would work, but watched her every move as she tinkered with the engine. Her small fingers worked quickly as she pulled on this and pushed on that. I couldn't wait to learn how to do all this myself.

I looked out over the water. The tide was moving in fast. The mud was already completely covered. Only the tips of the marsh grass were visible.

Lovie straightened and wiped her hands on her shorts again. "Okay, I think we're ready to see if it'll work." She crossed fingers for luck.

I smiled and crossed my fingers too.

Lovie bent over the engine and did one rapid pull on a cord. Instantly the engine sprang to life.

We looked at each other in shock, then fist-pumped the air.

"Yeah!" we both hollered.

"I can't believe it *actually* works!" she cried. "Okay Jake, you're getting your first lesson in boating." She pointed as she spoke. "Fuel line . . . choke knob . . . throttle handle . . . kill switch."

I hovered close and watched, listened, and learned. My blood was pumping like fuel through the rumbling motor.

Lovie lifted her chin. Her eyes were gleaming. "The engine's working. The tide is high. It's time to take her out and see what she's got." She looked at me. "I need a push."

"What?" I looked at her dumbly.

"A push. We need to get out of the mud."

It took me a minute to understand what she meant. "You want *me* to get in that mud? With all those bugs and crabs?"

"Uh, yeah. We can't go unless you do. *I* can't do it. I have to drive the boat."

"But . . . ," I sputtered, looking back at the marsh.

"Do you want this boat or not?"

I thought of the other things that could be lurking—like alligators and water moccasins. But I wanted the boat more.

"Okay," I said grudgingly.

"You'd better take your shoes off," Lovie said. "They'll get stuck in the pluff mud."

"No way I'm stepping in that muck in my bare feet."

Lovie merely shrugged. "Suit yourself. But don't say I didn't warn you."

With a grunt I climbed over the kayaks to the rear of the boat. Making a face, I said out loud, "Yuuuuuuck!"

Lovie giggled. "Oh, go on, silly. It's just mud."

Slowly, thinking of crabs, I eased myself over the side of the boat. First my toes, then my feet sank down deep into the slippery brown goo.

"This is so gross," I muttered. It felt like I was walking in slime. "Now what?"

"The front of the boat is called the bow. Go there."

The mud made a sucking, slurpy sound with each step I made. Step by step, I plodded through the thick mud as it got deeper. Then I raised my foot—and my sneaker was gone.

"My shoe!" I cried. "It came off."

"You'll never find it," Lovie called back. "Just keep going."

"But . . ."

"I tried to warn you."

I fumed but couldn't stop now. I was up to my knees in it.

"You sure this isn't quicksand?" I yelled back.

"It's just pluff mud, but it can suck you down . . . a bit. Don't worry, Jake," she called to me. "You're almost there."

I finally reached the front of the boat, lifting my knees high to plow through the mucky mud.

"I'm going to put the engine in reverse," Lovie called out. "When I do, you push hard. With all your might. Got it?"

I gritted my teeth and lowered my weight onto my left foot. I sank a few inches deeper into the goo, then stopped, praying it wasn't a bit like quicksand. "Hurry up!" I shouted. "I'm sinking!"

"Ready?" she yelled. "Now!"

I grunted and pushed with all my might as the engine rumbled low in the water. To my surprise—and relief—the boat slowly eased away from the muddy bank.

"Woot!" I called out, feeling the boat slide forward.

"Hop on!" Lovie called.

I tried to move, but my feet wouldn't budge. The mud was gripping my legs.

"Lovie, I can't move!" I called out. My heart was pounding fast as I imagined being sucked down into the mud, disappearing forever.

"Don't panic," Lovie called out, and put the engine in neutral. She hurried to the bow. "You can get out. Bend forward and try to lie on the mud."

"Lie on it?" I shook my head as fear licked my spine. "I'll sink faster."

"No, you won't. It's a trick. We all know it. Do you trust me?"

I nodded.

"Lie flat. Then slowly wiggle your legs out of the mud. Then crawl on the mud to the shore. The mud is harder there. You can climb back in the boat. Go on now, hurry!"

I decided to trust Lovie. She was my friend. And she knew a lot about living in the Lowcountry.

I leaned far forward till I was lying on my belly in the thick mud. I didn't sink! My face was getting coated with the stinky mud as I wiggled my legs. At last, one by one, I got them out from the mud's gooey hold. Without shoes!

I crawled a foot or two closer to shore and could feel the mud thicken. When I lowered my feet again, I was able to stand. I quickly reached out and grabbed hold of the boat before it drifted farther away. Lovie grasped my arms, and we groaned as together we dragged my body back into the boat.

"Ugh," I said in relief when I landed hard on the bottom of the boat. I was covered from head to toe in mud. Even my face was smeared with it.

Lovie released another high, trilling laugh. She hurried to the steering wheel and looked over her shoulder. "Look at you. You're covered in pluff mud."

"It smells like rotten eggs."

"You're now officially a Lowcountry kid."

I looked at my mud-caked legs and clothes and laughed too. I liked that title.

Lovie moved like a pro as she maneuvered the skiff into the deeper water of the creek. I have to admit, I was pretty impressed with her seamanship.

"Take a look and see if there's a leak," she called back to me. "We don't want to go far if we take on water."

"Aye aye, captain!" I moved the kayaks to get a good look at the floor of the boat.

"Looks good."

"Here we go!"

I held on to the side of the boat as Lovie accelerated. The little flat-bottomed boat took off down the creek, skimming over the water. Feeling the wind on my face felt so good I couldn't stop grinning.

"Let's get over to Macon's dock," I shouted. "He's going to flip out when he sees us!"

When we reached Macon's dock, Lovie slowed the engine to a low growl.

"Hey! You guys!"

We both turned to see Macon standing at the end of his dock, his hands on his head and his mouth wide open in shock.

"Told you he'd be surprised," I said.

"Look what we found!" Lovie shouted to Macon.

Macon ran up to us, his big feet pounding on the wooden boards. When he got close, I could tell he wasn't surprised. He was mad.

"What have you done?" Macon shouted. "You *stole* a boat?"

"We didn't *steal* it!" I called back. "We found it. It was abandoned."

"Mom's going to freak out when she sees this." Macon paced the dock, muttering to himself, then stopped short. "No. She *can't* see this. I can't let her get upset." He pointed to the boat. "Get this . . . thing outta here. Now!"

"Wait, wait," I said, trying to calm him down. "We're just leaving it for a little while. Until we figure out what to do with it. We'll move it. But come on. You've got to admit, it's pretty cool." I grinned wide.

Macon wasn't convinced. He looked at me covered in mud and raised his brow. Then he sniffed and made a face. "You stink."

I laughed and nodded. "Pluff mud. It's bad."

Lovie and I climbed up onto the dock. We all crossed our arms and stood side by side on the dock and looked out at the dirty little boat in tense silence.

"It can't stay here," Macon said.

"Okay, we should've asked your permission," I said. "But you weren't there and here we are."

"And out it has to go."

"I know you're mad," I said.

"You think?" he snapped back.

"Come on, Macon," Lovie said. "It's a real find. A treasure!"

"Oh sure, a treasure," Macon replied with sarcasm. "Are you looking at the same boat I am? This thing looks like it was pulled out of a dumpster and then pooped on by a flock of angry pelicans. Even *they* thought it looked bad. And it stinks!"

His comment triggered a burst of laughter from me and Lovie.

"Yeah, but it works," Lovie said smugly.

"Can we dock it here? Just till we find someplace else?"

"Please," Lovie begged. "If you let us keep it here, we'll clean it up and make it our own. Jake could get his boating certification. So could you."

This argument made a dent in Macon's resistance. I could see him considering that possibility. We'd talked a lot about getting our boater's licenses.

"Hey, it might be our only chance for it," I added pleadingly.

"We're actually doing a good thing," Lovie said. "We're cleaning up the creek. The boat was lying there. We're giving it a new lease on life."

"Come on," I said. "It can be *our* boat. All of ours. We'd be the crew."

"Fine," Macon said in a clipped tone. "I'm only agreeing to this because my mom is usually stuck in a bed or in a sofa chair by windows that don't face the dock. She won't see it. But let's be clear." He pointed his finger at each of us. "I have nothing to do with this stupid idea of yours."

"You don't want to own it?" I asked.

He shook his head. "If you did something like this back in the city, you can bet a cop would be knocking on your door asking a lot of questions."

"But we can keep it here?" I clarified.

"For a little while. Just till you find somewhere else."

"Thanks, Macon," I said, punching him in his shoulder.

"Yeah, yeah," Macon grumbled back. "And for the record, y'all are crazy people. And you need a shower. You smell like a giant fart."

Lovie drew near, her face serious. "We're sworn to secrecy, okay? This is our boat now."

Macon was doubtful. "I thought you said you found this boat."

"We did."

"Then why the secrecy?"

"'Cause after we fix it up and scrub it clean, we don't want someone claiming it, do we? After all our work?"

"Okay, I get that," Macon said.

"We'll make it shine," I said, feeling ownership of the boat already. It was my first boat, after all.

"We need to name the boat," said Lovie.

"How about the *Buzzard*?" Macon suggested.

We all laughed. The boat was covered in gray mud and looked like roadkill.

"No, it needs a noble name," Lovie argued.

"How about the *Fiddler Crab*?" I asked. "It was found in the mud, it's little, and it's quick."

"Perfect," Lovie exclaimed. "Now let's scrub the *Fiddler Crab* clean before we return the kayaks."

> Journal of Jake Potter
> A fiddler crab has one large claw. They got their name because when they wave the claw in the air, it looks like they are playing the fiddle. Nature is full of funny surprises.

CHAPTER 13

Crime and Punishment

Just when things start looking up, they all come crashing down again.

THAT NIGHT MY MUSCLES ACHED, AND I was so tired I could barely eat the hamburgers Honey fixed for dinner. She wasn't a fancy cook, but all the food was fresh, and to a starving man it tasted great.

I'd returned so dirty, I showered in the outdoor shower—twice—and removed my clothes before entering the house wrapped only in a towel. I didn't know how I'd tell Honey that I needed a new pair of sneakers.

After sunset, the night songs of insects swelled loud then soft, repeatedly. Their sounds seeped through the windows in the kitchen, where I sat writing another letter to Dad. I smiled when I wrote to him about finding the *Fiddler Crab* and capturing every amazing detail I had seen out on the water.

Honey came close and rested her hand on my shoulder. "Are you writing to your dad?"

"I just finished."

"That's fine. I started writing to him too."

I smiled up at her. She was really trying hard. The house was much cleaner after all the work she and Mrs. Simmons's maid, Miss Dana, did today. Honey had also showered and was wearing a pink shirt I'd never seen before.

"So, what do you have to show me tonight?" she asked me.

I was eager to show her my drawings. "We went kayaking today. I found a lot out on the mud." I moved my notebook closer to her. I showed her my sketch of the white bird rising from the mudflat. "I think that's an egret."

"I think you're right. Let's see what we can learn about it." Honey went to the guidebook and quickly located the snowy egret. She brought the book back to the table.

"It's an egret, all right. The egret is all white with black legs and those showy yellow feet. Years back, all the fine ladies wanted the white curving feathers of the snowy egret for their hats. So much so, the egrets were hunted to near extinction." She shook her head with sorrow. "All for women's hats. Thanks to the Migratory Bird Treaty Act, the egrets have been protected and the population has bounced back."

I thought that was a cool fact I could share with Macon.

"What else have you got there?" She turned the page and

chuckled. "A fiddler crab! Aren't they comical critters?"

Together, we laughed.

"You know, the male's the one with the lopsided claw," she said. "The females don't have the oversize claw. He waves that claw into the air to attract a mate. He uses it for fighting, too. But mostly for showing off."

I thought about our boat, the *Fiddler Crab*, but I didn't tell Honey about the boat or draw a picture of it. Macon, Lovie, and I made a pact to wait for the right moment to show everyone.

"You went kayaking in the marsh . . . ," she said wistfully.

"It's real pretty out there," I said.

"True enough," Honey said, settling into her chair. "The marsh is the mother of our three favorite foods: shrimp, crabs, and oysters. She bathes them and feeds them. And we love her for it. But looks can be deceiving," Honey warned with a raised finger. "You've got to be careful out in the marsh. The tides are the masters of the marsh and they don't suffer fools." She gave me a firm look.

"You should know. The water recedes fast and fills back up quick too. If you aren't mindful, you can find yourself stuck out there in the mud. Lots of folks do. They get lost, too. Have to wait to be rescued."

"Lovie told me that."

"She's a smart girl. Listen to her. She's lived here all her life. I want you to learn all about the Lowcountry too. Her beauties *and* her dangers."

"I already know about the pluff mud," I said with a wry grin. "It stinks."

Honey laughed. "I grant you, it's an acquired smell," she replied. "To me, pluff mud smells like home."

"I'm getting used to it."

"I thought you might. But mind you know what's lurking in the mud. You can get cut up by those razor-sharp oyster shells something fierce. They'll slice right through your boots."

I swallowed hard, thinking of walking around in the mud in my bare feet.

"And that muck can suck you in, good and proper." Honey chuckled. "You won't smell too good when you finally get out."

"Nope," I said, and shook my head.

The phone rang and we startled. We looked at each other, and I knew we were both thinking it was my parents. Honey rose to answer the phone and I trailed close behind.

"Hello?" I heard the tension in her voice. Then the surprise. "Why hello, Chief Rand. What?" Her smile fell and she glanced again at me. "Yes, all right. We'll be right over." She hung up the phone. "That's odd. Fire Chief Rand said there's a little problem and he needs *you* at the station right now." She raised an eyebrow. "What's going on?"

I swallowed hard but only shrugged. I had a very bad feeling about this.

"Well, hurry and get your shoes on. We'd best go."

"About my shoes . . ."

≈

We drove the golf cart in a silence as dark as the sky. The trees felt like towering, beastly shadows hovering over us. Honey maneuvered the cart carefully along the dark roads. No speeding tonight. We could see only as far ahead as the headlight beams.

When we arrived at the fire station, the big garage door was open. I saw a small group of people clustered in front of the red fire truck. No one was smiling. Their stern facial expressions made my stomach flip-flop like a fish on land. We parked and approached the group. I spotted Lovie first, her head hung low. She was standing next to her Aunt Sissy—a tall woman with short hair the color of sand.

"Hello, Sissy," Honey said as we approached.

"Well, Helen Potter," Aunt Sissy said with a smile of recognition. "It's nice to see you again. How are you, neighbor?"

They hugged and Honey replied, "I'd be better if I knew what was going on."

Aunt Sissy's lips were tight with worry. "I was just told to bring Lovie here."

I walked up to Lovie. "Did you have to come all the way from your mom's house on Isle of Palms?"

Lovie shook her head. "I was so tired, I asked my aunt if I could spend the night." She leaned closer and lowered her voice. It shook as she spoke. "Do you think this is about the boat?"

"I don't know." I could tell she was as scared as I was. "Where's Macon?"

Lovie shrugged. "I don't know. But his cart is here."

Fire Chief Rand was standing in the crowd with his arms crossed. I couldn't read his face to tell if he was mad.

We waited a few more minutes in tense silence before Macon came out from a side room of the fire station. He was followed by a tall man in a suit that I guessed was his father. He was stone-faced, but it was Macon's expression that really had me sweating. His face was set in a furious frown, and he wouldn't even look at Lovie and me.

Behind them was a police officer. Lovie and I looked at each other, our eyes wide with fear. Last came a short, bearded man with a pot belly, a torn T-shirt, and wearing only one white rubber boot that was caked in crusty mud. He didn't look one bit happy.

Rand cleared his throat to get our attention. "I'm sorry to call y'all out here at night, but it appears we've had a theft on the island. The Isle of Palms Police Department dispatched Officer Doyle here to follow up on the incident."

My dinner started churning like waves in my stomach as Lovie and I exchanged nervous glances.

"This gentleman"—Rand gestured toward mud man, who stood with crossed arms and a scowl—"is Oliver Middleton. Better known as Oysterman Ollie to some of you. He reported his boat missing late this afternoon. He'd left it on the back side of the island after running it aground at low tide. He waited onshore till the next tide to see if he could get it unstuck."

Honey turned to the mud-caked man. "Ollie, where's your other boot?"

A short laugh escaped, and I slapped my hand over my mouth.

"I don't think *any* of this is funny," said Oysterman Ollie, glaring at me.

"No sir," I replied, looking down at my spit-shined Sunday shoes.

Oysterman Ollie took a step forward, then wiped his mouth with his hand. "I was checkin' on my oyster beds, and my boat got stuck in the mud. It happens," he fired off as the men glanced at each other while holding back smiles. Everyone knew it was poor seamanship to get stuck in the mud at low tide.

"My boat was gone! As if that weren't bad enough," continued Oysterman Ollie, "I done lost a day's work *and* my boot!"

"But Ollie," Honey said, "what has this got to do with the children?"

Ollie pointed at us children with a mud-encrusted finger. "These water rats done stole what don't belong to them. I demand they return it!" He stomped his bare foot, causing a few clumps of dried mud to flake off his leg.

Honey's gaze swept over Lovie and Macon before landing on me. "Explain yourselves."

Lovie was the first to talk, but it was almost impossible to understand her through her sobs. "We . . . we didn't know it was his boat. We . . . thought it was abandoned."

"I told them so," muttered Macon.

I glanced at Macon. The muscle on the side of his jaw moved as he clenched his teeth.

Ollie stepped closer to Lovie and peered into her face. "You're Darryl's young'un, aren't you?"

Lovie paled and stared back at him, not answering.

"I see the ol' apple doesn't fall far from the tree," he jeered at her.

"Excuse me!" Lovie's Aunt Sissy protested. "That's uncalled for. Mind your words, or you'll hear from me."

I looked at Lovie and thought she might crumple. "We're really sorry, sir!" I said to the oysterman. "We didn't mean to steal anything. Honest. We really thought it was abandoned. I mean, it was just a junky ol' boat sitting there, all covered with mud and bird poop. No one was around."

I heard a few muffled guffaws slip out from the adults crowded around us. Oysterman Ollie cut them a sharp look.

"Mr. Middleton," the police officer said in a calm voice, "we've gotten statements from all three of the children involved. You got your boat back. In fact, the boat's in better shape than you left it."

The oysterman snorted at that remark. "What about my being bothered? Lost hours lookin' for it."

"Mr. Simmons has offered to reimburse you for your inconvenience and any work time that was lost." The officer nodded toward Macon's dad.

Oysterman Ollie only grunted and rubbed his jaw.

The police officer rocked on his heels. "Let's settle this and get you and your boat back home. I'm sure you're eager to get home and cleaned up after your long day."

"These kids should get jail time," Oysterman Ollie muttered. "Thieves, the lot of 'em."

Chief Rand spoke up this time. "Come on now, Ollie. You don't really mean that. We were kids once too," he said, then he turned toward us. I stood taller, at attention. *Could we really go to jail for this?* I wondered. My lungs ached from holding my breath.

"Let me be clear, kids," Chief Rand said. "What you did was stupid. And *wrong*."

The police officer leaned in with a dead-serious look. "This man has every right to press charges against you for stealing his personal property. And if he did, you'd have to go to court and let the judge issue your punishment, hear?"

"Yes, sir," we all whispered in unison.

"Good. If you see an abandoned vessel, you report it to the authorities. Don't take it yourselves. Now, luckily, Mr. Middleton is not pressing charges, thanks to Mr. Simmons."

I glanced over at Mr. Simmons. He stood tall, shoulders back, his face stern. I could see why Macon was nervous about making his dad mad.

"You kids better steer clear of me and my boat from now on!" Oysterman Ollie yelled. "And I better not see any of ya in my oyster beds, either. Or I won't be so . . . agreeable next time."

The police officer said with a warning in his voice, "No

threats, Ollie." He turned to the adults. "I think we're done here. I'm going to escort Mr. Middleton to get his boat. Good night."

Oysterman Ollie mumbled under his breath as he walked away with the officer.

Some of the tension in the room lifted.

Fire Chief Rand put his hands on his hips. "Kids, you stay right here a minute while we grown-ups figure out what to do with you."

We watched, wide-eyed, as the adults stepped into the adjoining room and shut the door.

This was the moment Macon was waiting for. He looked fit to explode.

"I knew it!" he hissed, eyes flaming. "I knew I shouldn't have let you two convince me to help you with that stolen hunk of junk." He pointed at Lovie and me. "Y'all stole it—and I got the blame for it."

"*You* didn't get the blame," Lovie argued. "We all did."

He scowled at her. "Oh yeah? Whose dock was the boat found at? Whose house did the police visit? *Mine!* Do you know how scared I was? I mean, I don't know what would have happened if my daddy hadn't come home today. My mom's real upset. And now he's royally mad at me. Because of you two!" He jabbed his index finger our way.

"I . . . I'm really sorry," Lovie said. Tears brimmed in her eyes. "I'm not a thief. I . . . I didn't mean to steal it."

"Come on, Macon. We didn't know. It was an honest mistake," I added.

"You just don't get it. You just don't get it! You're not the one who had the police show up at your door. You're not the one taking the heat for someone else's stupid idea. You're not the one whose parents are super upset!" He backhanded his mouth and took a deep breath. "This is your nice, safe town. You should know. Things like this don't always end so nice in the city. Especially not for a Black kid. It's a good thing my dad is a lawyer. If it wasn't for him, we all might be headed for juvie." He snorted. "Me, for sure." Macon lifted his hands over his head. *You stole a freaking boat!*" He shouted the last part. Then he walked away—as far away from us as he could get.

The hum of the overhead lights filled the silence between us. I wrestled with what to do next. He totally hated us now. Sure, Lovie said the boat was abandoned, but I totally went along with it. I was just as stupid as she was. I didn't think Macon would ever forgive us. I glanced over to where Macon was standing alone by the fire hydrant, head bent and hands in his pockets.

A metal door squeaked open. Fire Chief Rand, Mr. Simmons, Honey, and Aunt Sissy stepped out, their faces grim.

"Gather round," Chief Rand said, waving us closer.

When we gathered in front of the adults, they all looked at us with serious expressions.

Chief Rand put his hands on his hips and gave the three of us kids a long stare. We each straightened as we looked back.

"Mr. Middleton didn't press charges." Rand turned toward

Macon's dad. "Mr. Simmons saved your tails with his generous check to Oysterman Ollie."

"Thank you," we all replied in hushed voices.

Mr. Simmons nodded in acknowledgment.

Honey spoke up. "Mr. Simmons, I hope you'll allow us to pay our portion of whatever you paid Ollie."

Mr. Simmons smiled at Honey, then at Aunt Sissy. "I wouldn't mind another one of those fine pies."

Honey grinned and brought her hands together. "You've got it. With my gratitude."

Chief Rand spoke up. "Just because a police report wasn't filed doesn't mean you are off scot-free." He gave us kids a stern look. "The fact remains that you were in the wrong."

In his pause I heard Lovie choke back a sob.

"We adults have discussed the situation and agreed that you children need to learn that actions have consequences. You will be held accountable. Starting tomorrow morning," Chief Rand said, "you will begin island community service."

I sucked in my breath and looked at Macon, but he kept his eyes on the ground, his fists clenched at his thighs. He was definitely giving me the cold shoulder. Not that I blamed him.

"For the next six weeks," said Chief Rand, "you will work together to help the Dewees Island Turtle Team. Helen Potter has agreed to be your supervisor."

I looked at my grandmother with surprise. She nodded with a no-nonsense expression and stepped forward.

"Okay then. Eyes up here," Honey began. She waited until

all our eyes were on her. "You three children are responsible for arriving at the gazebo each morning at six thirty sharp."

When she saw our faces, she added, "That's why it's called the *Dawn Patrol*." She pointed at us. "Don't be late. Every morning we will walk the high tide line on the lookout for loggerhead turtle tracks. Don't worry, I'll teach you all you need to know about how to spot them." She moved her hands to her hips and glared. "No grousing or grudges. No show-offs. You will work as a team. And your nest reports must be done by seven a.m. That's every morning, seven days a week, hear? Turtles don't know the meaning of a weekend."

"Ughhh," I moaned under my breath.

"My summer is officially ruined," Macon grumbled.

Out of the corner of my eye I caught Lovie doing a little fist pump. She was happy about the sentence! And she definitely was the only one of us who felt that way.

CHAPTER 14

Dawn Patrol

What's life without hope?

DAWN PATROL BEGAN—NO SURPRISE—AT dawn.

The sky was dusty gray when I awoke, brightening to soft pine while I ate my cereal. I grumbled as I chewed, but Honey gave me a no-nonsense look.

"You better keep that grumbling to yourself, young man. You brought this on yourself. And remember, I'm getting up early too. Helping you out," Honey said, then took a sip of her coffee.

In truth, Honey didn't look put out. She looked cheerful at the prospect of getting up early and back out on the beach.

Honey had told me last night that she used to be the leader of the Dewees Island Turtle Team. After my grandpa died, she'd stopped.

"I haven't worn this old uniform in ages," Honey said.

She didn't look any different to me. She had on a green SEA TURTLE PATROL T-shirt, khaki hiking shorts, a wide-brimmed hat, and Teva sandals.

"If you're ready, let's go. We can't be late."

Macon and Lovie were waiting for us at the gazebo. Honey pulled out a paper bag from the cubby in our cart. She handed me, Lovie, and Macon green T-shirts.

"These are your Turtle Team shirts. I think I found the right sizes. I have another to give each of you. Nice blue ones. It's your uniform out here every day, okay? It's a way of letting people on the beach know who we are and what we're doing."

She paused as we all looked at the shirts.

"Well, what are you waiting for? Put them on."

Immediately we all pulled the shirts on over our other shirts.

She reached again into the bag and pulled out two black-and-white composition notebooks, just like the one I'd been using.

"These are your nature notebooks. You can use them to write down all you see, all you find, all you learn. Especially about the turtles. There's a lot to learn out here, a lot to get excited about. I'm going to share some of what I know. To help you understand what a special place on earth we are lucky enough to live on. I'm hoping when we're done, you won't see these excursions as punishments, but you'll be glad for this time we share."

When none of us spoke, she straightened and said more firmly, "Someday, you'll thank me. Any questions?"

"Thank you!" Lovie exclaimed. She was beaming down at her new shirt.

Honey smiled and slipped on her sunglasses. "Okay then, Dawn Patrol. Let's go!" She began walking down the narrow beach-access path.

Macon shot me and Lovie a look. He didn't need words to tell us he was annoyed. He marched ahead of me and Lovie, his heels digging deep into the sand.

When we reached the beach, I felt the familiar welcome breeze on my face and caught the salty scent.

I'd never seen the beach this early in the morning. The sun was rising over the ocean, spreading pink light across the sand. The water was calm and gentle, and rose-tipped waves seemed to whisper *shhhh shhhh* as they lapped the shoreline. The sand was smooth, unscarred by footprints. Even the birds were quiet. It felt like the world was awakening.

"Kids, this is the best time of the day to come to the beach," Honey said, taking in a deep breath and staring out at the sea. "I near forgot this." Then she seemed to collect herself and pointed to a long line of seagrass, shells, and dirt that ran parallel to the dunes.

"See that line of wrack?"

"What's wrack?" I asked.

"That's the line of seaweed and bits of broken shells, stone, and loose material that the tide carries in. We call that the high tide line."

"What does high tide mean, exactly?" Macon asked.

"Good question. Well, sir, it has to do with the gravitational pull of the moon," Honey explained. "You know when you are at the beach and watch the water slowly creep farther up the sand? Then, hours later, the water level goes down again? That's the tides at work. It repeats twice a day on a regular cycle, every day. So, to answer your question, high tide is when the water level is highest, and low tide is when the water level is lowest."

Honey pointed to the beach. "See how smooth the sand is below the line of wrack? That's because the sea rose all the way up to that line, leaving everything below it swept nice and clean. When it went back out, it left all the debris, or wrack, it carried. That's what forms the high tide line. And that, children, is our marker for where to walk. Why do you think that is?"

Lovie eagerly gave the answer. "Because the turtle tracks get washed away by the sea below the high tide line."

"That's right. The tracks above the high tide line won't get washed away, so you'll spot them. If you're walking along the water, you might miss the tracks."

Honey said, "Turtle tracks are usually about two feet wide. Just holler if you see anything that looks like tire tracks. You'll get to know the difference right quick. Okay, let's move on!"

We walked along the high tide line as the sun rose in the east. Lovie sprinted ahead when she spotted her nest. The orange tape surrounding it was secure. Honey stopped and bent low to look at the nest carefully.

"I'm looking to check if any ghost crabs dug into the nest," she said.

I crouched low. I wanted to see the small, pale white crab. When I was five, my dad and I walked the beach at night on the hunt for ghost crabs. We'd see them scamper on their claws like tiny dancers across the sand while I tried to catch them with my net.

"See that hole there?" Honey asked.

"Yes," we all answered as we spotted the small hole about a foot away from the nest in the dune.

"Ghost crabs are one of many predators that eat hatchlings," Honey said. "Can you think of others?"

"Birds," I said.

"Right. They'll swoop down from the sky to gobble one up. What else?"

"Raccoons," said Lovie.

"Coyotes," said Macon.

"You're all correct. There are lots of predators for hatchlings on the beach. And once they reach the sea, other predators attack. Fish, dolphins, sharks will eat them from below. It's a perilous trip for our hatchlings. Only one in one thousand hatchlings will survive to adulthood."

Macon released a soft whistle of surprise that spoke for all of us.

"Why so few?" I asked.

"It's the way of nature," Honey replied. "Some animals have only one or two offspring, like humans, dolphins, birds. We nurture our young till they are strong enough to leave the nest and our care. Other animals lay lots of eggs all at once, like fish and reptiles. Turtles are reptiles, don't forget. The mother lays the eggs and often leaves them, not to return to care for them. This isn't bad. It's their way. Because there are so many eggs, it's expected some of them will get eaten. Other species need to survive too. Enough eggs survive and hatch, however, to keep the sea turtle species alive."

"So that's why turtles lay so many eggs?" I asked.

"Yes," Honey replied. "A mother turtle comes ashore and lays a lot of eggs. Then she goes back to the sea and won't return. And that," she said with a quick smile, "is why we're here to help."

"Yeah," said Macon with a fist pump.

Lovie and I looked at each other and smiled. Even though Macon might still be angry, he couldn't hide his enthusiasm.

"Well," Honey said rising, "everything looks good today. Let's keep moving!"

We walked on as the sun rose higher. The blue in the sky erased the pink. The heat was already rising too. I wiped the sweat from my brow as we marched on and checked on two more nests. Honey declared all was in good order. There were no new nests to report either.

I squinted, looking at a line in the distance that carved the sand from the shoreline to the dunes. I trotted ahead, eyes peeled. My heart started pounding faster as I grew closer. It sure looked like tire tracks to me!

"Honey! Come see!" I called out, and waved at her to hurry.

Macon and Lovie came running.

"Turtle tracks!" Lovie shouted when she reached me. She jumped up, clapping her hands, then sprinted toward the dunes, following the long line of tracks.

Honey arrived, a bit winded from the rush. She huffed and said, "Yep, sure looks like it. Let's check them out!"

Macon and I began running toward the dunes.

"Hold on, kids," Honey called, huffing a little as she followed the tracks higher up to the dunes. "Stay off the dunes. That's a big rule here. First, it's not good for the sea oats. But also, we can't mess up the field signs."

"What are field signs?" asked Macon.

Honey caught her breath and looked at the large circle of disrupted sand. "Well, now," she began. "Those are the signs we look for to find the eggs. We have to be like detectives, eh?"

That caught my attention. Macon and I drew near Honey as she pointed out the signs.

"The field signs are all the telling details that help the Turtle Team find the eggs. So careful where you step, hear?"

Honey pointed to the tracks above the high tide line. "Take a look. Those are the *incoming* tracks, where our mama turtle crawled out of the water. You can tell by looking at the direction that the sand is pushed by her flippers. Loggerhead tracks look like commas."

"They weren't washed away by the high tide," Macon said.

"That's right, Macon," Honey said, pleased with his answer. "Now, see how the tracks go up to that circle of stirred-up sand? That's where mama turtle stopped to lay her eggs. We call that the body pit. Let's check it out."

Macon was laser-focused on the tracks now as he followed Honey toward the dunes. He pointed to a second line of tracks. "If the other tracks were made by her coming in, then those must be the tracks she made going back to the ocean."

"Yes, indeed," said Honey. "You can tell by the difference in length that this turtle was up here for quite a while. And what do you think she was doing?"

"Laying eggs?" Lovie asked.

"Right again. I'll bet the team will find eggs in there, all right," Honey said, smiling. "Look carefully at that circle of sand. The turtle will dig with her hind flippers in a scooping motion to create the egg chamber. When she's done, she'll cover the eggs with her rear flippers and throw sand with her front flippers to camouflage her nest. Do you see any thrown sand?"

"Here!" called out Lovie, hurrying to sprayed sand near the nest.

"Right. Y'all make good team members."

I smiled but didn't reply. I was too busy drawing the tracks in my journal.

Honey put her hands on her hips and beamed with pride. "I'd say this is a great first day of turtle patrol for us. Now, let's measure the width of the tracks."

Honey pulled out a measuring tape from her bag and stretched it across the width of the tracks.

"Twenty-four inches," Honey called out. "Mark it down in your books, kids. Loggerheads are pretty much the only kind of sea turtle that nests on our beaches in South Carolina. I'm guessing this mama weighed at least three hundred pounds. Our work is done. Now it's time to notify the Turtle Team. We have to tell them of any tracks we find before seven a.m."

"We don't get to find the eggs?" Macon asked. I could see he wasn't ready to stop searching.

"Nope. You have to be permitted by the state to touch a turtle egg or get slapped with a huge fine." Honey pulled out a cell phone from her pocket.

"Wait. When did you get a cell phone?" I asked. "I didn't even know you owned one."

"Well, of course I do. For emergencies. And for when I'm on turtle patrol. Like now."

The three of us stood and waited. Macon was keeping a distance from me and Lovie. *This is going to be a long six weeks,* I thought.

Before long, we spotted two women wearing green Turtle Team T-shirts and backpacks walking toward us. One carried a red plastic bucket. The ends of the wooden stakes were poking out the top. The other had a long yellow pole with a handle that looked like the letter T.

"Hey there, Helen," they called out, and greeted Honey with hugs. "So glad to see you back out on the beach."

One woman with sandy blond, short hair, blue eyes, and a kind smile walked up to us. "Hey, kids! I hear you're helping us out this summer. Welcome! My name is Judy, and this is Alicia and Claudia."

The woman had long red hair pulled back in a ponytail. She smiled under her Turtle Team ball cap. The third woman had a big black camera hanging from her neck. "Congratulations on finding a nest on your first day out. Beginner's luck! Do you want to watch us find the eggs?"

We all said we did. We followed the women back up to the body pit. We stood out of the way with Honey and watched as Judy carried the yellow metal probe to the center of the mound. She studied it for a few minutes, then she bent at the knees and very slowly inserted the yellow probe into the sand. She pushed it a few inches down, then stopped. She moved the probe to another spot and pushed it until it stopped. Then another. Each time the probe stopped, she moved to another spot.

"Normally, the sand under the probe is hard," Honey explained to us. "When the probe hits hard sand, she'll look for another spot. When the sand is soft, the probe will keep going down. That's how she'll know the eggs are there."

Judy repeated the action six more times, in and out, bending at the knees as the probe slipped in the sand. Suddenly she froze, then removed the probe. She set it aside and lowered to her hands and knees.

Lovie sucked in her breath and leaned closer.

Alicia joined her kneeling on the sand and together they scooped handfuls of sand out of the nest, slowly and carefully. Alicia straightened and brought up one perfectly round, white egg in her hand.

"We've got eggs!" she exclaimed.

Honey cheered, and excited, we edged closer for a better look.

"The egg looks like a Ping-Pong ball," Macon said.

"Exactly like one," Honey agreed.

Alicia and Judy carefully put the egg back into the hole and replaced the sand, patting it down gently. They placed three wooden stakes in a triangle around the nest and wound bright orange tape around them to form a barrier. On the front stake Judy stapled an orange sign that marked the nest as protected by the federal government.

"Congratulations!" Judy told the three of us. "You found the nest, so I'll put your names on it."

"*Our* names?" Macon asked.

"Yes, it's your nest," Alicia said.

We all bent close to watch as Judy took a marker and wrote on one of the wooden stakes: POTTER, LEGARE, SIMMONS 6/24.

"Well, we may not have a boat," I said, "but at least we have a turtle nest."

Even Macon cracked a smile at that.

Journal of Jake Potter

Loggerhead tracks lead to nest.

Eggs look like a Ping-Pong ball.

The red bucket to move eggs

Probe stick

CHAPTER 15

Save the Nest!

Nature seems cruel sometimes.

EVERY MORNING WE WALKED THE BEACH in search of turtle tracks, but our beginner's luck seemed to be over because we didn't find any more.

But at least we were talking to each other again. It was impossible to carry a grudge after we found a turtle nest. Macon stopped glaring at us and joined in the conversations. I figured that was his way of saying he'd forgiven us, and it was enough for me.

Honey was looking better too, now that she was walking outdoors every day. And my drawing was improving. All in all, summer was picking up on Dewees Island.

Honey pointed out the wildflowers that grew on the dunes. We wrote the names and sketched them in our notebooks. She also told us the names of the different shells we found, and any ocean life that had washed ashore. Lovie was right: My grandmother knew a lot about nature. My notebook was filling up with names like "sea stars," "sea urchins," "primrose," and "crabs." We even found a baby shark swimming in the tide pool!

One day Macon found a sand dollar. "Hey, this one's all green!"

"Turn it over," Honey instructed him as she walked closer. "What do you see?"

He did so and made a face. "There's all these tiny wiggly legs!"

"That's right," Honey said, laughing lightly at Macon's expression. "Come closer and look. That sand dollar is *alive*."

Macon looked like he was going to drop it. Honey gently put her hand over his.

"Toss it back into the sea, Macon, and give that creature a second chance at life. Never keep the living sand dollars or sea stars, children. Carry them home to the sea." We were just getting into the routine of Dawn Patrol when—disaster struck. On our way to checking her turtle nest, Lovie stopped short with a gasp. We could see that the orange tape was torn from the sticks and flapping in the wind. I looked at Macon and we both grimaced. Not a good sign.

"Oh no!" Lovie shrieked, and took off running.

Macon and I ran after her. The sand over the nest had a gaping hole right in the middle. Broken eggshells lay scattered around it. Some of the shells oozed yoke.

Macon pointed to the sand. "Look! Animal tracks. Looks like a dog. Or probably a coyote."

Lovie stood, shoulders slumped, with tears rolling down her cheeks.

Honey caught up to us and sighed when she saw the carnage. She wrapped an arm around Lovie.

"Now this is a terrible sight, isn't it? Nature seems cruel sometimes." She dropped her arm. "But now you have to dry your tears. We've got work to do. Our job is to report what we find to the team. Then we'll see what we can save."

"*Can* we save some of them?" Lovie asked, hope ringing in her voice.

"We can try," Honey said.

Honey pulled out her cell phone to call Judy and the team. They talked a few minutes, and when she was done, Honey handed Lovie the phone.

"Lovie, take some photos of the nest. And be sure to get a few of the animal prints." Honey bent to study them. "Yep, sure looks like coyote tracks. Good eyes, Macon."

Macon grinned, pleased with the compliment.

"Could you run to the cart and fetch the red bucket?" she asked him.

"Yes, ma'am." He took off like the wind.

"Jake, you got your journal?"

I nodded and took my backpack off to retrieve it.

"Write what I tell you to write."

We watched in silence as Honey pulled plastic gloves out of her tote bag and slipped them over her hands. She got down on her knees by the nest and began scooping the damaged eggs out and laying them in piles of ten on the sand. Lovie finished taking the photos and stood beside me. She held tight to her silver turtle charm that was dangling from her neck, a sure sign she was nervous.

Honey's voice grew breathless as she worked at clearing out the ravaged eggs. "Coyotes don't typically eat all the eggs in the nest. A raccoon, on the other hand, will gobble them all up." She took a deep breath of the fresh air. "My, it's a bit pungent down there," she said before once more bending far into the nest. Her arm was nearly shoulder deep.

Honey's face lit up with triumph as she gingerly pulled out a perfectly round white egg. "Good news!" she exclaimed. "It looks like there are still a lot of eggs left."

Lovie clapped her hands and cheered in excitement.

Macon came racing back with the red bucket and handed it to Honey.

He bent over with his hands on his knees, winded. "What's up?"

"There are eggs to save!" Lovie told him, her eyes bright.

Honey put sand in the bottom of the bucket, then turned to me. "Jake, you mark the number of eggs I call out. Ready?"

"Ready."

"One," she began, placing one egg into the bucket.

One after another she carefully placed eggs in the bucket, calling out the number for me to record. At last, she put the final egg into the bucket. "Eighty-two!" she called out, straightening up. Honey put her hand to the small of her back and smiled, satisfied at the count. "Feel better, Lovie?"

"Yes, much. Thanks, Honey," Lovie replied, beaming down at the bucketful of eggs.

"Don't thank me yet. It's never good to have to move the eggs after they've settled, but we have no choice. Let's gather up the nest stakes and the sign, will you? I'll bury the ruined eggshells in the old nest. Don't want the scent to attract ants and worse. Then we'll move the good eggs to another spot a ways away from here. The team is already digging a new nest."

Honey carried the bucket back to the golf cart, walking slowly. "Macon, you sit in the front with me. You're the biggest, and I wager the strongest. You get the honor of carrying the eggs. Just please don't let them jiggle."

"I won't."

I could tell Macon was proud as he carefully held on to the red bucket. I knew there was no way he'd let those eggs jiggle.

Lovie, however, pouted as we hopped onto the back seat of the cart. I could tell she wanted to carry *her* eggs.

"Ready?" Honey called, and she slowly drove off, not at all speedy. She was being extra careful not to bounce. We didn't go far. Honey turned off on another beach path.

Judy and Alicia from the Turtle Team were waiting for us

on the dunes. Macon carried the red bucket of eggs as gently as if they were made of glass. When we reached the nest, Alicia took hold of the bucket, thanking him.

I walked to where Judy was finishing digging a nest. She used a large cockle shell to dig with, rather than a shovel.

"We like to use the cockle shells," Judy told me. "They scoop great and each one holds about a cup of sand, the same amount a female turtle digs up with her rear flippers. We try to do everything like the sea turtle does," she explained. "I dug this new nest about twenty-four inches deep, the same as the original nest." She looked up as Alicia settled the red bucket on the sand by the new nest. "Okay Jake, ready to record the eggs again? We want to be sure we have the same count going back in."

I pulled out my notebook and kept score as one by one, the two women very, very carefully placed each egg into the new nest.

"Eighty-two!" Alicia called out.

"That's the same number," Honey told them. "Let's cover them up."

Judy put sand over the eggs, and then she and Alicia marked the nest with orange tape and a federal sign.

"That should do it," Honey said.

"How do we know the eggs will be okay?" Lovie asked.

"We don't. But we did the best we could to give them a chance. Now it's up to fate and the good Lord."

"But we're not done yet," said Judy with a grin. "This time

we are putting a wire cage over the nest to protect the eggs against any more coyotes."

Honey put her arm around Lovie's shoulders and gave her a gentle squeeze. "We just have to hope, child. What's life without hope?"

Dear Dad,
What a day! Last week we found a turtle nest.
This week we saved one!
Lovie's nest was attacked by coyotes! They ate
more than twenty eggs. We don't know how many
exactly were laid, but there were eighty-two left. I
know because I counted them.
Honey was great. She sure knows a lot. She
moved the good eggs to a new nest, so now
they have a chance. She says she can't promise
they'll hatch, but me, Lovie, and Macon are

going to do all we can to protect them.

I'm really glad Macon and I are talking again. He started joining me and Lovie at the Nature Center again too. Glad that's over. He was mad at me and Lovie (long story), but we deserved it. We got him in trouble with his dad. I think Macon was mad not so much because he got in trouble. I think Macon was upset because his dad was disappointed in him. I get that. I don't ever want to disappoint you.

Anyway, I'm going to find a way to make it up to him. I hope you like my letters. I know you're trying hard to get well. I miss you.

Love, your son,

Jake

CHAPTER 16

Operation Coyote

A vision of red, white, and blue.

ANOTHER DAY. ANOTHER LETTER. I WAS sending one to Dad almost every day, along with my drawings. Mom called again to say my letters were arriving and how much Dad was enjoying them. They were the best medicine, she told me. It made me want to write more often.

I sat in the shade of the wraparound porch at the Nature Center, waiting for Macon and Lovie. It was hot and the tide was low, exposing the pluff mud. Its pungent smell filled the air, and as Lovie predicted, I was getting to like it.

I was getting to like the whole island a lot.

Learning how to identify the animals and birds, knowing their names, made all the difference. The white bird poking its beak in the mud was an egret. I knew that it was hunting for a meal—a fiddler crab, a snail, or a frog. I knew that a land turtle was called a terrapin, and I spotted a yellow-and-black-shelled fellow moving lazily along the salt marsh edge. A diamondback. Knowing the names of the wild things here made the island more like home. It was personal. I *knew* them.

My summer was different here, compared to the ones back at base. There, I spent a lot of time indoors playing video games. When I went out, I played team sports. On the island, I was more on my own. I could explore. Go swimming. Read. I could do whatever I wanted to do. And I was never bored! I was learning not just about critters and plants, but about myself.

And knowing these things, I started to trust my instincts. When I went out to explore the woods and beach, I knew to be quiet and keep my eyes and ears open. The animals came out of their hiding places while I filled my journal with drawings and notes.

I smirked, remembering how upset I'd been when I arrived on the island. I couldn't imagine what fun I'd have here. I didn't know yet the mysteries of the wild. Or my new friends, Macon and Lovie.

At the sound of footsteps, I turned to see them charging up the staircase toward me. I smiled seeing my friends.

"I won!" Lovie shouted with triumph, and panting.

Macon rested his hands on his head. "Why . . . do you always make it . . . a competition?" he puffed out. Drops of sweat rolled from his hair down the sides of his face.

Lovie hoisted herself up on the porch railing to rest, grinning with satisfaction.

"Jake! Check this out!" Macon slung off his backpack and pulled out a book. "It just came in the mail. It's a book of animal tracks." He opened it to a page he'd marked, already full of underlined words. "What do you think?"

"Let me have a look," Lovie said, squeezing in between us.

We all leaned in to read the page together.

Coyotes are opportunists and scavengers. They eat rodents, insects, birds, fruits, and vegetation.

"And turtle eggs," Lovie added to the list.

Macon pointed to one photograph. "Don't the tracks in this picture look exactly like what we saw around Lovie's turtle nest?"

"Yeah," I said, impressed. "It sure looks like it definitely was coyotes that tore up Lovie's nest."

Lovie stroked the ponytail draped over her shoulders. "Do you think the coyotes will come back and tear up the nest again? Or the other ones?"

"If they're hungry, for sure," Macon said, pulling another book out of his backpack and setting it on the ledge of the porch.

"You got *another* book?" I asked.

"My mom said I should have guidebooks to look up things, like your grandmother does." He snorted. "Old-school."

"But you have internet," I said.

Macon glowered. "Not allowed to use it. Thanks, bro."

I made a face. "Sorry."

"It doesn't matter. I like looking things up in books." He fingered through the pages. "I think what we've got to do is arm the nest."

"Arm it?" Lovie asked with doubt ringing in her voice.

"Yeah. You know, protect it," said Macon. "I looked up things that could scare off coyotes. Here," he said, pointing. "It says that loud noise works. And whistles." He looked up. "I figure we could use noisemakers."

"What about water guns?" I asked.

"It doesn't say anything about water guns."

"All animals hate water," I said. Then I looked at Lovie. "Don't they?"

She shrugged. "Worth a try."

Macon closed the book and stepped back. "So, guys, what do you think?"

"Let's have a stakeout!" I blurted out. "We can keep guard over the eggs."

Macon's eyes brightened. "Yeah. We'll take shifts."

"But Jake," Lovie said. "Turtles usually hatch at night. Real late at night. We'll be at home, in bed."

"Then we'll stay up all night," I replied, feeling braver than I typically was.

They both looked at me like I was crazy.

"Like, every night?"

"Maybe not every night. But we can arm the nest and do a stakeout to see if our plan works. Plus, we know the date they're supposed to hatch, right? We'll camp out then, too. I'm sure our families will let us. They're the ones who said we're supposed to be spending time outdoors, right?"

"I don't know . . ." Macon hedged.

"It'll be fun," I urged him. "You're not afraid of a little ol' coyote?"

"Yeah, right," Macon said with a wave of his hand.

"Well, I am. A little," Lovie said.

"I read that coyotes are afraid of people," Macon said.

"Then I'm in!" I said. I looked at Lovie. "Come on. Don't be a scaredy-cat."

Lovie crossed her arms over her chest and squinted her eyes at me. "I suppose we could sleep in the gazebo. It's all screened in and we could shut the door."

"That's a great idea," I said. "Like a fort. Now we have to make a list of the things we need for the stakeout."

"Are we really going to do this? Camp out with coyotes out here?" she asked.

"That's the plan, yeah," Macon said as he pulled a pencil and his journal from his backpack. He ripped a piece of paper from it. "First, we need noisemakers to scare the coyote away." He tapped his pen. "I've got a loud toy kazoo at the house. I can bring that."

I nodded. "That'll work. I could borrow some of Honey's metal cake tins to clang together. And a pot. I could bang on those with a spoon."

Lovie giggled. "Y'all sound like you're making a little kiddie band, not a stakeout."

"You got better ideas?" asked Macon. Then he added, "We need something that will make noise even if we're sleeping. To keep them away."

"I know!" Lovie said, jumping in. "Pinwheels. We have a whole bunch of them for the Fourth of July celebration. They don't make a racket, but they'll whirr around in the breeze. Aunt Sissy puts them in her flower box to keep the deer away."

"Let's do it," I said, and smiled at Lovie, glad she was getting caught in the enthusiasm. "Honey brought home some of those little American flags on wooden sticks. They'll flap in the breeze too."

"If nothing else, we'll at least have a very patriotic nest!" Macon said.

We all laughed at that one.

"I have some water guns," said Macon.

"Sweet! Bring me one," I exclaimed.

"I could bring my aunt's walkie-talkies," Lovie said. "They're long-range ones and maybe they'll come in handy."

"Bring 'em!" I shouted. We were really getting into it.

We added sleeping bags, water, and snacks to the list. It was getting long.

"I think we've got all we need." Macon held up the list.

"Wait! Bug spray," Lovie said. "And guys, be sure to cover up. Long pants and long sleeves. The mosquitoes can be awful at night. And the no-see-ums are even worse. Those are teeny, tiny gnats that my aunt calls 'flying teeth.'"

"Okay, guys," I said, looking them in the eyes. "This is it. I'll pick you up in my golf cart at eight o'clock. Are we all in for Operation Coyote?"

I stretched my arm out in front of me, palm down. Macon and Lovie each put a hand on top of mine and replied in unison, "All in!"

Just before sunset, or 2000 hours in military time, Operation Coyote began. I picked up my comrades and drove us to the gazebo, or as we referred to it, base camp. Our families gave us permission to camp out at the beach.

But we didn't mention the part about coyotes.

Our fortress—the gazebo—had a perfect view of everything: the boardwalk, the empty beach, and the darkening forest. We took turns showing off what we'd brought for supplies. Macon's bag was overflowing. He started pulling things out.

"Water guns." Macon wriggled his eyebrows. "Already loaded with a solution of water and vinegar. I also brought this cowbell." He gave it a jiggle, and it could really clang. "And six cans of Silly String. To eat," he continued, pulling things out of the bag, "chocolate chip cookies. Jelly beans. Chips. Soda. Oh, and a pack of beef jerky. My favorite." He sniffed it dramatically and tucked the package into a pocket of his pants. "A midnight snack," he said, patting his leg.

Lovie snorted. "I thought this was a stakeout, not a party."

Macon pushed out his lower lip in an exaggerated pout. "Hey! We need food to survive. What did *you* bring?"

"Glad you asked," Lovie said smugly, slinging her backpack to the ground and unzipping it. "Bug spray. You're welcome," she said, tossing it to Macon. "Walkie-talkies, a headlamp, an old coffee can filled with coins." She shook it to show how loud it was. "And for nibbles, I packed peanut butter and a bag of apples."

Macon and I groaned.

"Hey, it's healthy," she shot back. "And look what Aunt Sissy gave me. Glow sticks!"

"What are we going to use those for?" I asked.

She took one slender stick out of the box and bent it in half. Instantly the stick lit up neon green. She wrapped it around her wrist. Then she took another, snapped it, and put it around Macon's wrist. This one glowed neon yellow. Finally, she snapped a third and slipped it onto my wrist. Neon blue.

"This way we can easily see each other in the dark," she said.

"Very cool," I said. "Here's what I brought." I unzipped my backpack and pulled out a long flashlight, an empty squirt bottle, plus two metal cake pans and wooden spoons. I lifted a pan in one hand and clanged it with the spoon to show how loud it was.

"Pretty good," Macon said with a grin.

"And here's what I found in my dad's room. I think it's pretty cool." I pulled out a silver whistle. Then, with wriggling eyebrows like Macon, I showed him my ace.

"A slingshot!" cried Macon. "Nice find!"

As Macon began testing out the slingshot, I grabbed my food. "I have some juice boxes, oatmeal cookies, and a super-size bag of potato chips."

"This is quite a stash," Macon said, looking at all the items we'd brought.

"Let's set up our sleeping bags and head out to the beach," Lovie said. "We have a lot to do before it gets completely dark.

We were arranging our sleeping bags when we heard a distant yipping sound. We froze. My skin prickled at the sound of a faint, short howl, followed by more yipping.

"Coyotes," said Macon.

"Now what?" I whispered. My adventurous spirit had fizzled into fear.

"Gear up," Macon commanded. He stuffed a can of Silly String in one pocket and the kazoo in the other. Then he picked up his water gun. "Ready."

I grabbed the slingshot and my whistle. "Ready."

Lovie put on her headlamp and grabbed the tin of coins. "Ready."

We stood guard at the gazebo's screen, staring out at the beach, afraid to breathe so we wouldn't miss a sound. Nothing.

Only the occasional bird cry and dog bark. After what felt like forever, Lovie finally broke the silence.

"I think it's gone," she whispered.

"Yeah," Macon agreed. "And I'm kind of hungry."

"We'll eat later," I said. "It's almost dark. First we've still got to arm the nest."

"What are we waiting for?" asked Lovie.

"Okay, let's go," I said.

We grabbed our supplies and walked in single file toward the beach.

It was strange being out on the beach at night. It felt so different from the day. In the daytime, we would have to speed across the hot, dry sand to avoid scorching our feet. At night, the sand felt soft and cool underfoot, like walking in flour.

Suddenly we heard high-pitched squeaks. We stopped short and craned our necks toward the sound. It looked like birds flying overhead in dizzy, zigzag patterns.

"Are those birds?" I asked.

"No, those are bats," Lovie shrieked. "I hate bats." She put her hands over her head and began running toward the nest.

I yelped and ducked my head as one veered in close. "Wait up," I called as I raced after her.

Macon walked calmly as he followed. He didn't seem the least bit worried about them. In fact, he seemed to be into them.

"I wonder what species they are?" Macon asked when he caught up. "I read in one of my books that there are more than forty species of bats in the United States, and fourteen of them can be found right here in South Carolina."

"Do you know if they'll suck my blood?" I called over my shoulder.

Lovie ducked her head as one bat swooped down close to our heads. "It'll get stuck in my hair!"

"Nope. Not true," Macon said. "They're not after us. The bats are chasing insects. They use echolocation. That's like radar."

"I know what that is," Lovie replied a bit haughtily. She was embarrassed for acting like a baby with the bats. "Dolphins use that."

"Yep," said Macon. "Mr. Bat makes high-pitched sounds that bounce off an insect back to the bat's ear. Then he swoops in and snags dinner." He looked up into the night. "Feast on those mosquitoes, Mr. Bat!"

"Says Mr. Google," I teased.

We finally reached the turtle nest. It was undisturbed, thank goodness. We set down our gear, then worked together in friendly silence to arm the nest as the sun slowly set around us. We put all the pinwheels and the small American flags around the perimeter of the nest. The sun had almost disappeared by the time we stood back and looked at our creation.

The soft breeze started the pinwheels spinning and the small flags flapping. The nest was a vision of red, white, and blue.

"It's working," I said, grinning.

"That there is an all-American turtle nest," Lovie said with a giggle.

I put my hands on my hips and sighed. Man, I was epic proud of that nest.

"Now we wait!" Macon said.

CHAPTER 17

The Stakeout

Survival of the fittest.

WE WERE SET UP NEAR THE TURTLE nest, sitting on towels on the sand. Even though we were covered in bug spray, the no-see-ums and ants were biting. While we talked, we kept slapping our ankles, necks, and arms. But we kept our coyote gear close at hand.

Clouds were moving in. Not storm clouds, just the wispy kind that floated across the sky like longboats. When they passed over the moon, the night was suddenly cloaked in blackness. We sat side by side at the bottom of the dune, staring out at the black sea. It felt like *something* was going to happen tonight.

"I've lived on the islands most of my life," said Lovie, "but I've never seen a coyote. I've just heard stories about how they roam neighborhoods, eating people's cats and little dogs."

"Come on, really?" I asked with doubt.

"Really. Folks are up in arms. They want to kill all the coyotes."

"That's harsh," said Macon.

"I don't know," I said, raking the sand with my fingers. It was cool to the touch. "I've always wanted a dog. My mom says we move around too much for a dog." I tossed a bit of sand. "I think that's lame. She just doesn't want the mess. But if I ever had a dog, I'd love it a lot. And if a coyote ate my dog . . ." I shook my head.

"Still, killing *all* the coyotes? I mean, they've got to make a living too," Macon said. "Nature's nature. Survival of the fittest."

"What do you think *we're* doing here?" I asked him. "We don't want them eating our turtle eggs. So we're stopping them."

"We're trying to scare them," Macon said. "Not kill them. Anyway, they're definitely on the island. I read about it in the Island Community Information booklet."

"They're not *all* bad," said Lovie. "I mean, they eat mice and rats. That's a good thing, right?"

"As long as they don't see *us* as dinner," I said with a snort. All this talk about coyotes was making me nervous. "Let's go over the plan one more time. If a coyote shows up, we have to act *real* aggressive. And loud. Wave your arms, shout, and bang the tins."

"I'm going to shoot this vinegar water right in their eyes," said Macon, hoisting up his squirt toys.

"That reminds me. I have a plastic water bottle I have to fill up," I said, climbing to my feet. I started walking and realized I was alone. "Anyone want to come with me?"

"Nah, you go ahead," Macon said.

"I'm good. But don't go too far into the ocean," Lovie said. "You know what they say about the ocean at night."

"No. What do they say?"

"Feeding time for the sharks." Lovie made pretend smacking noises with her lips.

I shrugged her off and walked alone across the beach toward the water. A cloud drifted over the moon, cloaking the beach in darkness. I felt a shiver of fear, and looking over my shoulder, I could hardly see my friends. Their shadowy bodies blended into the dark maritime forest behind them. If it wasn't for the outline of the gazebo in the distance, I might not be able find my way back. I wasn't sure if I was more afraid of the coyotes or the sharks.

The water of the ocean loomed large and as black as tea. It sure was dark. I stuck my hands in the shallows. And it was blood warm. *How shallow do sharks go?* I wondered. Taking a breath, I walked in. The gentle waves slapped at my ankles . . . then my calves . . . then my knees. So far so good.

I bent down and began filling up the water bottle. I could hear the slapping of water against my legs and the squishy sand beneath my toes. I was twisting the squeeze-top lid on when *BAM!*

"Yoooowwww!" I felt a blinding, hot white pain on my ankle.

Howling, I raced out of the water. Through my tears I saw Lovie and Macon racing toward me.

"What's the matter?"

"Did a shark bite you?"

"My ankle!" I cried. "It feels like it's on fire!" I fell onto the dry sand and gripped my ankle, lifting it in the air. "It burns so bad!" I gritted my teeth.

Macon put the light of his flashlight on my leg. "Your leg, it's all red."

Lovie clicked on her headlamp. "It's not blood."

I howled again, clutching my leg. "Jake," said Lovie, "it looks like a jellyfish got you."

I could barely pull myself up to look. In the narrow beam of light, I could see angry red lines raised around my ankle like it was hit by a whip.

"What do I do? It hurts! So bad!"

Everyone was as scared as I was, I could tell.

"I read something once about how to treat jellyfish stings." Macon squatted down in front of me and said in a softer voice, "You're not gonna like it, though."

"Anything," I moaned as I rolled on my back. It felt like a thousand red-hot needles were stuck all over and around my ankle.

"Lovie, turn around," Macon said.

Lovie's eyes bugged. "Aw, no. Please tell me you are *not* going to do what I think you're going to do."

"I don't want to, but if it's going to help, I'm doing it," Macon said.

"What are you going to do?" I asked, grimacing.

"I have to pee on it."

That pierced through the pain. "Have you lost your mind?" I shouted back.

"It'll help. Really."

Lovie shook her head. "That's totally bogus. And gross."

"Hey, it works."

"You guys!" I yelled. "For once can you stop fighting? I'm the one in pain here! Do it!" I cried.

"I'm telling y'all . . . this is not what to do. Mama uses vinegar; just saying!" Lovie said, while turning her back on us and covering her face with her hands.

I turned my head and squeezed my eyes shut. The pain made me desperate. "Just do it."

A warm stream hit my ankle. I didn't know which was worse, the pain of the jellyfish sting or the fact that I let someone pee on me.

"How do you feel now?" asked Macon. "Better, right?"

I hoped it would work, but the prickly pain surged.

"It feels worse!" I gagged. "I'm gonna hurl."

Lovie grabbed Macon's squirt toy. "This one has vinegar in it, right?" she asked him.

Macon nodded sheepishly. "Yeah."

Lovie drew near and without a word poured the vinegar-and-water solution over my ankle. It still hurt, but not as bad as before.

"Now we have to take out the tiny stingers," Lovie said.

"No!" I howled. "Don't touch it! Nobody touch it!"

"We've got to get the stingers out."

"I don't think that's right," Macon said dubiously.

Lovie turned on him. "Said the boy who peed on his friend."

"Guys!" I called out to stop the arguing. "I want to go home. Honey will know what to do."

"I'll take you," Lovie offered.

"I'm not staying out here alone," said Macon.

"Who's going to keep guard?"

"You keep guard," Macon said. "I'll take Jake."

I couldn't listen to those two at it again. I scrambled to my feet and began hobbling up the beach. "You guys just keep fighting. I'm getting out of here."

Lovie and Macon stopped arguing and ran after me.

Not a great start for Operation Coyote.

Honey couldn't stop laughing when we told her what happened.

"It's not funny," I said with a pout.

I was sitting on the side of the bathtub with Honey by my side. She'd been pouring vinegar water over my red welts for a long time. But it wasn't feeling any better. I was gritting my teeth, determined not to cry. Especially not with my friends nearby. I looked over my shoulder. Macon and Lovie crowded the door, eyes wide.

"The pain isn't funny," Honey agreed as she poured more vinegar and water over my ankle. "At least you had vinegar on hand. Maybe you should've tried that remedy *first*," she said with a short laugh and head shake.

"But I read it was the right thing to do," Macon said.

"That, child, is what is known as an old wives' tale. Right up there with not swimming after eating."

"That's not true?" asked Lovie.

"Nope." Honey set aside the vinegar solution and dried her hands. Then she gave me the no-fooling look. "Tell me, Jake. Do you feel light-headed or dizzy? Any nausea?"

I shook my head. "I did before, but I think I was"—I sneaked a glance at Macon and Lovie and lowered my voice—"I was a little scared. But I'm okay now. Except it still hurts. A lot." I grimaced.

She patted my shoulder. "I'm sorry. It will hurt for another hour or so. Pretty bad, I'm not going to lie. But I'll put some cream on it that will help. First, though, let's get those stingers out. Can you be brave a little longer?"

I gritted my teeth and nodded.

Honey slipped on her reading glasses and picked up the credit card she had waiting on the bathroom sink.

"Can you put your ankle up in my lap? That'll do." Honey bent over my leg with the credit card. "I can see some of those tiny stingers in there." She waved Macon and Lovie a little closer.

"Jellyfish will drop hundreds of those stingers on your leg, but pouring the vinegar on it helped. Good job, Lovie," Honey said. "Next time—though I pray there won't be a next time—make a paste of wet sand and put that on the sting. Then take something flat, like this credit card, and very gently scrape the sand off the skin. That should take off most of the stingers with it. Watch carefully," she said, then began scraping the welts with the edge of the credit card, like she was shaving my leg.

I reared back and clenched my teeth, but it didn't hurt much more than the sting already did.

Macon and Lovie hovered, watching with wide eyes.

"Done," Honey exclaimed. "That wasn't too bad, was it? The stingers are out. You'll feel better soon."

Honey had me soak my ankle in a bucket of warm water. "Keep your ankle in it for ten minutes," she said. "I'll be right back."

I heard her laugh again in the kitchen. She returned with a glass of water. "Here, take this," Honey said, offering me some ibuprofen. My friends sat on the side of the tub and the toilet, keeping me company.

Lovie giggled. "I won't tell anybody about the jellyfish thing. But, for the record, I tried to stop you two," she teased.

Macon and I snorted a short laugh.

"What happens on the island, stays on the island," I said.

We laughed again. Then again. Suddenly we were all laughing hard, the hold-your-belly-because-it-hurts kind of laughing.

"That was so sick!" I cried.

"Totally," Macon managed to get out between laughs.

As we laughed, I felt the fear and worry in my chest lessen. Even the stinging hurt less.

By the time Honey returned, I knew I was on the mend. She dabbed antibiotic cream on the sting.

"This will help make it feel much better. Now," she said, screwing the lid back on the tube, "there's nothing left to add but a tincture of time. Let's bring you out to a comfortable chair."

What a night! I was glad to be safe and sound in the Bird's Nest with my foot resting on a cushion on the sofa, surrounded by my friends. It was late, and I could tell everyone felt as tired as I did. Even Honey looked weary as she carried a plate of cookies into the room.

We ate our cookies hungrily. We'd never had the chance to eat all those great snacks.

"I guess we should get back to the nest," Macon said when the last cookie was gone.

"Yeah, we've been gone a long time," said Lovie.

My ankle was still killing me, but I knew my friends were eager to get back to the stakeout. "Yeah. I guess the worst is over." I lowered my ankle and began to slowly rise from the sofa.

"Hold on, young man," Honey said, putting her hand out.

I sunk back into the cushion.

"You're not going anywhere tonight," Honey said. "Your ankle needs to rest. As for you two." She looked at Macon and Lovie. "It's late and I don't think you two should be setting up camp. You should be in bed."

"But the turtles!" cried Lovie.

"The turtles will have to survive on their own. They've done so for millions of years; they can do it one more night. You armed the nest. Trust your work. Honestly, I've never known a more protected nest. And . . ." She clasped her hands together with excitement. "Tomorrow is the Fourth of July. Dewees does the holiday up proper! There are going to be so many fun activities on the island for y'all to get involved in. You'll need your energy to enjoy them all. So let's get a good night's sleep. Okay?"

We kids shared a glance, then nodded.

"Good. I'll drive you home. But before you go," Honey said, holding up her hand, "there's one final thing I want to discuss." She waited until she had our full attention. "Jake, we have rules. And one of the biggest ones is not going into the ocean at night."

I sat straighter. "I didn't go into it. Not really," I said. "I mean, not to swim."

"Did you go into the water?"

I nodded. "Yeah."

"Did you get hurt?"

I nodded, shamefaced.

"Enough said. I'll let you off this time. But know this: A jellyfish sting is not the worst that could've happened to you. You're never to go in the ocean again at night, hear? At least not while you're under my care."

"Yes, ma'am."

She looked at Macon and Lovie.

"Yes, ma'am," they echoed.

"Okay, then grab your stuff and I'll drive you home. We'll pick up your supplies from the gazebo tomorrow morning."

Honey paused at seeing our surprised faces. "What? You thought there was no Dawn Patrol? Turtles don't know it's a holiday!"

STAY AWAY!

Jellyfish

CHAPTER 18

Independence Day

The truth shall set you free.

THE FOURTH OF JULY WAS ALL FRIENDS, family, and fireworks on Dewees. Everyone was invited—and everyone came.

I awoke early as usual for Dawn Patrol. We all raced to Lovie's nest first. Boy were we relieved to find it safe and sound. No turtle tracks on the beach meant we could go home early.

After we collected our supplies from the gazebo, Macon, Lovie, and I headed back to see a boatload of people arriving on the ferry. Golf carts were zipping along the dirt roads, people calling out greetings. My sleepy island was bubbling over with families and guests of the residents. The three of us looked at one another and smiled. We could feel the excitement thrumming in the air.

The pain was gone from the sting. All that was left was an annoying itch I wasn't allowed to scratch. So Honey kept me busy.

"Just don't think about it!" she said.

Honey and I dressed in red, white, and blue. Honey even had a scarf that looked like the American flag. Every day she seemed a bit cheerier and brighter, like the clothes she wore. Together, we decorated the golf cart with leftover American flags and pinwheels and lots of red, white, and blue crepe paper. On the roof of the cart she strapped down a humongous inflatable sea turtle. It hung over the sides and looked so ridiculous, it was actually funny.

"I think you could spot that turtle from an airplane!" I told her.

"You're on the Turtle Team now. Consider this festive team spirit," Honey said, tugging on the bungee strap to make sure the float was secure. "I named this turtle *Caretta caretta*. You know why?"

"Duh. It's the scientific name of the loggerhead."

"Bingo! Now for the best part." Honey went to her small workshop under the garage and pulled out a large poster board sign. She turned it over for me to read. There in bright green letters was DAWN PATROL.

I groaned and put my forehead in my palm.

"What? I worked hard on this sign. I was going to ask you to draw a turtle. But we're out of time. Just give me a minute to tie this up on the back of the float."

A few minutes later Honey had the big sign strapped to the back of the cart.

"Hop on!" she called, climbing behind the wheel. "I told Tessa we'd pick up Macon for the parade."

A few minutes later we arrived at Macon's house. He was waiting for us on the front porch dressed in navy shorts and a red-and-white striped T-shirt. He also had a Fourth of July ball cap with stars and stripes. His eyes widened when we pulled up, and then he shook his head.

"Oh no! I'm not riding in that!"

I know, I mouthed.

Honey leaned back in her seat. "Last I recall, you were on Dawn Patrol. Well sir, this here is the Dawn Patrol float. So, hop on! We've got a parade to catch."

Macon slapped my outstretched hand and hopped onto the back seat. It was a short drive to the main field across from the fire station. My jaw dropped. There were so many people! Dozens of carts were parked there, each decorated in crazy red, white, and blue everything!

"I didn't know *this* many people even lived out here!" I said.

"Everyone who has a house likes to return to the island for the holiday. Lots of folks have their families visiting too," Honey explained. "It's the biggest holiday on Dewees. The more the merrier."

"There's Lovie and her aunt." I pointed toward their golf cart.

Honey swerved past two people walking, dodged a dog running across the field, and managed to pull up next to them.

Lovie and Aunt Sissy were wearing matching red shorts and white ruffled tops. Lovie's hair was in a ponytail decorated with oversize red and blue trailing ribbons. Their cart was draped with stars and stripes bunting.

Lovie clapped her hands when she saw the turtle. "Oh my gosh! That is so awesome!"

"You have to ride with us," Macon called out to her. "This is the Dawn Patrol float."

Aunt Sissy laughed and gave Lovie a gentle nudge forward. "Go ahead," she told her. "I'll catch up with you later."

With a quick squeal, Lovie ran to our float and hopped in the back with Macon.

The fire truck blasted its horn, and the surrounding golf carts began honking their horns. Lovie handed out kazoos and the three of us blasted them.

"The parade is beginning!" exclaimed Honey with excitement. She started the engine and joined the golf carts as they scrambled like bugs to line up in single file behind the fire truck.

When the fire truck's siren began sounding, we were off! Call it corny. Call it old-school. But it was a blast! I'd never been in a parade before. The carts bumped along the dirt road in single file to the music of Bruce Springsteen's "Born in the USA" on a wireless speaker. Anyone on the island who wasn't riding in a golf cart stood at the end of their drive and waved an American flag as the parade passed.

The parade wound around the entire island as the music changed from one patriotic song to another. It ended to cheers and applause at the high dock along the creek. Colorful beach chairs lined the wide, long dock, and signs welcomed all to the Fourth of July creek float.

The sun had risen during the parade, and I had a sheen of sweat on my brow. I looked out and saw adults and kids already in the water—swimming, lounging on inflatables, paddleboards, and kayaks. The water looked great. Lovie and I looked at each other, eager for Honey to park the cart.

"I can't wait to get in!" I said, excited to jump into the water.

Macon's mood shifted and his smile fell.

"Are you okay?" I asked.

"Yeah," he replied. But it didn't sound like the truth.

We watched some older teenagers jump off the edge of the dock—whooping and hollering as they splashed into the water below.

As soon as the cart was parked, Lovie and I hopped off and raced to the dock. Macon followed more slowly.

"Come on, y'all!" called out Lovie. "Let's jump in together! We'll do a Dawn Patrol jump."

Macon quickly jerked away from her grasp. "You go ahead. I'll take a pass."

Before we could argue, he turned his back and headed toward the main path, away from the dock.

Lovie scrunched up her face. "Why's he being a dud?"

I didn't know, so I just shrugged.

The tide was high, and the greenish-blue water sparkled under the cloudless sky. Lovie and I got in the long line to jump.

We watched, breathless, as one by one the kids took off running down the dock to cannonball into the creek. The folks sitting along the creek, young and old, always cheered and waved flags.

When our turn came, Lovie and I held hands and looked at each other with huge grins. "Ready?" I asked.

"Ready!"

"On the count of three.... One. Two. Three. Dawn Patrol!" we cried as we took off, hand in hand, running to the end of the wooden dock. For a moment we were suspended in midair. Her hand in mine.

Then *SPLASH!*

The water felt instantly cool against my hot skin. Under the water, among the bubbles, we let go of our hands and kicked our way up to the surface. Applause and cheers greeted us as our heads surfaced for air.

Lovie's face was pink, and she squealed, "Again!"

"Okay!"

We swam to the side and climbed up the rope ladder, eager to get back in line.

"Hello, Jake!"

Turning my head, I spotted Honey waving from her seat in the shade. She looked so happy, it made my own heart happy too. I waved back, then cast a quick glance around for Macon. But there was no sign of him.

Lovie and I swam till our arms grew tired from fighting the creek's current. We grabbed on to the rope ladder to rest and catch our breath.

"Look, there's Macon," she said, craning her neck.

"Where?"

"Standing near the ice cream stand." She waved her arm in a wide arc over her head. "Macon!" she called out. "Come on in, it's awesome!"

Macon was leaning against a tree, eating an ice-cream cone. He lifted the cone and shook his head no.

"What's his deal?" Lovie asked me.

"I don't know. But I'm going to find out." I gripped the ladder and climbed out from the creek. Lovie was right behind me. Water dripped from our bodies as we raced, barefoot, across the dock to where Macon was standing under a craggy oak tree.

"What's up? You okay?" I asked him.

"I'm fine." Macon licked his cone.

"Why won't you join us?" I asked.

"Because I don't want to."

I stared at my friend and wondered if he could possibly still hold a grudge about the boat fiasco. But that was so long ago.

"Macon!" Lovie said. "What's wrong? Why are you acting this way?"

"What way?" Macon challenged her.

Lovie softened her tone. "Why won't you come in the water?"

"I just don't want to. Okay?"

"You *never* want to get in the water with us," she argued.

"You scared or something?" I joked.

Macon's eyes narrowed. "Shut up!" he said, shoving my shoulders.

The force of it knocked me flat on my butt. First, I was shocked. Second, I was mad. A rush of heat ignited inside me.

"What's your problem?" I yelled, jumping to my feet.

"I don't have a problem," he said, standing chest to chest with me. "You're the ones who won't leave me alone."

"We just want you to hang out. But instead you're over here . . . acting like a jerk!"

"Just leave me alone," Macon said through clenched teeth, and marched away.

Lovie and I looked at each other, confusion in our eyes. We both heard it. Macon wasn't mad. He sounded more . . . hurt.

"Wait here," I said to Lovie. I trotted to catch up with Macon, calling after him. "Hey, wait up!"

Macon stopped short and spun around to face me. His lips were scrunched up, like he might cry.

"Hey, bro. What's bothering you?" I asked in a friendlier tone.

"I can't swim," Macon blurted out.

I blinked, not sure I heard him right. "Huh?"

"I. Can't. Swim."

My mouth dropped open.

"There! You happy now?"

"Hey, I . . . I didn't know. I mean, who doesn't know how to swim?"

I was sorry the minute I said the words. I didn't mean it the way they sounded. But it was too late. Words have power, and these hit their mark.

"I'm outta here." Macon turned on his heel and took off

running. His bold blue sneakers flashed against the brown of the dry dirt path.

Lovie hurried to catch up to me. I could tell by her face she'd heard everything. All the happiness we'd felt earlier had fizzled like air from a balloon. When we turned around to walk back, I was surprised to find Honey standing nearby. She met my gaze and I knew she'd heard everything too.

"If I heard correctly, Macon shared something that's a very big deal for him."

"How were we supposed to know?" I asked defensively.

"Why didn't he just tell us he didn't know how to swim?" Lovie asked.

Honey gazed up to the towering pines as if the answer to the question hung from a branch. "We all have little secrets or fears that we don't feel comfortable sharing with others . . . even our closest friends."

I understood what she meant. I didn't talk about the worries I had about Dad. Honey didn't share her secret of loneliness. And Lovie didn't tell anyone about her biological dad in prison. I scratched my leg, trying hard not to scratch my ankle as I thought. The guilt I felt for embarrassing my friend itched my conscience every bit as much.

"We didn't know," Lovie said. "It doesn't seem fair that he's mad at us now."

"Unintentional as it was, the fact remains that you two were being insensitive. Macon told you he didn't want to jump in, and you kept pestering him. You wouldn't take no for an answer."

"We just wanted him to join us," I said, and kicked a pebble.

"I know," said Honey. "In times like these, you have to put yourself in the other person's shoes. How do you think Macon felt?"

"Embarrassed." I knew the answer to that one.

"Left out," Lovie added.

Honey looked into our eyes, one after the other. "So, what's the solution?"

That answer came quickly. "To apologize," we both replied.

"You three make great friends," Honey said with a soft smile. "And sometimes, a simple 'I'm sorry' is all that's needed to start anew." She reached out to pat our shoulders.

"Now go on. The truth shall set you free."

CHAPTER 19

The Long Walk

*It's never good for a secret to come
between friends.*

WE WENT ON FOOT TO MACON'S HOUSE,
walking along the lagoon path. Lovie toyed with her
sea turtle necklace charm and chewed her lower lip.

"You thinking about what to say?" I asked, trying to break
the quiet between us.

She shrugged without glancing at me.

Snap.

The loud sound of twigs cracking made us freeze. We
scanned our surroundings. Just off the path to our left, we
quickly spied a family of deer munching on leaves and twigs in
a tangle of overgrown bushes.

"They're so close, I feel like I could touch them," I whispered.

"Never touch a wild animal, remember," she whispered back.

I rolled my eyes. "Duh. It's not my first day on the . . ."

Another movement in the bushes made us go silent again. In a flash, the deer bolted. Something new was moving from the forest toward the path. This sound was heavier, like something was dragging. Something big.

Lovie linked her arm in mine, squeezing it. I leaned into her too, but I hoped she couldn't feel my heart trying to pound itself out of my body.

"What's that?" Lovie whispered.

"An otter, maybe?"

"Maybe. My aunt said she saw two on the island."

We watched, not moving, not even taking a breath, as the tangle of brambles and bushes and weeds rattled.

"Umm, that would be a *big* otter, then," I replied, pulling back on Lovie's arm. We took a few slow, cautious steps backward.

The underbrush slowly parted and then, with barely a sound, a massive leathery brownish-black snout poked out. Its long mouth was in an upturned grin. Two big, sharp, upper teeth pointed upward.

Lovie sucked in her breath.

Another step forward revealed its massive head.

"Big Al!" His name fell from my lips with a mix of wonder and fear.

The alligator eased its impressive thirteen feet from the

shrubs with a slow swagger, as if the creature knew he was king of the island.

"He's huge!" Lovie whispered, terror making her voice tremble.

The gator paused, giving us a full view of his profile. I swear, he looked as long as a truck.

"Let's get out of here," I whispered, tugging her arm.

"Don't run," Lovie said in a shaky voice.

Al began moving again. And again, we froze. The alligator looked away from us, as though we weren't even there. Then with a step, he sauntered across the dirt path on his way to the pond.

Lovie said in a low voice, "Just keep walking backward. Nice and slow."

I didn't need any encouragement. We started inching our way back, lifting our feet higher so as not to make noise, our eyes peeled on Big Al. He'd already reached the pond and was slipping soundlessly into the dark water. I felt sorry for the birds wading there but didn't shout out. Instead, we turned heel and took off running.

"Feet don't fail me now!" I called out, laughing in relief as we ran down the road.

We were still laughing by the time we got to Macon's house. We couldn't wait to tell Macon about Big Al. He loved alligators. He even had a poster of them on his bedroom wall.

When we reached Macon's front door, Aunt Sissy answered the door. "Well, this is a surprise," she said. She'd changed from her red shorts and white top and was wearing tan pants and a white polo. "Come in before we let all the air-conditioning out."

"Aunt Sissy, what are you doing here?" Lovie asked.

She ushered us into the Simmonses' spacious front hall. "I'm officially helping Macon's mom now that she's getting close to her due date." She shut the door behind us.

"I'm guessing you're here for Macon."

"Yes, ma'am."

"Sorry to say he's not here. He was here for a short minute, then he left again. Hold on a second. I'll ask his mother if she knows where he was headed."

"Where do you think he went?" Lovie asked me when her aunt left the room.

"Beats me. It's getting close to dinnertime. Not like Macon to miss a meal." I looked over my shoulder, then said, "Is your aunt working for Mrs. Simmons now?"

"Sort of. She checks in on her now that Mrs. Simmons is getting close to her due date." Lovie looked up when her aunt returned to the front hall and waved us in.

"Mrs. Simmons asked if she could speak to you. Do you have a minute?"

The living room was up another flight of stairs, higher up where the windows overlooked the trees to see clear to the ocean. Honey once told me she thought the Simmons house had the best ocean views on the island. Boy, was she right.

It was a big, sunny room in cheerful, bright colors, like

the clothes Mrs. Simmons wore. She was stretched out, her head wrapped in a colorful scarf. Her belly had grown since the last time I was over. It looked like she had a basketball under her tunic.

"Hi, guys!" Mrs. Simmons called out in greeting when we entered. Her smile was as bright as the sunshine.

"Hi, Mrs. Simmons. How are you feeling today?" I asked politely.

"Big!" she replied, and gave her rounded abdomen a gentle rub. "You're here to see Macon? He's not here right now, but I'm glad you came over. Could you come on over here please. I'd like to ask you a question about something while Macon is gone." She gestured to the chairs nearby.

Lovie and I looked at each other warily. I had a sinking feeling we were going to get in trouble for pestering Macon. We obliged, each slinking onto a chair. Lovie sat straight and held her hands in her lap, real tight. Her aunt stood by her side.

Mrs. Simmons smiled again, and I could tell she was trying to make us feel comfortable. "Happy Fourth of July," she said. "Macon told me you had a real fine parade. I peeked out the window, but I couldn't see much. But I heard you!" She laughed lightly. Then she looked at her hands while we sat quietly. "Macon also told me about what happened at the creek." She looked up at us. "He told you that he couldn't swim."

I squirmed and nodded my head. *Here it comes,* I thought.

"That was a big secret for him to share," she told us.

"We didn't mean to make him mad," Lovie blurted out. "We didn't know."

"He wasn't mad," Mrs. Simmons said kindly. "He was more . . . embarrassed. He knew you both loved swimming. He didn't want you to find out."

"I'm sorry for what I said to him," I said.

"I know you are, Jake," Mrs. Simmons said kindly. "The thing about secrets is that they can be difficult to keep. Some secrets are good, like surprises or gifts. Some secrets are not so good. No adult should tell you to keep a secret if you think it's wrong or it makes you feel uncomfortable. Trust your instincts and tell your parents." She paused and looked out the window a moment. When she turned back to us, she smiled sweetly.

"And then there are the secrets that hide something we're embarrassed about. You didn't know why Macon didn't want to go in the water with you. This was a secret that was Macon's decision to share. And I'm glad he did. It's never good for a secret to come between friends."

"I'm just glad he told me," I said.

"Exactly. Now, since we're confessing secrets," Mrs. Simmons said, "here's mine. I don't know how to swim either."

I looked at her, surprised. I didn't know anyone, grown-up or kid, who didn't know how to swim. Now I knew two people.

"Swimming wasn't important in my family," Mrs. Simmons explained. "My mama and daddy didn't know how either. I grew up in these parts, near the water. I love the ocean, the rivers, and creeks. I can look out this window all day and my heart just sings," she said, staring out at the brilliant ocean shining under the blue sky. "South Carolina is home for me. Water is a part of the landscape I grew up with. But swimming?" She shook her head. "To be honest, the water scares me. I don't even like getting in the shallow end of a pool." Mrs. Simmons readjusted herself gingerly in her recliner.

"When Macon was four years old, I wanted him to learn how to swim. I overcame my fears and signed him up for lessons at our local pool. He liked to swim. I was so proud of him. He could blow bubbles and was a strong kicker." She smiled. "You know how strong he is."

"Yeah," I said.

"He was doing really well. Jumping in and getting to the side of the pool all by himself. Truth is, I thought he could swim better than he actually could." She smoothed her hand over the rim of her belly. "And I let down my guard."

Her voice grew soft and I leaned in to hear better.

"It all happened so fast. It was a crowded day at the club," Mrs. Simmons continued. "I was sitting outside the pool, talking to a friend. Macon was beside me sitting on a towel, playing with a toy. One minute he was there. And the next minute, when I looked up, he was gone. I was frantic. I leaped from my chair, calling his name. I'd never been so afraid."

She paused to rub her belly again and took a short breath.

Aunt Sissy drew close to her. "Are you okay?"

"Just a twinge," Mrs. Simmons said. She took another short breath and exhaled. Then she returned to her story. "It couldn't have been more than a minute or so, but it felt like forever. When I spotted him, he was in the pool. Underwater. Struggling." She shook her head. "I couldn't even jump in to save my own baby."

"What happened?" Lovie asked, at the edge of her seat.

"We were blessed," Mrs. Simmons replied. "The lifeguard heard my cries, and in a flash, she jumped in and grabbed him. She lifted Macon out of the water, and I will never forget the sound of that huge breath my baby took, his mouth wide open, like a fish. I wrapped him in a towel and hugged him to within an inch of his life. We got there just in time. He didn't swallow any water. But . . ." Mrs. Simmons shrugged. "Another minute and it could've been a very different story. That incident confirmed my fears of the water. We left the pool that day and never returned. Macon never took classes again. Never entered a pool. Never swam. He never said he didn't want to, but he never said he did, either. I never encouraged him."

"Didn't you go to the beach?" Lovie asked disbelievingly. I knew she couldn't imagine a life away from the beach.

"Sure we did. We traveled to islands on vacations. We just did things other than swim. We played on the beach, and there was golf, tennis. In the city, swimming isn't a big deal. It's not a sport Macon's ever been interested in." She paused. "Until this summer." She looked out the window again. "I suppose I should've seen it coming, living on an island." She laughed lightly.

"Do you think he wants to learn how to swim now?" I asked.

"Yes, I think he does. Especially with you two as his friends. He feels a bit left out."

"He could take private lessons at Huyler House," said Lovie. "That's where I learned how to swim."

Aunt Sissy added, "That's a little community center here on the island. It has a nice swimming pool. And I know an excellent instructor I can ask."

Mrs. Simmons smiled. "That's a wonderful idea. I'd feel safer knowing that he could swim." She looked again at me and Lovie. "I knew you two would have a good idea. Why don't you go talk to him about it?"

"Where is he?" I asked.

Mrs. Simmons smiled. "He said something about a stakeout."

Aunt Sissy prepared sandwiches, drinks, and cookies for us to take with us, reminding us that there would be free hot dogs at the creek if we wanted more.

"I'll call Honey and let her know what's happening. Have a good time, children!"

The gazebo was empty when Lovie and I arrived. We picked up our pace as we walked toward the beach and the turtle nest. The sun shimmered off the ocean water, making me squint beneath my ball cap. A woman with her dog on a leash trotted by close to the tide line. It was late in the after-noon, and everyone had packed up their towels and headed home for barbecues and fireworks.

We found Macon sitting alone on the sand near the nest. His knees were bent, and he had his arms wrapped around them as he looked out at the sea. His backpack was beside him. I thought he looked sad and lonely, and that made me feel sad too.

"Hey, Macon!" I called out.

He spun around at my call, surprised to see us.

"What are you guys doing here?"

"We came looking for you," Lovie said.

We reached his side and let our backpacks hit the sand.

"Anything happening?" I asked.

"Nope," he replied.

I spread out my towel beside Macon. Lovie did the same. We joined him at the nest, legs crossed. It felt good for the three of us to sit together again, side by side.

"I'm sorry, man," I said.

"Me too," Lovie said.

"It's okay," Macon said.

"No, it's not," I said. "I pushed you to admit you couldn't swim. I'm sorry, But . . . I'm glad you told me."

"Us," Lovie chimed in.

"Right. Us. We're a team. The Dawn Patrol." I let my fingers drag the sand. "What did you think we'd say?"

Macon picked up sand and let it trail through his fingers. "I thought you'd laugh." He looked at me and there was accusation in his eyes. "You *did* laugh."

I jerked my head over to look at him. "No, I didn't."

Macon's eyes flashed. "You said you couldn't believe anyone didn't know how to swim," he fired back.

"Oh yeah," I said, ashamed. That did sound mean. "I'm sorry. I didn't mean it like that."

"Whatever." He looked at his shoes.

"I'm glad we know," Lovie said. "A lot of things make sense now. Why you didn't want to kayak or go in the waves."

"I didn't want you guys to think I was, you know . . . weird. Besides, it just seemed easier not to tell you."

"I don't know," Lovie said softly. "Sometimes secrets are the hardest thing to keep inside."

I looked at her, knowing she was talking about her dad.

"I guess I was embarrassed I didn't know how," Macon said. "I mean, I'm almost twelve."

"We all have something we're embarrassed about," Lovie said. "Afraid to let other people know about. In case they laugh."

"Yeah," Macon said.

Lovie took a deep breath, then looked at Macon. "I know what that feels like"—she paused to twiddle with her sea turtle necklace again—"to feel embarrassed."

Macon furrowed his brows in confusion. "What do you mean?"

She shifted her body and looked down at her flip-flops, which were coated with sand. "I have a secret. But I don't want to have a secret between us."

Macon sat quietly, listening.

"My daddy . . ." She paused. "Not my real daddy, but my

199

biological father," she explained. She paused again to bite her lip. "He's in prison."

Macon's chin dropped. "Really? For how long?"

"A long time. Since I was in kindergarten."

"That's tough," said Macon softly.

"Yeah. Everyone at school knows. I'm *that* girl. The one with the bad dad. I hear them talking about me behind my back."

"How come you never told us?" Macon asked.

"Why didn't you tell us you couldn't swim?" she asked.

"Yeah, okay. I get it," Macon said.

"Your mom told us about what happened to you when you were little," I said to Macon. "How you almost drowned."

His eyes widened with surprise. "She did? When?"

"We went to your house looking for you and she told us," Lovie said. "That had to be so scary."

Macon nodded. "I still remember that day," he said. "I had on green swim trunks, my favorite. They had these little frogs all over them." He leaned back on his arms. "It was weird being underwater and looking up and seeing blurry colors above me. I kept kicking and reaching, but no matter how hard I tried, I couldn't get out. My chest hurt. Then, in a flash, this lifeguard was yanking me out of the water. I remember my mom's face. She was screaming and crying." He shook his head. "That's what scared me the most."

"You almost drowned . . ." The words fell out of my mouth.

"Yeah," Macon said, and blew out a plume of air. "It gave me nightmares for a long time."

"But you're not scared now, are you?" I asked.

"No," Macon said quickly. Then he shrugged. "I don't know."

"You could learn how to swim now. You can learn right here. At Huyler House," said Lovie.

Macon looked up from his shoes at her. "Yeah?"

"Yeah," she told him, filled with the excitement of a fisherman who hooked a fish. "They have classes."

"Isn't it kind of babyish? I mean, I don't want to be the big kid in a class with a bunch of four-year-olds."

Lovie replied quickly. "There's hardly anyone in the class. I mean, we're the only kids. This is our island, remember? Who's to watch? Your mom said she'd like it if you could swim. She'd feel better about you living around all this water."

"She did?" he asked.

Lovie said, reeling him in, "You'll learn how to swim in no time. You're so strong."

Macon smiled at that.

"I know: You take a swim class," I told him. "I'm taking boating lessons starting next week."

"What about me? What class should I take?" Lovie asked, never liking to be left out.

"I don't know. What do you want to take?"

She shrugged. "Maybe art. I'm trying to get better in my notebook." She paused. "Yeah, I'll take an art class," she decided in typical quick fashion.

"I guess that means we'll all be in summer school," I said.

"Don't call it school," Macon said with a roll of the eyes. "It's summer *cool*!"

I snorted a laugh at his joke, glad that he thought swimming classes would be fun. "I'm all for that," I said. "If you promise to learn how to swim, I promise to get my boater's license. How awesome would that be?"

Lovie moved to sit on her heels, excited. "At the end of summer, we'll all go out on my boat for a ride together."

I extended my right hand toward Macon in a handshake. "Are you game?"

He stared hesitantly at my hand.

I extended my hand a little farther. "Come on, man. What's there to think about? You know you want to. I can see it in your eyes. And . . . my arm is getting tired."

"Yeah," Macon said, and took my hand.

Lovie wrapped an arm over each of our necks, completing the circle.

We stayed out until the sky grew dark, waiting for the fireworks to start on Isle of Palms. We ate the sandwiches, adjusted the pinwheels and flags, filled in the ghost crab holes with wrack, told stories, and hunted for shells until the first explosion of color burst into the sky. It caught us by surprise. We all jumped up and down and cheered.

Then for no reason other than joy we took off running along the beach in single file, our arms stretched out like the wings of pelicans. Our feet skimmed the shoreline, spraying the air with droplets of water that sparked in brilliant colors, the fireworks mirrored in the water. I felt the wind in my hair and the water on my face as we ran.

I led the pack, veering toward the beach, and still the fireworks exploded overhead. The sudden bursts of sound were a drumbeat and we danced wildly. Overhead the fiery lights zigzagged across the sky in staccato.

We whooped and hollered at the top of our lungs. We were the only ones on the beach. We could act goofy. Jump and sing and dance and laugh out loud the way we couldn't if we were home, or at school, or anywhere else than this beach.

Our beach.

CHAPTER 20

Our Lucky Day

Be fearless.

THE FOLLOWING NIGHT, OPERATION COYOTE was back on. I picked up Lovie and we were on our way to meet Macon at the nest. We crossed the wooden bridge by the gazebo. It sounded like a thousand frogs were in the bog below. We couldn't see them, but their croaks and squeaks pulsed so loud it drowned out everything else.

"Stop! What's that?" Lovie pointed to the edge of the path.

I hit the brakes and leaned forward, squinting. "It's some kind of dead animal."

We hopped off the cart for a closer look with a flashlight.

"It's a dead rabbit." I gently nudged the lifeless animal with the tip of my shoe.

"Or what's left of it," she said.

We stepped around the bits of flesh, fur, and blood surrounding the carcass.

"Coyote," Lovie whispered.

Our walkie-talkie crackled to life, making us jump.

"Guys. Come in. Guys!" It was Macon and he sounded scared. "Where are you? Come in! Over."

I ran back for the walkie-talkie in the golf cart cup holder and pushed the talk button. "Macon! We hear you. Over."

"I think the coyote's near," he said softly. "I heard a bark and some whining. Close. Where are you? Over."

"Close. We can reach the rendezvous in just two minutes. Over."

"Ten-four. I'm standing guard at the end of the boardwalk. Over."

Lovie and I leaped back on the golf cart. I stepped hard on the pedal and took off. We sped down the boardwalk and screeched to a halt next to the gazebo, our tires spitting sandy gravel and broken shells. Jumping off, we sprinted the rest of the way toward the beach and Macon.

Suddenly Macon's scream pierced the ocean air. "Help!"

Lovie shouted, "We're coming, Macon!"

Our feet dug into the sand as we raced. The light from Lovie's headlamp bounced on the sand. I caught sight of Macon standing frozen, arms outstretched.

"Macon! Wha . . . what is it? What's wrong?" Lovie called out.

"A coyote!" Macon pointed, his hand shaking. "It's right there! Staring at me! I can't move."

Lovie came to a sudden stop a few feet behind Macon. I crashed smack into her.

"I see it!" she said in a loud whisper.

"Where?" I said. Panting, I searched wildly around for something . . . anything.

She pointed to the shadowy shrubs farther up the dunes. I squinted and leaned forward and then I saw it too. The hulking shape of the coyote was standing beside the tall grasses. In the dim light it was shadowy, but I could tell it was thin and scraggly. I felt my blood drain from my face and the hairs on my body stand straight up.

"What do we do?" Lovie asked.

Macon didn't move his head but spoke in a loud whisper. "Retreat."

"Okay. Start stepping back toward us. Real slow," I said in a low voice. "We don't want to spook it."

"What about shouting and screaming?" Lovie asked.

"We don't have our stuff! On the count of three, step back. Then we all start screaming and run for the gazebo together. Okay?"

Macon nodded his head. I could feel Lovie's hand clutch my arm.

Macon took one step back.

The animal took one step forward.

He took another step.

The animal took another step. Again and again until Macon stopped moving.

"It's not working!" Macon cried. "It's after me!"

My body pulsed with fear. All the plans we had made suddenly seemed so stupid. This was real. *What do I do?*

My mind flashed back to a time my dad and I were walking in a park when suddenly a mangy-looking dog approached us. It lowered its head and growled threateningly. I wanted to run, but Dad warned me not to turn my back. "Be fearless," he told me. Then he waved his arms out and roared like a beast as loud as he could. The dog backed away.

I took a deep breath and raised my arms. Then I started waving them and growling like a monster. I yelled to my friends, "Run! Run to the gazebo now!"

Macon turned and sprinted across the beach. Lovie ran by his side.

The coyote's ears pricked up when it saw them run off. Then it began trotting toward me. I still had a flashlight in my hand. As the animal drew near, I stepped forward with another loud "Aaarrgh!" and swung my flashlight. I missed. The animal stopped, nose in the air.

I turned and ran as fast as I could, my fists like pistons at my side. My heels dug into the sand. I was fast.

But so was that coyote. It stayed hot on my heels.

Macon and Lovie were inside the gazebo banging the tin

pans and shaking the coin canister, making a loud racket.

"Hurry!" Macon screamed.

"Run, Jake!" called Lovie.

I ran so fast my chest felt like it would explode. Macon stood at the gazebo door, holding it open. His flashlight shone a path to guide me. I ran inside and he slammed the door. We stood staring at one another, wide-eyed and panting. Sweat poured down our faces.

Suddenly, *bam!* The coyote leaped up on its hind legs, its front paws against the screen. Macon and Lovie screamed and ran to the opposite side of the gazebo. I spun around and growled as fierce and loud as I could. I shone my flashlight right in its eyes.

"Grrrrrrrrr!" I shouted as mean and growly as I could.

But . . . the coyote wasn't growling back. Or gnashing its teeth. It wasn't clawing to get in. It wasn't acting mean or scary at all. It was licking the screen and whimpering.

Confused, I stopped shouting and took a step closer to peer into the darkness. Something shiny caught my eye.

"Jake, get back here," Lovie cried in panic. She shook the can of coins again.

Macon ran to my side, aiming his vinegar-filled squirt gun at it. "Jake, stand back!"

"Hey, wait!" I put my hand on the squirt gun. "Look! It has a collar."

Macon lowered his gun a little, his eyes doubting me. He was ready to spring. "It has a *what*?"

"A collar! What kind of coyote wears a collar?"

"Maybe it's an animal tag," Lovie called out from the corner. "They tag animals in the wild."

The animal whined, then lowered to a sit outside the screen door. The sounds of its pants sounded loud in the hush.

I shone my flashlight in the animal's face. In the beam of light, I saw a black-and-white rounded muzzle. A plump black nose. Floppy ears.

Macon took a step closer to peer through the screen. "Coyotes don't have floppy ears."

Lovie stepped nearer, hesitatingly.

"You guys," I said, wonder filling my voice. "This isn't a coyote."

Lovie leaned in and exclaimed, "It's a *dog*!"

"That dog absolutely cannot sleep in the house. It's filthy! And it's probably covered in fleas and ticks," Honey exclaimed.

"We can't abandon him. Please . . . ," I pleaded. "He has nowhere to go."

"And he's starving," Lovie cried. "We gave him the rest of our food, but he's so skinny."

We were standing at the foot of the stairs of the Bird's Nest with a piece of rope slipped around the dog's neck. The dog did look mangy. It was the size of a small Labrador retriever and not bad-looking. Brown hair, sad brown eyes, and a mass of dirty, matted, wiry, brownish fur. He looked like a big Benji, from the movie. And he stank like sweaty socks.

"We can't let him loose," I said. "That'd be mean. He could get attacked by a coyote. Besides, I don't think he'd run away anyway. He'd just be here in the morning."

"Fine. He can stay on the screened porch. Just for tonight. But don't you go getting any wild ideas of keeping him. I'll call Chief Rand to come by tomorrow morning and take him to a shelter."

The dog pressed against my leg. I stroked his head.

Even though it was late at night, word traveled fast on the tiny island. A neighbor came to drop off dog shampoo, a leash, and a bag of dry food. Honey mixed in leftover hot dogs and hamburger from the holiday. She put her hands on her hips and watched as the dog ate it all up.

She seemed pleased that he licked the bowl clean. "Poor thing. He's near starved and covered in those awful sand-spurs. Jake, go in my junk drawer and grab me some needle-nose pliers."

The dog didn't yelp or snap as Honey carefully plucked out one sharp, pointy sandspur after another from his hair. He just stood there. I sure knew how those spurs could hurt.

"These spurs hurt like the devil," she muttered as she snipped a knotted-up spur from the hair with scissors. "We call them the revenge of the Carolina parakeet."

"The what?"

"The Carolina parakeet was a fancy-looking parrot, native to America. Used to fill the skies around here. Their favorite food was sandspurs . . . these tiny round prickly things. Some folks call them cockleburs or sandburs. No matter what you call them, they hurt like the dickens when they prick your skin. Ouch!" Honey plucked one off her finger.

"Well, we humans drove that beautiful bird to extinction, in part because farmers were afraid they were eating their crops." She frowned as she kept working on the dog's fur. "Now the Carolina parakeets are no more. Extinct." She shook her head. "And we're stuck with the seeds of these devils. There, I think that's the last one."

She rose and patted the dog's head. He whimpered gratefully and put his paw on her leg.

She cracked an unwilling smile. "I have to admit, he's a good-natured creature. That had to hurt. He'll sleep better tonight. But tomorrow, he gets a bath." She waved her hand in front of her face. "This dog stinks!"

Carolina parakeet

RIP

CHAPTER 21

A Boy and His Dog

*Sometimes life makes decisions for you, and it's
best not to fight it and just to go along.*

WHEN THE MORNING SUN SHONE
through my round window, I raced downstairs to
see if the dog was still in the screened porch. I
swung open the door. There he was, lying on the makeshift
bed of blankets we made for him. The minute he spied me, he
sprang to his feet to greet me with whimpers of excitement. I
petted him, then fed him more dog food and filled his water
dish. When I turned to leave, the dog trotted behind me.

"I'll be back," I told him. "I promise."

The dog tilted his head and his big eyes looked up at
me, trusting.

It killed me to hear him whimper and scrape at the door when I left. I begged Honey to let me off Dawn Patrol just this once, but she wouldn't allow it. "A dog is all about accepting responsibility," she told me. "And being old enough for a dog means you're willing to accept responsibility."

Macon, Lovie, and I raced through our turtle patrol duties, then rushed back to the Bird's Nest.

The dog barked and whined and jumped all over us, he was so happy to see us. His tail wagged so hard and fast that his butt wiggled.

"He's so cute," Lovie said.

"He's so dirty," said Macon with a frown. "I'll bet he's covered in fleas."

"You're just in time to help with the bath," I told them.

"I have no clue what to do," said Macon. "I've never had a dog before. Or any pet."

"It's easy," said Lovie. "First we need a hose."

"This way," I said, and led the dog to a spot under the house.

"Jake, you hold on to the dog while I spray him gently with the hose," Lovie said. "And guys, prepare to get wet. Ready?"

The dog wagged his tail all the more and his tongue hung out of his mouth, happy for the attention. In the summer, the water from the outside faucet was as warm as bathwater. Macon squirted soap all over the dog, and Lovie and I took turns lathering him up with our hands. I could have sworn I saw the dog smile. By the time we rinsed him off, we were as wet as the dog. When he shook his wet fur, he sprayed all three of us. We stepped back, laughing.

Macon and I patted him dry with a towel, and Lovie brushed him.

"You know, with all the pluff mud and sandburs gone, he's a pretty good-looking dog," said Lovie.

The dog licked my face. "He's beautiful," I said.

"I wonder what his name is," Macon said. "Did you check the tag?"

"It's just a rabies tag," I answered.

"Let's give him a name," Lovie said. "How about Bubba? That's a good Lowcountry name for a dog. Or maybe Bo? No, scratch that. Buster!"

"Too common," I said. "He needs a special name. Like Braveheart. Think of how brave he had to be to live out in the wild by himself."

"We don't know how long he was out in the wild," Macon said. "Maybe it was one night."

Lovie lifted her chin. "How about whoever gets to keep him gets to name him?"

Macon and I looked at her, mouths open. She'd said aloud what we were all secretly wanting.

"I want to keep him," I said. "I'm the one who figured out he was a dog. And he's at my house."

"We all found him," Lovie fired back. "Plus, you have to go back to New Jersey at the end of the summer."

"But I've always wanted a dog," I told her, feeling suddenly defensive.

"So did I!" she said.

Macon said morosely, "I wish I could keep him. But Mom says with the baby on the way, she can't allow a big dog in the house."

I was surprised that Macon had already asked permission. I had not worked up the courage yet to ask Honey.

"Well, we can't get our hopes up anyways," I said. "He obviously belongs to someone. He has that collar."

We all fell quiet while petting the dog, who was now flopped out on the driveway with his long pink tongue hanging out of his mouth. His watery brown eyes looked at us with relief and joy. I thought about how scared the poor dog must've been.

A fire department pickup truck rolled up to the house. It was one of the very few vehicles allowed on the island. We watched as Chief Rand stepped out of the truck. He wiped his brow and looked around, then, spotting us, he waved and walked toward us.

"So, here's the furry mischief maker," Chief Rand said, bending down to pet the dog. "Sounds like it was a pretty crazy night for you kids and your four-legged hostage."

"He's really nice," I said, feeling the need to defend him. "We just gave him a bath and he didn't nip at us or bark. Not once. Not even when Honey pulled sandspurs off him."

"Well, I yelp when I get those prickly suckers on me." Chief Rand gently held the dog's face with his hands. "You did a real good job cleaning him up." He ran his hands down the length of the dog's body. "He's a skinny thing. Likely been lost for a while. I'd say he's one lucky dog to have survived in the wild with coyotes around too."

"Does he belong to someone on the island?" Lovie asked.

Chief Rand shook his head. "I put the word out, but no one here's stepped up to claim him. Plus, I think I know every resident dog on the island. I've never seen this guy."

"Well then, how did he even get here?" Macon asked.

Rand stood up, stroking his bearded jaw in thought. "It's possible he swam over from Capers Island. It's a short distance from here. Deer do it all the time."

"They do?" I tried to imagine the sight of deer swimming across the inlet.

"Yep. This poor fella probably got left behind from a boating trip—on purpose." He shrugged. "He likely smelled food on Dewees and swam over."

The chief looked down at the collar tag and read it. "It's good to know he's up-to-date on his rabies. That's one less worry. And it shows he belonged to someone."

I looked into the dog's liquid brown eyes. Something inside of me shifted, and I just knew this dog was going to be mine . . . somehow.

"Do you have to take him away?" I asked.

"We all love him already," Lovie said, wrapping her arms around the dog's neck.

Chief Rand's face softened. He reached up to scratch his

beard again. "Tell you what," he said. He spoke to all of us, but his eyes were on me. "I'll take him to the vet on the mainland, to check for a microchip and make sure he's healthy. Then I'll report him to the local animal shelters to see if this dog is on any lost pet list. If I come up empty-handed, I'll bring him back here. I don't see much point in him having to stay in a cage at a shelter when he could be living the good life out here on the island with you kids."

We jumped to our feet, cheering. The dog jumped to his feet too and barked.

"Thanks, Chief Rand!" I exclaimed.

"Hold on now!" Rand motioned for us to calm down. "We have a lot of hoops to jump through first. And I have to know your grandma agrees to all this. What she says, goes."

"She'll say yes!" I didn't know what I'd have to do to convince her, but I'd figure something out. I just had to.

"Then say goodbye for now. Hopefully, I'll have this dog back to y'all soon. What's his name, anyway?"

My friends and I looked at one another. I remembered what Chief Rand had said when he first saw the dog. *I'd say he's one lucky dog.*

"His name is Lucky," I said, and looked to Macon and Lovie for agreement.

Lovie and Macon both smiled and nodded.

Waiting for Lucky to return seemed like the longest day of my life! The three of us tried to pass the time catching a meal. We hung out at the crab dock armed with long-handled nets and a bucket. But we were quickly run off by curious alligators, only the tops of their heads and dark, bony ridges of their backs visible as they drifted lazily toward us like logs in a pond.

Lovie suggested a cart ride to the northern end of the island to fish. But the bright afternoon sun was zapping our energy and would keep the fish away. July was the hottest month of the summer in South Carolina, and this felt like the hottest day.

So we retreated to our usual hangout . . . the Nature Center. Inside, the air was chilled and a fan circulated it in a gentle breeze that cooled our skin. We got out our journals to recap the wild experiences from the last twenty-four hours. Each of us had our own best way of telling stories. Macon's notebook had lots of cool facts and he wrote long paragraphs about what he saw, and more about what he felt about it.

I could draw. I felt good about my skill after a month of practice. My details were better. Honey told me frequently how good my powers of observation were. She said I was a born naturalist.

Lovie's drawings were not as detailed as mine, but, well, prettier. More like paintings. Her art classes were paying off. She filled her pages with color. I was jealous of the way she could draw faces that actually looked like the people she drew. Her drawing of Lucky was just plain beautiful.

≈

When I returned to the Bird's Nest, the fire truck was parked in the driveway. My heart skipped a beat. I darted up the stairs and raced into the house. Chief Rand and Honey were talking at the kitchen counter, coffee cups in their hands. I searched the area, panting, but I didn't see Lucky.

Honey looked up, saw my face, shook her head, and smirked. "Go on to the porch. That lucky mutt is back."

I dashed to the back porch. There was Lucky, sitting like he belonged there, wearing a brand-new red collar. I slid open the sliding glass door, and in a flash I had the dog in my arms. I gave him head scratches and belly rubs, and I wasn't ashamed of the tears.

Chief Rand and Honey stepped out onto the porch.

"So far so good, Jake," Rand said. "He isn't microchipped, and the vet gave him a clean bill of health."

"And flea medicine," Honey added.

"I posted Lucky's picture at the local community centers, and on the ferry," Chief Rand added. "I also ran a check of the local animal shelters. So far, no one's posted a lost dog of his description. And no one has claimed him."

"Yet," Honey warned.

"I just know no one is going to claim him. He belongs here." I gave Honey my most desperate, pleading look. "Pleeeeeease, can we keep him?"

"You can stop the begging," she said with a wave of her hand. "I already told Rand that Lucky could stay here. *Temporarily*. We have to wait seventy-two hours for someone to call about the dog. After that, we can discuss Lucky's future."

Chief Rand winked at me. "Animal control is not coming out to us, so the way I see it, possession is nine-tenths of the law."

I smiled and buried my face in the dog's fur. As if Lucky heard my thoughts, he put his paws on my lap and started licking my face. It tickled and I couldn't help but laugh.

Chief Rand chuckled and said, "A boy and his dog."

Honey crossed her arms and sighed. "Sometimes life makes decisions for you, and it's best not to fight it and just to go along."

Dear Dad,

You're not going to believe this, but we have a dog! Honey just doesn't know it yet.

😃

His name is Lucky. We had our stakeout last night for the turtle nest. We thought he was a coyote, but we saw it was just a scared, lost dog. And hungry. He probably smelled the beef jerky tucked in Macon's pocket.

I know you've always said no pets for as long as you and mom are active duty. But he needs a family. And I think we could all use some luck in our lives, don't you?

PLEASE write to Honey and tell her I can keep him. She'll do anything you ask. I want him so bad. I don't think I ever wanted anything more.

(Except you getting better.)
Here's my best drawing of Lucky. I promise he looks way better than that. Can we keep him? PLEASE?
I miss you.
Love,
Jake

Lucky

CHAPTER 22

The Tests

Your dad would be proud.

THE SUMMER DAYS FLEW BY AND THE JULY weather kept getting hotter. Quick afternoon pop-up storms raced across the island on their way to the Atlantic Ocean, adding to the humidity. The bugs sure loved it. At night the songs of the cicadas swelled and the frogs bellowed. The mosquitoes were bigger and hungrier than ever. Honey joked that the mosquito was the state bird!

The Turtle Team was super busy now. In the mornings we looked for turtle tracks and nests, and in the evenings the early nests were beginning to hatch!

Best of all, no one ever came forward to claim Lucky, so he

got to stay with me. Lovie was okay with that. She was happy to see the dog every day. Honey wouldn't admit that we were adopting him. But I could tell Lucky was winning her over. He couldn't climb the ladder to my loft, so he slept on a mat in the main room. Every morning Lucky scratched at Honey's bedroom door and whined to wake her up. Up in my loft, I could hear her croon to the dog as she made her coffee. Lucky also put his head on her lap for attention and dropped toys at her feet to play.

Mostly, though, Lucky was my sidekick. I was in charge of feeding and walking him. He sat on the golf cart with me while I did my chores. And he was officially part of the Dawn Patrol.

The big shift for the second half of my summer was the classes we were all taking. Macon was signed up for private swim lessons at Huyler House. Lovie met a retired artist on the island who agreed to give her art lessons. Me? At last I was taking my boater education course.

I'd passed the written part of my boating test. Now I just had to pass Honey's test. She said she wouldn't let me operate a boat unless someone she trusted could agree that I knew my way around a boat. Chief Rand volunteered for the task on his day off.

On the big day, Lovie was waiting for me at the end of the dock. She'd helped me practice on her boat and was as eager for me to get my license as I was.

"Good luck," she said. Her eyes were bright.

"Thanks," I said.

Then, taking a deep breath, I turned and walked to the end of the dock, where Chief Rand was standing wide-legged in a boat named the She Crab. His beard was as red as a channel marker. He waved his arm high above his head and tossed me a tube of sunscreen.

"Lesson one: Always protect your skin."

"You sound just like Honey," I replied, while removing my Army ball cap and slathering lotion on my face and arms.

"Let's get this show on the road, or should I say water." He chuckled. "First, untie the boat." He pointed to the metal cleat on the dock.

I scurried to release the rope.

"Hop aboard!"

I tossed the rope into his arms, then jumped aboard the boat.

Chief Rand said, "What's the front of the boat called?"

"Bow," I yelled out.

"Correct," he said, and tossed me a life jacket. "Back of the boat?"

"Stern." I felt confident as I snapped on my orange life vest.

"What's the difference between starboard and port side?"

"Port side is the left side of the boat and starboard is the right."

Chief Rand playfully slapped down the bill of my cap. "You've been studying, I see. All right then, I'm ready to help you captain your own vessel." He clapped his hands together. "This here is a sixteen-foot Boston whaler. It's my pride and joy. Had it since I was a teenager. I bought it with my own money, too." He rubbed his hand across the upper edge of his boat.

That's the gunwale, I said in my head, still thinking about all the parts of a boat.

"A little TLC and you can enjoy a boat like this for decades. There are a lot of good memories here. You should ask your dad to tell you some stories about our times out on the *She Crab*."

"Yes, sir!"

He grinned at my enthusiasm.

"Okay, fire her up, Jake!"

I licked my lips, dried my damp hands, and scurried to the engine. I quickly got it growling. I couldn't help but throw my shoulders back and grin.

"Well done! How much practice have you had taking off from the dock?" Chief Rand asked.

"Uh, none, sir."

My proud moment was totally over. Luckily, Rand was a patient teacher. I followed his every command, and under his guidance, managed to slowly steer the boat away from the dock.

"You're a quick learner," he said as I eased the motor's tiller handle to follow the creek.

A breeze rippled across the sparkling water. The green tips of cord grass swayed in the high tide. The creek snaked lazily from left and right. Every bend revealed hungry birds fishing for their meal.

"It's like riding a bike, Jake. Once you learn, you'll never forget," the chief said. His eyes were hidden behind reflective wraparound sunglasses. "Every Lowcountry kid should know how to operate a boat."

"Yes, sir," I said, keeping my eyes on the water.

"Did you know your dad and I learned how to drive a boat together one summer?"

"No sir."

"Your dad and I spent practically every day together on the island. We were best friends, back in the day," he said, looking off at the water. Suddenly he shouted. "Whoa! Cut the engine! Dolphin, starboard."

I followed his command and scanned the dark water. Suddenly a smooth gray dorsal fin emerged. I gasped and pointed.

"Dolphin at two o'clock!" I called out, using the clock as a marker, the way my dad had taught me. I just spotted the dorsal fin before it slipped beneath the surface again. "Are you sure it was a dolphin and not a shark?"

"Definitely not a shark. A dolphin's dorsal fin has a very curved edge like this." He curved his fingers on one hand. "Sharks have a straight dorsal fin. Plus, watch the way they swim. A dolphin arches in and out of the water. A shark glides in a zigzag pattern." His head jerked up. "Dolphin . . . three o'clock!" Rand shot his arm out.

I scanned the water and spotted a dolphin arching in the water.

"Look! Another one!" I yelled.

"Two of them! No, three of them," Rand said, shaking my shoulder with excitement. "They're checking us out."

When they surfaced again, I spotted one with a damaged fin. "Look at that one." I pointed. "Part of its fin is missing."

"Dorsal fins are like fingerprints for humans," Chief Rand said. "That's how we identify them. I've spotted that one a few times over the years. It's likely a resident dolphin that got hurt, either from a shark bite or boat propeller strike. Boats sometimes speed too fast in these waters, without a thought to the animals they might hit."

I felt sorry for the dolphin and kept my eyes peeled. I didn't want to hit a dolphin or a turtle.

We bobbed quietly on the water, trying to guess where the dolphins would appear next. Suddenly a loud puff cut the

silence. I spun around to the bow of the boat. I couldn't believe it. A dolphin was right by the boat! Its blowhole was just above the surface. Then it rolled over a little on its side so it could look right at me.

"Someone's feeling curious," Rand said softly.

"It looks like it's smiling at me," I said. I leaned over the edge of the boat, and my eyes locked on the dolphin's eyes. I wasn't imagining it. In that instant, I felt a connection. Like we were talking, without words.

Then it slid over and disappeared into the water. *Come back*, I wished in my mind.

"That right there is the sign of a very good day," Chief Rand said, interrupting my thoughts. "Every time I see a dolphin, it feels like a gift. Especially up close like that."

"Yeah," I said. I couldn't believe my luck. I wanted to write my dad.

"What do you say I bring us back in?" asked Chief Rand.

"Aye aye, sir!"

"Grab your hat," Chief Rand told me as he stepped in to take the wheel.

I did so just as he powered up the engine. Within a minute, we were skating over the water. Big white wakes spread out behind us, and I couldn't stop the ear-to-ear grin across my face. I felt the salt water flowing through my veins. I was more of a Lowcountry kid than I thought.

When we neared the dock and entered the No Wake zone, Chief Rand throttled back the engine and stepped aside.

"Now bring us in," he said.

I grabbed the wheel. This would be the hardest part of my test. I couldn't believe he was trusting me to bring in his beloved Boston whaler.

"Rule one: Line up your approach," Chief Rand told me. "How's the wind or current?"

"Behind me."

"Good. Then come in shallow to stay off the dock."

"Aye aye."

"Rule two: Come in slow!"

I slowed the engine to a crawl.

"Never come into a dock faster than you're willing to hit it."

I swallowed. "Yes, sir."

"Rule number three: Time your swing. That means aim for the center of the dock where you want to tie up."

I followed his instructions.

"Good," Chief Rand said. "Now give the engine a little bump. That's right. Finally, rule number four: Roll the wheel all the way back to port. That, young man, is what we call the flourishing finish. Yep, that's good. Turn off the engine!"

I did so. Suddenly the air was quiet.

"Let the breeze carry you into the dock." Chief Rand stood behind me, hawking my every move.

I wiped the sweat from my brow and listened to the water lapping at the sides of the boat. We floated the final few feet parallel to the dock. I concentrated on my entry, then exhaled and let my shoulders relax. I did it! And I didn't crash the boat.

Chief Rand hurried to the side of the boat, stretched far out, and grabbed the rope lying on the dock. He pulled us close to the dock.

"Okay, you're all set to tie up."

This was the final test. I leaped from the boat, and grabbing the rope, wrapped it around the base of the cleat. I made a figure-eight with the rope over the horns of the cleat. Finally, I tucked the line under and pulled tight. Done!

I straightened and waited for Chief Rand to inspect.

He climbed from his boat and stood beside me, hands behind his back, and inspected my knot. "A good cleat hitch. Job well done!"

I released a stream of air.

Chief Rand patted me on the back. His voice lowered and he spoke with emotion. "It was my honor to teach you. Your dad would be proud. Congratulations, skipper."

Rand shared the news with Honey. With great ceremony, she presented me with my official boater education card. It had my name, birth date, and Honey's address on it.

"You did it, Jake. I'm proud of you. Keep that in a safe place. You'll need it whenever you're the captain of a boat."

With the card hot in my hand, I raced to Macon's house.

"I did it! I can captain my own boat!" I shouted when he swung open the front door.

He slapped my back and hooted out loud.

"I can't wait to tell Lovie!"

"Congrats! One problem, though."

"What?"

"You still need an actual boat."

I punched him in the arm. "Ha. Ha. Funny. Really, though . . . I've already been thinking about that. I'm going to start saving up every dollar I get. How much do you think a boat would cost?"

"Way more than you got in that skinny wallet of yours."

I sighed and opened up my wallet wide. I counted seven dollars and an old movie theater ticket. "I'm going to need a job."

"More like *multiple* jobs," he joked. "You're coming back to Dewees next summer, right?"

"You bet I am."

His face eased into a grin. "Then I'll help you draft a business plan. Something we can do together right here on the island. Dude, I'll *help* you buy a boat! A decent boat, not some muddy piece of junk. I'll even get my boater's license. And you know what? You can dock it at our dock."

I laughed, thinking we'd come full circle. "Said the guy who wouldn't even get in a kayak!"

Now it was Macon's turn to pass his test. Low clouds raced across the afternoon sky as Lucky and I hurried to Huyler House for Macon's swim test.

I spotted Lovie and we sat together by the pool with Lucky between us. Macon's instructor was a young college girl with blond hair pulled back in a ponytail. She wore a dark blue Speedo swimsuit, the kind team sport swimmers wear.

"Here they come," Lovie said, and walked to the porch railing to watch the Simmonses' golf cart pull into the parking lot. "I don't believe it! Mrs. Simmons left the house!"

I hurried to stand beside her. There she was, in her flowing colorful caftan. On one side was Aunt Sissy. Holding her other arm was Mr. Simmons. I guess he'd flown in for the event. I swallowed hard. This was only the third time I had ever seen him. And the last time wasn't under good circumstances.

Macon ran up the stairs ahead of them to greet us.

"Dude, your mom's here," I said in a low voice.

"Yeah." He was beaming that his parents had come. "It's against the doctor's orders. But my mom said nothing was going to stop her from coming out here to watch her son swim."

"You'd better do good."

"I got this," he told me with his wide grin.

Macon wore reflective goggles and bright green and black board shorts. His parents waved at us, then settled in chairs under a big umbrella with Aunt Sissy.

Macon eased into the pool. It was so hot, I wished I could jump into the pool too.

Lovie and I returned to our seats. Lucky trotted over to lie in the shade. I scooted to the front of my chair. Lovie jiggled her foot. We looked at each other, and with a smile, lifted our hands to show each of us was crossing our fingers for luck.

The instructor joined Macon in the pool and led him through his challenges. He didn't seem at all nervous. He took a deep breath and eased himself under the water, all the way. I shifted my eyes over to Macon's mom, who had a death grip on Mr. Simmons's arm. I could feel her tension ease when Macon popped back up.

That was easy. Next was freestyle. Macon never cracked a smile. We watched his strong, long arms cut through the water with the power and grace I admired in the dolphins. He easily completed a full lap.

"He's killing it," I said to Lovie.

"I know, right? He wouldn't put a toe in the ocean a month ago," she whispered back. "And now he's a regular Cullen Jones."

Macon completed the different basic strokes—the front crawl, the backstroke, the breaststroke, and the sidestroke—with ease. He finished his test with the survival float and a sixty-second treading-water test. When he was done, Macon lifted his arm over his head in a fist pump.

We erupted in applause and cheers. Macon climbed from the pool, and his instructor presented him with his swimming certificate. Macon held it up over his head with a triumphant smile, then raced over to show it to his mom and dad.

"Macon, we're so proud of you!" His mom had tears in her eyes as she wrapped him in a towel.

"Thanks, Mom," he said. "It's not a big deal, really."

"No big deal?" Macon's dad shook his son's shoulders gently with his big hands. "This right here *is* a big deal. You overcame a fear. And you achieved your goal—in record time. We're so proud of you. And next summer we're going to get your mom in this pool," he added, turning his head to smile at his wife.

Mrs. Simmons laughed and nodded. "And baby, too!"

CHAPTER 23

The Emergence

Pick out the biggest, brightest star to wish on.

JULY TURNED INTO AUGUST. THE DAYS AND nights grew steamy and hot. There was no escaping the near 100-degree temperatures, not even in the shade. We spent our afternoons swimming in the Huyler House pool or going out on Lovie's boat. I couldn't get enough of the water.

Macon, Lovie, and I were tighter than ever. We could almost finish one another's sentences. Along with Lucky, we had truly created our own pack. Sometimes we called ourselves "the Three Musketeers." Or "the Scribes," because of our journals. Macon liked "the Water Rats," the name Oysterman Ollie called us. I came up with "the Coyotes," but we all agreed Lucky had enough of being mistaken for a coyote. Lovie said we had to wait until we found the absolute best name . . . the one that fit us.

"We'll know it when we hear it," she told us.

We were hanging out on the wooden Adirondack chairs on the porch of the Nature Center. We had our favorite table beside a shelf the center had provided for us to house our summer collection. Judy and Alicia, Honey, and Lovie's Aunt Sissy walked up the stairs, surprising us.

"Hey, kids," Judy called out with a wave. Her blue eyes were sparkling. "We have some news."

The three of us exchanged worried glances. *What did we do now?*

Judy laughed. "Good news. Your community service is officially over!"

Lovie's face crumpled, but Macon and I high-fived.

Alicia added, "We are very proud of everything you've done to help the team this summer. You did a great job." She looked at Honey. "I think you should say a heartfelt thank-you to Miss Helen for all she did to teach you these past six weeks."

"Thank you," we all chimed, and clapped our hands. I even hooted.

Honey beamed. She looked like her old self—tanned, fit, full of gumption. I laughed to myself, thinking how Honey was always telling us kids to play outdoors. I guess getting out every morning was good for her, too.

"Can we still help the team?" Lovie looked worried.

"Of course. In fact . . ." Alicia turned to Judy.

Judy stepped forward. In her hand she carried a canvas bag. "We've made you Dewees Island's first official Junior Turtle Team members." She handed us each our own Dewees Island Turtle Team ball cap. "These are special caps. Look at the name on it."

We all looked at the lettering on the front of the blue ball caps. In big lettering were the words DAWN PATROL.

We slapped our caps on our heads and checked one another out approvingly.

Honey turned to us. "I'm game to keep on going till the end of the season. What do you say?"

Lovie jumped up and down, clapping her hands. "Yes!"

Macon and I looked at each other and nodded. "Sure!"

"Good to hear," Judy said. "The mother turtles may be leaving, but the hatchlings are still coming. There's a lot of action out on the beach. We've got a nest hatch happening this week."

"As a matter of fact," Alicia said, looking at Lovie, "the next nest due to hatch—is *yours*! The nest you've all worked so hard to protect."

A few days later, Honey and I had finished my favorite dinner of fried fish and collard greens. Honey was in her blue chair, her feet up, reading a book. I was reading too, lying on the sofa with Lucky across my legs.

I'd already read most of the books from my dad's bookshelf. I was currently halfway through *Hatchet*. I could relate to the thirteen-year-old character Brian Robeson. In the book, Brian's plane crashed in the wilderness, and he had to survive on his own with only his hatchet.

I looked at the ceiling and wondered if I'd be able to survive if that ever happened to me. When I arrived at the beginning of summer, no way I could have. But since then, I'd learned a lot about animals and plants, the land and the sea. And about myself, too. I thought that maybe I could manage in the wild alone.

The phone rang and both Honey and I swung our heads to look at it. I moved to answer, but Honey waved me back.

"I'll get it. I think I know what this might be."

I hawked her every movement, her facial expressions, as she said, "Uh-huh . . . uh-huh . . . okay then."

When she hung the phone up, her eyes gleamed. "Get your backpack, Jake. It looks like there's a nest tonight!"

Lucky felt the excitement and leaped to his feet with a bark.

"Lucky can't come this time," Honey said firmly. "No dogs at the hatchings."

"But it's his nest too. I mean, he found us at that nest."

"It's a firm rule. No exceptions."

"Sorry, boy," I told my dog, feeling bad when he looked at me trustingly. I gave Lucky a dog bone to enjoy before we headed out the door.

Honey sped along the dirt roads and reached the beach

in minutes. She could really move fast when a turtle nest was hatching.

"We're in luck," she said to me when she parked the cart. "Full moon!"

The moon glowed bright, lighting the beach like a theater. Honey handed me a special flashlight that had a red light.

"This is your Turtle Team flashlight. It has a red light, not white. Only red light is allowed on a nesting beach. White lights confuse the hatchlings," she said. "Their instinct tells them to go toward the brightest light. In the wild, that would be the light of the moon and the stars over the sea." She handed me a beach chair.

"But electricity changed everything. Now we have to worry about the light coming from the houses and the streetlamps. If hatchlings emerge from the nest and see the white light, the babies wouldn't know better and would head straight for the streets instead of the sea. And their certain death." She grabbed the bag of Turtle Team supplies.

"The same with flashlights. That's why it's important for people to turn off their lights along the beach and for the team to only use red lights." She looked up again at the full moon. "But the moon is so bright tonight, we don't need any flashlight. Our eyes will grow accustomed to the dim light." She hoisted her bag on her shoulder. "This way, Jake," she called out, and led the way down the beach path.

The sand on the path seemed to glow in the moonlight. Honey was right. Soon my eyes could see the figures and shapes in the distance. When we reached the beach, I saw that Judy and Alicia were already at the turtle nest. They flicked on and off their red-tinted flashlights to guide us to where they sat.

Honey set down her chair, then walked directly to the nest. "We have our fingers crossed on this nest," she said to me. "The coyote disturbed it and we had to move it, so we have to face the fact that this nest might not hatch."

"Okay." I wondered how Lovie would feel if the nest didn't hatch.

Honey bent over to inspect the nest, then turned her face toward mine. Her eyes gleamed like the stars.

"Oh, it's happening, Jake!"

I felt my heart beat quicker and squatted down for a closer look. All I saw was sand. "I don't see anything."

"Look closer. See how the sand is caving in a little?"

"Yes."

"That's a sign the turtles are sitting there, waiting to emerge."

"So, it *is* going to hatch?"

"It sure is."

I beamed. I couldn't wait to tell Lovie.

Honey lowered her voice. "When the eggs start to hatch deep in the nest, they all work together. The turtles on the top scrape the sand, the ones below them push the sand down, and they all rise to the top like an elevator."

I imagined all these tiny turtles crammed in a little elevator, rising to the top. *What floor, please?*

"When the hatchlings reach the top," Honey continued, "they stay there for several days while their shells straighten. That's where they are right now. And they can even hear us."

"They're all just sitting there? Why don't they just come out?"

"They're waiting for the sand to cool. That's their first clue. Then instinct tells them the right moment to run home to the sea. We don't know what that trigger is."

"We'll be right here, waiting. Won't we?"

"Oh yes. We'll stand guard over them as they crawl to the sea."

"From the ghost crabs," I said fiercely.

Honey laughed at my reaction. "Indeed. A few of us turtle ladies have a saying. 'The only good ghost crab is a dead ghost crab.' I delegate *you* for crab duty. Just keep them away."

Honey opened up her folding beach chair. "Now we just sit and wait for the hatchlings to emerge. It might be a while, so get yourself comfortable. If you need more bug spray, let me know."

"Jake!" Lovie came racing across the beach, a rolled-up beach towel tucked under her arm. Macon was right behind her with his own towel.

"What did we miss?" she asked, breathless.

"Guys, the nest is hatching!"

Lovie squealed and hurried to the nest.

"Does that mean exactly all eighty-two eggs will hatch?" Macon asked, peering down at the nest.

"I don't know. But for sure some will." I pointed to the concave circle. "Wait a minute. Something changed." I called over my shoulder. "Honey! There's something sticking out of the nest!"

With mutterings of surprise, the three women scrambled from their chairs for a closer look.

"Why, that's a flipper," exclaimed Honey.

"Are they coming now?" Macon asked, holding his hands tightly together.

"Soon," Judy answered. "Waiting on turtles to emerge from a nest is like waiting for a baby to be born. It can go fast. Or it can take forever. You might as well get comfortable. You know what they say. 'A watched kettle never boils.'"

Macon, Lovie, and I laid out beach towels not far from the nest. Time passed slowly as we waited and waited. The only action was the mosquitoes trying to feast on us.

"Is it possible to die from too many mosquito bites?" I whined, smacking one of the little suckers on my arm.

"You should have worn a long-sleeve shirt. Haven't I taught you anything?" Lovie said jokingly.

"Tell us an interesting fact," I said to Macon. I was desperate.

Macon scratched his head. "Did you know the loggerhead got its name because of its big head?"

"Yes," I groaned. "Everyone knows that."

Macon thought for a minute. "Did you know sea turtles have their own GPS?"

I looked over at him. "No. Really?"

"Yep. They use the earth's magnetic field."

"Okay, that's a cool fact," I told him.

"Speaking of turtles, what's taking so long? Do you think the turtles are okay?" Macon asked.

"Honey said it could take a long time."

Macon pulled his phone from his backpack.

"Mom's getting close to having the baby. I have to check in with her. I've got the emergency plan outlined in here." He started scrolling down his screen.

Lovie continued to bury her feet in the sand, using a large rounded cockleshell as a shovel.

The moon climbed higher in the sky as the hours passed. It was now high above us. Macon checked his phone over and over. The glow from the phone lit up his face. His brows were scrunched in worry.

Judy walked over to us and handed Macon a red sticker. "Hey, kiddo, turtles are coming. Put this on your phone. Or turn it off."

"Thanks, but I think I should get back home. I hate to miss this, but it's getting late and Mom's all alone," Macon said.

Judy smiled. "She's waiting on her own hatchling, isn't she?"

Macon snorted at the joke. "Yeah. Just like the turtles, it's taking forever. I've got to go. Sorry, guys."

"It's good to trust your instincts. Just like the sea turtles do," Honey said. She eased herself up out of her beach chair. "I'll give you a ride back home." She looked at me and Lovie. "You two stay on guard, okay?"

Honey consulted with her friends, then began the long walk across the beach with Macon. We watched until their silhouettes disappeared into the dark.

I pushed a button on the side of my watch to see the time: 11:32 p.m. glowed on the face of it. I yawned. I couldn't remember ever staying out on the beach this late.

Lovie stretched out her legs on the beach towel and leaned back on her elbows.

"Jake?" Her eyes were fixed on the millions of stars above us.

"Yeah," I replied, then stretched out my legs too.

"I don't want this summer to end," she said wistfully.

We watched long wisps of clouds float lazily in front of the moon.

"Me neither." I dug my toes into the sand. "I'm not sure I know where I'll end up when it's over. Mom called and said everything is up in the air, because of my dad's injury."

"Will you stay here?" she asked hopefully.

I shook my head. "Doubt it. I'll probably be heading back to New Jersey. I have to start seventh grade. That means another new school."

"Are you nervous?"

"Kind of. But I'm used to being the new kid in school." I scooped sand in my hand and let it slide out between my fingers. "I hear there's a lot of homework. But I guess it'll be nice to see my old friends. It's funny, but I haven't thought about them all summer."

Lovie didn't say anything.

I found a moon shell in the sand next to me and handed it to Lovie. "You and Macon are my best friends now."

Lovie held the shell gently in her fingers, then lay back on the towel and looked up at the stars. "You're my best friends too."

Her eyes shone in the moonlight. I lay back on my towel. Side by side we stared up at a billion stars shimmering in the night sky.

"There!" Lovie pointed to a twinkling star. It was larger and brighter than the rest. "That's the wishing star."

"That's the North Star," I corrected her. "See? It marks the tip of the handle of the Little Dipper. My dad taught me that if you can find the Big Dipper, you can find the North Star." I turned my head to look at her, but all I could see was her profile. "Besides, isn't a wishing star the *first* star you see at night?"

"Out here on the island, you can see *all* the stars. So I pick out the biggest, brightest star to wish on." She stroked the thick braid of her hair. Then she said softly, "Jake, what do you wish for?"

I watched the red blinking light of a faraway plane. "I wish I was on that plane, going to see my dad." I turned to look at her. "What about you? What's your wish?"

She didn't answer. I only heard the rhythmic sound of the waves rolling ashore.

Lovie sat up and brushed away the sand. "Never mind. Wishing on stars is for babies, anyway."

I couldn't understand why her mood had shifted suddenly.

"Jake," Lovie said, peering into the dark, "someone's coming."

I bolted upright and saw a familiar shape walking toward us from the boardwalk. "It's Honey!"

Judy and Alicia flashed their lights and waved.

Honey approached, her breath coming in short pants. "Did I miss anything?"

"Nope. Just mosquitoes and sand gnats," Alicia said with a laugh.

Honey walked to the nest, then crouched low. "I don't know about that," she called out in a singsong voice. "The pot is bubbling. Y'all better get ready for a boil!"

We all jumped up and scrambled to move our towels and chairs out of their path toward the sea.

Lovie and I kneeled close to the nest, shoulder to shoulder. I couldn't take my eyes from it. The widening circle in the sand looked like a big chocolate chip cookie with all the little brown bumps popping out. We watched, almost holding our breath, as one lone hatchling, dark brown and only three inches long, wiggled its flippers and pulled itself from the nest. Without pausing, the hatchling began digging its flippers into the sand as it headed straight for the sea.

"It's so cute," said Lovie in an excited whisper.

"Look at that tiny turtle track," I said with a short laugh. It was so small compared to the two-foot-wide tracks of the adult sea turtle.

"That's the scout," said Honey. "The rest won't be far behind."

Suddenly the little brown bumps in the sand began to heave, like something from beneath was pushing them upward. Then the bumps in the sand became flippers and heads as dozens of little hatchlings began pushing out of the nest all at once.

Judy moved the front wood stake out of the sand to clear the way. "Heads up! Here they come!"

Boy did they! Tiny brown hatchlings were wiggling and pushing as they climbed up and over one another to escape from the hole in the sand. There were a lot of them. They were crazy, scrambling wildly with their flippers waving. They couldn't wait to get to the sea, where they would spend the rest of their lives. They had to hurry to get there alive.

"Look at them go!" I shouted.

It was hard to imagine how someday those tiny creatures would grow to over three hundred pounds.

"You're going home, babies!" Lovie cried. I could see how happy she was to witness *her* sea turtle nest hatching. I was just sorry Macon was missing this.

When the last hatchling scrambled out of the nest, we all rose to guard the turtles as they crawled across the beach. The moon lit up the shore, so we could see nearly eighty tiny turtle tracks crisscrossing the smooth sand. Everything from footprints to driftwood to wrack were obstacles for them, but nothing stopped them.

"Never give up. Never surrender!" I called out with excitement.

As the turtles neared the water, they fanned out across the beach. From a distance, they looked like dark stones on the wet sand. We followed beside the hatchlings, on the lookout for ghost crabs.

We slowly walked toward the shoreline, careful of our every step. At the water's edge, we watched the first of the hatchlings dive into the waves and quickly disappear into the dark water.

"Where do they go?" I asked Honey.

"They'll swim for three days without stopping to reach the giant masses of seaweed beds called Sargassum in the Gulf waters." Honey stepped out of the way of two hatchlings that had gotten close to her feet.

"They won't see their mother again, right?"

"No," Honey replied kindly. I knew she heard the loneliness in my voice for my own mother. "The hatchlings work together in the nest. But once they reach the sea, they're lone swimmers. Instinct and luck are their guides now."

"Goodbye!" I called out. "Good luck!"

I felt Honey's arm slide across my shoulder. "I always feel a twinge in my heart when I say goodbye."

"My mama says only a lucky few will make it to the Sargassum," Lovie said, coming to stand beside us at the water's edge.

"True," Honey said. "But each of the female hatchlings tonight who survives and grows to adulthood will come back here and lay her own eggs. That will be in twenty-nine years."

She squeezed our shoulders. "I might not be here to welcome her back. But you might."

We stood at the edge of the shore until the last baby turtle caught the outgoing tide. The moon created a ribbon of light over the water that looked like a golden path for the hatchlings to follow.

I thought about how they were all gone now. They'd left the island and were swimming toward their new life.

Soon, I'd be leaving the island too.

CHAPTER 24

The Magic of the Full Moon

We're all in it together!

THE WHIRRING OF AN APPROACHING helicopter drowned out the sound of the ocean. I looked up to see a white-and-blue chopper flying low—straight over us.

Judy squinted in the blowing sand. "That's the ambulance helicopter!"

"To the cart, kids! Quickly," Honey yelled. We scrambled as fast as the hatchlings to collect our towels, chairs, and bags. As one, we hustled through the soft sand toward the board-walk.

"A helicopter only comes to the island at night if someone

needs to be medevaced to the hospital," said Honey.

She looked over at me. I knew we were both thinking the same thing: Mrs. Simmons.

Honey drove the cart through the darkness. The moon that lit up the beach lit up the road. We skipped the turn to the Bird's Nest. Honey made a beeline for the fire station.

Lovie and I sat on the back seat, gripping the cart. The chopper's propeller was beating the night air as it landed. The whipping sound was so loud it was frightening. We climbed out of the golf cart and hurried closer as a team of medics jumped out of the chopper. A few other neighbors' golf carts were arriving to watch the excitement.

"Surprised to see all of you up at this hour," Chief Rand said.

"Turtle nest boil," Honey said curtly. "Is it Tessa?"

"Yes, but everything's fine. She had her baby!"

"The baby!" Lovie and Honey exclaimed in unison.

"Wow," I said. "Macon's instincts were right."

"Is the baby okay?"

"Yes, everyone appears fine, but we have to get mom and baby to the hospital to get checked out. Baby Girl Simmons came a little early. It turns out your friend Macon saved the day. When he saw his mother was in trouble, he called your Aunt Sissy," Chief Rand said to Lovie. "She raced over and helped her through the labor. Macon called the fire station and we requested the helicopter. They'll be transported to the hospital by air."

"Macon sure was cool under pressure," Honey said. "I'm so proud of him."

Honestly? I wasn't sure I would be under those circumstances.

"Here they come," Chief Rand said, and saluted a farewell.

Lovie grabbed my arm again as we watched the team pushing Mrs. Simmons toward the helicopter on the gurney. She clutched the baby in her arms. Macon walked behind them. He didn't turn or wave to us. His eyes were on his mom. At the helicopter, the medics lifted Mrs. Simmons and the baby on board.

Then they pulled Macon into the passenger side of the helicopter. Lovie and I looked at each other, wide-eyed.

"Macon!" Lovie and I yelled out, and waved over the sound of the engine and rotor blades that were still spinning.

He turned our way. We waved wildly at him. He flashed us a big smile that seemed brighter than the stars and moon combined.

"The nest hatched," Lovie yelled out at him.

What! he mouthed back, shaking his head.

"The. Nest. Hatched!" Lovie and I yelled together.

Macon gave two thumbs-ups and disappeared into the helicopter.

The door shut, but we continued to wave at the chopper as its landing skids lifted off the ground. We watched the chopper rise above the trees, then head toward Charleston.

When the sound of the helicopter faded into the distance,

a noisy yawn escaped me. Suddenly the excitement of the night drained out of me.

Lovie yawned too.

"Time for us all to head home," Honey said. "I think we had enough excitement for one night."

We said our good-nights. Lovie headed for home with her aunt. Honey pulled me close as we walked back toward the golf cart.

"Can you believe it?" she asked. "A turtle nest boil *and* a baby's birth on the island. All in one night!" She shook her head in happy disbelief. "Must be the magic of the full moon."

Dear Dad,

What a night! I saw my first turtle nest hatch. It was the nest that Lovie found and we protected. So it was special. It looked like most of the seventy-six hatchlings all came out. Lovie called it a boil because the hatchlings look like they're all boiling out of the sand.

Then, Macon's mom had her baby. At home! It sure was a surprise. The best part was a helicopter landed on the island to take her and the baby to the hospital. Macon got to ride in it too. I was pretty jealous!

Honey said it was magical that we had a nest hatch and a baby born on the same night. I think a lot of magic happens here on the island.

Come home quick.

Ha! I just saw that I wrote the word "home" for the island. I guess I really do love it here. Like you did.
Love, your son,
Jake

Three days later Macon was back on the island—just in time to join us for the turtle nest inventory. We all had on our Turtle Team T-shirts and our Dawn Patrol hats. As we trekked across the warm sand to the nest, Lovie and I told Macon everything that happened the night of the boil.

"Ready for your first inventory, kids?" Honey asked when we reached the nest.

"Why exactly do we look inside a nest that's already hatched?" Macon asked.

Lovie and I smirked. Macon always liked to know *exactly* what was happening.

"We count the hatched and unhatched eggs to see how the nest did," Honey said.

"Jake, go in my bag and get the sticks. You have to keep track of the egg count. Do you remember the drill?"

"Yes, ma'am."

Honey put on latex gloves so she wouldn't pass on germs, then began to dig into the sand where all the turtles came out. A few passersby stopped to watch as Macon, Lovie, and I crouched close. Honey scooped handfuls of broken eggshells out of the nest and set them in a pile.

"Oh! Look at this, kids!" She pulled her arm out of the hole and held up a small misshapen egg. "Here's an undeveloped one. And there's more in there. These just didn't make it."

"Oh no," Lovie said with a sigh.

Honey put her right arm back into the nest hole and retrieved two more eggs. She put these in a separate pile. In another pile she collected the eggshells that were broken. The hatchlings had burst out of these. She handed us a shredded shell to feel.

Macon rubbed it between his fingers. "It feels leathery."

In the logbook, I was making tally marks in different categories to keep up with everything Honey was finding.

The next time Honey put her arm back into the hole, her eyes widened. "Lovie! Bucket!"

Lovie swiftly ran to retrieve the red bucket and set it beside the nest.

We were all wide-eyed now.

Honey turned to Macon and said, "Looks like you didn't miss all of the action after all. You ready for your lucky day?"

Macon nodded expectantly.

With care and precision, Honey pulled her arm out of the hole. "We found a hatchling!"

In her hand was a sand-covered baby loggerhead. Its flippers waved wildly, ready to race across the beach. In the daylight, we could see the turtle more clearly than we could in the dark. It looked like a mini-me of a full-grown turtle, scutes and all.

We all leaned in for a closer look.

"A baby turtle!" Lovie exclaimed.

"Can I hold it?" Macon asked.

"Oh, no sir. Only those with permits can. You know that." Honey lowered the tiny turtle into the red plastic bucket. "We don't find live hatchlings every time we do an inventory. This is always a treat."

She reached her arm back down into the loggerhead nest. Her eyebrows shot up high. "Another one!"

"Why didn't they come out with the others?" asked Macon.

"They either got trapped in there, or they hatched later than the rest of the group." She added this one to the bucket. "If we didn't find them, I don't know that they would've made it. And here's another."

Lovie squealed and clapped her hands at the sight of each hatchling.

I recorded three unhatched eggs and seventy-six eggshells.

"With three live hatchlings, that brings us to the total of eighty-two," said Honey. "The number of eggs we moved into this nest. After all this nest has been through, we can be very, very pleased with that result."

"Operation Coyote was a success," I said.

"That's kind of a stretch," Macon said. "I mean, we caught a dog."

"Sure, but there were no coyotes!" I replied, and we all laughed.

Inside the bucket the three tiny, sandy hatchlings were scrambling around and around in a frenzy.

"They sure look ready to go," Lovie said.

"It's time to let them follow their destiny," Honey said. She pushed all the eggshells back into the nest and covered it with sand. Then she looked out at the ocean. "The tide's going out. That's good timing for the turtles. Macon, since you're the new big brother, you can carry the bucket to the water."

Lovie walked beside Macon, fussing over his every step. "Be careful. Don't drop them."

Honey had us stop ten feet before the water's edge. She stood by Macon.

"Gently now, tip the bucket so the hatchlings can tumble out."

"Why don't I just put them by the water?" he asked.

"It's important for them to crawl on the beach so they can remember it. The females return here when they're mature to lay their eggs. It's called imprinting."

Macon's face was serious as he tilted the red bucket on the sand. The three hatchlings tumbled out. As soon as they hit the sand, the turtles took off toward the sea.

"Look at them go!" Macon said.

"They're so cute," Lovie cried. Macon and I smiled at each other. Lovie thought all animals were cute.

As we followed the three little hatchlings, it was clear one of them had a deformed front flipper. The hatchling couldn't walk straight. It turned around in circles. I wanted to help it, but Honey said we could not interfere.

"Give it some time. It'll adapt."

It was hard to watch the little turtle with the bad flipper

struggle. But Honey was right. The turtle finally straightened its path and hobbled its way to the ocean. Despite the hatchling's deformed flipper, the turtle's instinct was strong. Nothing was stopping it from getting to the sea.

The first two turtles reached the sea. The minute they touched salt water they began swimming, pushing their flippers even harder than before.

"That's the dive instinct," Honey said. "Over a hundred million years old. One minute they're comical, scrambling across the sand. The next, they're swimming."

I nudged Macon in the ribs. "No lessons required."

He laughed and shook his head. "Nope."

The turtle I was cheering on finally reached the shoreline. No sooner did its flipper hit water than a wave came in and the turtle was tossed back, tumbling over and over.

"Aw, man," Macon said as Lovie sighed beside him.

"This poor little turtle isn't going to make it," Lovie said.

"You can do this," I told the turtle. I watched the hatchling get back up and try again. Its wonky flipper dug into the sand, pushing it forward. Another wave rushed in, but this time, the hatchling rode the momentum. Its flippers—including the stubby one—pumped fast and furiously into the deeper water.

I couldn't help but think of my dad. He had lost his leg. Getting around was going to be hard for him, too. But the turtle made it, right? So could he. My dad had good instincts too.

I followed the hatchling into the ocean, up to my knees. Macon and Lovie strode through the water to my side. Waves splashed us, soaking our shorts, but we didn't care. We couldn't take our eyes off the sight of the three tiny dark bodies barely visible on top of the water. We watched until they disappeared.

"Good luck, little dudes!" Macon called out.

"Macon!" Lovie said. Her brows arched with surprise. "You're *in* the ocean. *With* us!"

"Yeah!" he shouted, looking a bit surprised himself, and then raised his hands in triumph. "I'm *in* the ocean!"

I threw one arm over Macon's shoulder and my other arm over Lovie's. "We're in the ocean. Together!"

stubby flipper

CHAPTER 25

The Letter

Things work out best for those who make the best
of how things work out.

DUMP GARBAGE. CHECK.
Deliver recycling. Check.
Fill water jugs. Check.
Fetch the mail. Check.

I zipped from point to point like a pro. Lucky barked happily as we passed golf carts or bicycles. This was my neighborhood now. I knew all the shortcuts.

I climbed the stairs of the Bird's Nest, sifting through Honey's mail. There was the usual junk mail—weekly coupons, real estate flyer, credit card advertisement. One white envelope made me stop moving. It had my name on it. I stared at it in disbelief.

The letter had Dad's handwriting on it!

I ran up the remaining stairs, Lucky at my side. I pushed open the door, tossed the other mail on the table, hurried to the sofa, and jumped on it. Lucky joined me, settling by my feet with a soft grunt.

My heart was pounding. I stared at the envelope a minute, trying to take it in. This wasn't the journal, something my dad had written years ago. This was a letter. And the postmark date was only a few days old.

I tore open the envelope and pulled out a folded sheet of white paper. Leaning over it, I began to read.

> Dear Jake,
>
> I wanted to write you a letter, since you have written me so many letters this summer. I'm sorry I didn't write back. I was working hard to get better. I had to get used to living with a new leg. It hasn't been easy, but your mom's been a great help. And so have your letters.
>
> I'm learning a tough lesson. Things work out best for those who make the best of how things work out.
>
> I can't wait to see you. I hope to be coming home before long.
>
> Love always,
>
> Dad

I read the letter over and over.

"Dad's coming home," I said to Lucky. "And soon!"

I hooted out loud. Lucky cocked his head and lifted one

floppy ear. I leaned forward and got licked on the face. Laughing, I wrapped my arms around him and rubbed his back.

"I can't wait for you to meet Dad! You're going to love him. And I just know he's going to love you too."

Then I bolted off the couch and ran across the house to Honey's room.

"Honey!" I shouted with joy. "Dad's coming home!"

Later that afternoon, thick, dark clouds rolled in, blotting out the sun. In the distance, thunder rumbled deep in the clouds.

Macon, Lovie, and I took shelter at Huyler House. The ground floor was a large screened-in area with wooden picnic tables and rocking chairs. Faded posters of the daily tides, local fish species, and island event reminders were stapled to the tall round pilings. There were board games, a Ping-Pong table, dart boards, and foosball.

"So, your dad's coming home," Macon said, smiling. "That's awesome news. We'll finally get to meet him."

"Yeah. That's great," said Lovie, but her voice was too soft to be excited. I wondered what was bugging her.

"Hey, Lovie," I said, trying to think of a way to cheer her up, "bet I can beat you." I waved a Ping-Pong paddle in front of her. "I'll even let you use the blue one," I added, hoping I could lure her with her favorite color.

"Nah, I'm good," she said. She plopped into a hanging hammock chair and pushed herself off to swing.

Now I knew something was wrong, because Lovie never

turned down a dare. Another rumble rolled through the sky. I turned to Macon. "Are you game?" I pointed the paddle at him.

"Sure. Prepare to get beat!" He snatched the red paddle off the table and started pretending he was playing Ping-Pong with an invisible ball.

"Don't be so sure of yourself," I warned. "My dad and I have played a lot of Ping-Pong together. He says I have a pretty mean serve."

Then I paused. *Will Dad and I still be able to play Ping-Pong together? Or will everything be different?*

A flash of lightning was followed by a crack of thunder. The clouds burst open and rain poured down in sheets, so heavy the outside world was blurred.

Macon and I played three rounds of Ping-Pong. I won the first match, but he beat me the second time. I won the final match, but just barely.

"What's the matter with her?" Macon asked, looking over at Lovie.

Lovie was still sitting in the hammock fidgeting with her necklace. I signaled to Macon and we each pulled up a rocking chair near her.

"Hey, Lovie. We know something's bugging you. What's up?" I asked gently.

She only shrugged and continued rocking.

"Did we do something wrong?" asked Macon.

"No," she replied quickly. "It's not you. You're going to think I'm so lame."

"Nah, we're friends," I said.

Macon nodded. "You can tell us anything."

Thunder rumbled again. This time it sounded farther away.

"I was just thinking how . . . summer's almost over." Lovie tucked her legs into the hammock.

"Yeah," I muttered, suddenly feeling the storm in my heart. "You're thinking we're all gonna have to say goodbye soon."

"It's just weird, seeing us all hang out together like it was just another day," she said. "But it isn't. It's a day closer to when it's all over."

"But it's been a great summer," I said, trying to cheer her up. "The best."

"Well, we never saw a coyote," Macon said with a half smile.

I laughed and was glad to see Lovie crack a smile.

"We heard them," I reminded him.

"Yeah," Macon said, brightening. "Best thing: I learned how to swim this summer."

"Best thing: I got my boating certificate," I added proudly.

"What have *I* done?" Lovie said, her brow crinkled. "I haven't accomplished anything. And in a week everyone will be gone, and then it's back to school. And . . ." She shook her head and kicked her legs out of the hammock to get up and walk away. "Sorry, guys. I sound like such a baby right now."

I stood up to follow her to the porch's edge. "You did stuff. You found a loggerhead nest. You taught this military brat and that city boy about this wild place. You made the island fun."

Lovie turned and searched our faces with wonder. "I did?"

"Yeah," Macon agreed, joining us. "I'm pretty sure I wouldn't have learned to swim if it wasn't for you."

"'Cause I dared you?" she asked.

"'Cause you nagged me."

Lovie choked out a laugh. "It's not just that," she said, walking over to sit on top of the picnic table. "Jake, you've been waiting to hear from your dad all summer. And today you got your letter." She looked at her hands. "I'm so happy for you. I really am. But I guess it just reminded me of my summer wish . . ." She shrugged.

"What was your summer wish?" Macon asked.

"Macon . . ." I tried to catch his eye.

Macon got it. "Was it about your bio dad?"

Lovie nodded. "It's the one thing I most wished for this summer. To talk to him. See what he's really like."

"But Lovie, you can't just sit around and wait for it to happen," I said.

"What do you mean?"

"I wrote to my dad almost every day this summer. That's why he wrote me back. It didn't just happen. I bet your bio dad would be surprised to get mail from you."

"Just write him a letter," Macon said. "What are you waiting for?"

Lightning flashed again, cracking the sky. Lovie stared at me, her blue eyes brimmed with tears.

"But . . ." She wiped away the tear from her freckled cheek. "I . . . I can't."

"Why not?" I asked, flopping my arms up with frustration.

"It's just . . . I'm scared."

"Scared? About what?"

"About what I might find out. What if I'm just like him? He went to prison for stealing. I got in trouble for stealing the boat. You heard Oysterman Ollie. He said . . ." She sniffed and wiped her nose. "He said the apple didn't fall far from the tree. He knew my dad." She wrapped her arms around herself.

"You're no thief. That guy was just being mean. You can't listen to him. Listen to us. We know you."

"But what if it's in my genes? You know, my destiny?"

Macon said, "Your destiny is not set by chance, but by choice."

Lovie and I just stared at him.

Macon shrugged. "I read it on a poster hanging up in my classroom."

Lovie snorted. "Thanks."

"Hey, it's true," Macon said. "You didn't steal that boat. We all know that. I'll bet even old Mr. Oysterman Ollie knows that."

Lovie sighed. "Thanks, Macon."

"Don't mention it."

"What . . . what would I say?" she asked. "In the letter?"

"Doesn't matter. Whatever you want," I said.

"Uh, let's be honest. You've never been at a loss for words before." Macon playfully bumped his shoulder into hers.

"I don't even know what prison he's in. My mama never talks about him. She acts like it's taboo to say his name."

266

"You have to talk to your mom about it," I said. "I mean, even if she hates him, he's still your dad, right?"

The thunder quieted and the rain stopped. Tree frogs began to croak, celebrating the passing of the storm.

"Do you think he'd actually write me back?" Lovie asked.

"What else does the man have to do?" Macon asked. "I mean, he's got a lotta time on his hands."

I cut him a look to signal that it wasn't the right time for jokes.

"What have you got to lose?" I asked.

"You're right, guys. What do I have to lose?" She puffed out a long plume of air. "Okay then. My big accomplishment this summer will be to write my dad a letter."

Behind her back, Macon and I held up crossed fingers. *Please write her back.*

CHAPTER 26

A New Beginning

Trust your instincts.

"JAKE, WAKE UP!"

"What?" I blinked heavily. Honey was hovering over me. "Honey? Is it time for Dawn Patrol?" I asked sleepily.

"No. It's ten o'clock. Wake up, sleepyhead. Your mom's on the phone."

My eyes flashed open. "My mom? Is everything okay?"

"Why don't you talk to her and find out?"

I scrambled from my bed and practically slid down the ladder from the loft. Lucky leaped up my legs when I landed on the floor, but I pushed past him to the phone.

"Hello?" I held the receiver tight.

"Jake? It's me."

"Hi, Mom!" I yawned.

"I'm sorry to call so late, but I didn't want to wait. I have some news."

I didn't speak. I held my breath.

"We're coming home!"

My heart rate zoomed. "You *and* Dad?"

"Yes. He's being released from the hospital."

I began pacing with excitement. "When?"

"We should arrive on Dewees August fifteenth. I'll send all the details later."

"Oh Mom, I can't wait. I've missed you. Both of you." I swallowed hard. I didn't want to cry. "That's the best news."

"I've got more good news. I got transferred to a new base."

I swallowed hard. "We're moving? Again?"

"Yes."

"Where?" My joy dimmed at the thought of moving to another new town.

"To Charleston."

I blinked. "Like Charleston, South Carolina?"

"That's right." I heard the joy in her voice. "That's where my new base is located. We'll look for a place in Mount Pleasant."

"But that's near Dewees Island," I said in disbelief.

Mom was laughing now. "That's right!" she said again.

I turned to see Honey watching me, Lucky by her side.

She was smiling and I could tell she had already heard the good news.

"Aw, Mom. I can't believe it."

"It's true. Believe it! Goodbye, son. I miss you and we will see you soon!"

"Bye, Mom. I love you."

I hung up the phone and swung around with a hoot.

"Honey!" I exclaimed. "We're going to be neighbors!"

Honey laughed and brought her hands to her face. "I know!"

"I can't believe it. I'll be able to come back to the island to visit you."

"And I can visit you."

"I wonder where I'll go to school."

"I imagine you have a million questions. And you'll get those answers. For now, let's just think about the best news of all. You'll soon be seeing your father again. Finally. After so much waiting and praying."

"We both will."

"Yes," she said, her smile stretching across her face.

I walked a few paces as my thoughts spun wildly in my head. "I'm nervous, Honey."

"About what?" Her smile slipped away, replaced with concern.

"Everything," I confessed. "Everything's changing."

"You'll like Mount Pleasant," she tried to reassure me.

"No, not that. I mean . . . my dad."

"Ah," she said with a slow nod of understanding. "You're afraid he's not going to be the same, is that it?"

I looked away, afraid to answer.

"Because he lost his leg," she finished.

I sucked in my breath. She said the words aloud.

"Yeah."

"Truth be told, I'm nervous too. Not about your dad being different. I'm worried about the physical and mental challenges he must face. It's not going to be easy."

"He wrote that in his letter."

"What are you afraid of?" she asked, walking to my side.

I had thought so much about this all summer that my worries came rushing out. "Is he going to be able to walk? Or will he be in a wheelchair? Will he be able to do any of the same things with me the way he used to?"

I felt my heart pounding fast as I told Honey my most secret fear. "Is he still going to be my dad?"

Honey reached over and pulled me close in a tight hug. "Oh, dear boy. I don't know the answer to a lot of your questions. But I am sure of this. You father is still the same man who loves you with all his heart. No loss of a limb could ever change that." She released my shoulders. "Come sit beside me a minute, will you?"

She led me to the wood table, and we both pulled out a chair. I saw she had a cup of tea she was working on beside an open copy of the *Charleston Post and Courier* newspaper. Honey leaned closer to me.

"When your dad was young, he taught himself how to ride a bike, climb trees, catch fish, and carve wood. There wasn't much that Eric Potter couldn't figure out how to do. That's his nature. Do you think for one minute that he's not going to master how to use an artificial leg?"

I thought about that. "No."

"But it's going to take time for him to get used to living with a false leg. The change is not just physical, but mental. Do you know what I mean?"

"I think so. He's not going to be able to do the same stuff he used to do."

"Right. And that's going to make him sad some days. And frustrated. You too. Jake, you'll have to accept him for the man he is today. That's your challenge. Are you up to it?"

I nodded, not knowing what to say next.

"Here's what I know about *you*, Jake Potter. You have good instincts. You don't give up. You persevere. That's your nature. You're also curious. And kind. You have what's called compassion. You care about others, not just yourself."

My eyes widened at this compliment.

She lifted my chin to meet her gaze. "Trust your instincts, and all will be just fine."

CHAPTER 27

The Farewell

The Islanders

I TOOK ONE LAST LOOK AROUND THE LOFT. This was my dad's childhood room on the day I arrived on the island. But over the course of the summer, this small space became *my* room. I looked over the long shelves filled with my dad's collection of treasures, and mixed among them were my own. There was the row of books I'd read too. My journal lay on the wooden desk next to my dad's.

And the big round window. *My Heidi window,* I thought. So many nights I lay on my back and stared out of it, noting the stage of the moon, counting the stars, watching the clouds drift by. In the mornings I observed birds flying from tree to tree. And every day I sent out silent prayers for my dad to survive and come home.

I zipped up my duffel, picked up my bag, and climbed down the ladder for the last time. Lucky was waiting for me, as always. His tail wagged and his dark eyes were fixed on me, ears alert. He knew something was up.

Honey was in the kitchen. The countertops were shiny, and a vase of fresh flowers sat on the table. The air smelled of fresh-baked cookies she'd made for Dad's arrival. I grinned. Things sure had come a long way since day one. I might be leaving, but the Honey I knew and loved was back.

I set my duffel bag by the front door. I noticed a box of books resting there.

"What are the books for?" I asked.

Honey spun around. "Good morning, sunshine. Special day!"

I saw that her eyes were moist from crying. "Honey, are you okay?"

"Of course I'm okay," she replied with a short laugh. She sniffed. "These are just a grandmother's tears for the grandchild she's going to be missing."

I rushed to her side to give her a big hug.

"I'm going to miss you too. But I'm not going far, remember? I'll come for visits. Lots of them."

She wiped her nose with a tissue. "You're right, of course. These are happy tears. I see a lot of boat trips off the island in my near future." She dabbed at her eyes. "I've just gotten used to having you here every day. And this furry guy too," she said, stroking the top of Lucky's head.

Lucky gave a wide smile, letting his tongue flop out.

Honey laughed at that, then sniffed and straightened. "I just have to remember we've got lots to look forward to. Just think, Jake. We can celebrate all the holidays together. Maybe some right here on Dewees." She nudged me like she was telling me a secret. "Guess what? I'm having an elevator installed here for your daddy."

"That's great! For sure he'll come."

"That's the plan."

I looked over at the box of books again. "But what's up with the books? Those are all your research and guidebooks. You're not giving them away, are you? I'm coming back. I'll need them."

"I'm not giving them away," Honey assured me. "Not exactly. You inspired me, Jake. After we spent so many hours this summer looking up animal and plant facts for your journal, it occurred to me that there were many children who might want to learn the names of the wildlife when they visit. Adults, too. I have the books and a lot of time."

"And . . ."

Her eyes sparkled. "I'm donating the books to the Nature Center. *And*, I'm going to be the librarian! I'll volunteer a few afternoons a week. I'll take care of the collection, help adults, and teach kids of all ages. Who knows? I might even start an Island Journal Club."

"That's a great idea," I said, and meant it. "You're perfect for the job. You're the best teacher I've ever had."

Her face softened, and she playfully wiped a lock of hair from my forehead. "You certainly were my favorite student."

Honey glanced at her watch. "Look at the time! We best get going. We don't want to be late for the ferry!"

I felt I could fly down the stairs, I was so excited. This was the day I'd been waiting for all summer. My parents were coming!

We loaded up the golf cart with my duffel bag and Lucky's supplies. I tapped the bench seat for Lucky to jump aboard. "Good boy," I said, giving him a big hug.

As we pulled away, I turned and looked out at the Bird's Nest one last time. *My house high in the trees,* I thought. Late-afternoon light glowed across the windows, and leaves from the trees rustled in the wind, as though they were waving goodbye.

Honey drove in her wild and crazy style to the boat landing. She still managed to hit most every rut in the road. I gripped onto Lucky with one arm and held tight to the edge of the cart roof with the other. We were all smiling.

"Look, Honey!" I called, and pointed to the covered wooden ferry dock landing. I couldn't believe it. It was decorated like it was the Fourth of July all over again. Red, white, and blue bunting hung from the railings, and American flags lined the cart parking zone. A huge sign was stretched across the floating platform: WELCOME HOME, CAPTAIN POTTER.

"Oh my," was all Honey said.

A small crowd of people from the island gathered at the dock. I spied Chief Rand. Then Macon and Lovie. They waved when they spotted me and ran across the gravel to greet us.

"Guess we're not the only ones excited to see your dad," Macon said.

Emotion clogged my throat, so I could only offer a tight-lipped grin. My stomach started flip-flopping like a fish on a hook, knowing that the ferry was on its way with my mom and dad on board.

It was going to be a short visit. The plan was to celebrate with Honey at the Nature Center. There was an elevator there. We had to face the harsh fact that my dad couldn't get inside the Bird's Nest. Then, after the party, my parents and I would catch an outgoing ferry. We were going to live in a temporary condominium near the base. Mom said we would make do until they found someplace better. I didn't care what the house looked like. I'd be with my mom and dad again.

"Now, this is a hero's welcome," Aunt Sissy said, giving Honey a hug.

"You must be so proud," Lovie said. Her blond hair was parted into two long braids, each with blue ribbons that matched her shirt.

"What's that?" I asked, pointing to an envelope in her hand.

She leaned closer and smiled shyly. "It's the letter."

My eyes got big. "For your dad?"

"My bio dad," she clarified. But she was smiling. This was her big summer moment.

"Well, what are you waiting for?" Macon asked. "Put it in the mailbox."

"I was just going to," she said, lifting her chin.

"Then do it," Macon said.

"What's the hurry?"

"Tick tock."

"Guys!" I called out, and rolled my eyes in exaggeration. "Stop arguing."

We all burst out laughing.

Lovie lifted her chin and walked across the dock to the mailbox. Her long braids waved in the air behind her. She looked over her shoulder at us. Then she gave the envelope a quick kiss and dropped it into the outgoing mail slot. She didn't turn around right away.

Macon leaned close to me and whispered, "Do you think she'll hear back?"

"I sure hope so. I mean, it's Lovie. He'd be one crazy dad not to write back. Right?"

"Yeah."

Lucky trotted around the main dock, greeting everyone

with a wagging tail. The anticipation on the dock was mounting by the minute.

"Here he comes!" someone from the crowd shouted.

In one movement all heads swung to look out beyond the field of marsh grass to the sea. I stretched up on my tiptoes and caught a glimpse of the white double-decker ferry coming straight toward us.

My heart pounded against my ribs. I tried to remember what it had felt like that first day I'd been on the ferry, alone, coming to the island. Honey was standing where I was at this moment. Was it really two months ago? I'd thought the summer would last forever. Now the ferry was carrying my mom and dad to the island. My summer vacation was over. It went so fast.

I scanned the crowd. Where was Honey?

I spied her walking up to the landing with Macon's parents, their baby, and Lovie's aunt.

"Honey! They're almost here!" I called out, waving my arms. Then I turned and ran through the crowd, down the metal plank to the floating dock, Lucky at my heels.

The ferry blew its horn—*bwaang bwaang!* The people waiting at the dock burst into cheers. The big boat's motors chugged and gurgled as the captain brought the ferry in. I felt the vibration through the wood. I arched up, but couldn't see anyone yet. Only the American flag flapping on a pole.

Feelings of love, excitement, worry, relief, and fear slapped inside of me like the salty water that splashed the dock. My stomach was so tight I felt a little sick. I spread my feet wider to steady myself on the floating dock, rocking with the boat's arrival.

Would it be weird to see my dad again after so long? What would he look like without a leg? Should I hug him? Could I?

I felt Honey's hand on my shoulder. I looked up and smiled at her. Her happiness helped me feel better.

At last the ferry docked, and the captain opened the doors and stepped off the boat onto the dock. He searched me out, gave me a big wink, and called out, "You ready to see my special guests?"

"Yes, sir!"

Lucky jumped to his paws, his tail wagging.

The first mate jumped off the boat to help the captain lay a board down across the threshold of the boat to the dock.

Mom stepped off first and started walking up the dock toward me. She was wearing her green flight suit. Her brown hair was neatly pulled back in a bun, and her smile was wide and bright. She looked thinner and tired, but happy.

I couldn't hold back. I ran straight to her, with Lucky at my heels. In a rush I felt her arms around me, felt her lips on my head. I squeezed hard. She smelled like Mom.

"I missed you so much," she said close to my ear.

"Me too," I choked back.

She pulled back to look me in the eyes. "Are you ready?"

I squeezed my lips tightly and nodded nervously.

Mom returned to the boat. A moment later, a man stepped out. He stood a moment, getting his balance on the rocking deck.

I squinted in the bright afternoon sunlight, trying to make out each detail of the man I had pictured in my mind these past months. He was the same tall build but a whole lot thinner. He was dressed in his military uniform.

Dad made his way slowly down the wooden gangplank, gripping a black cane. Once he was on the dock, applause erupted from the crowd. My dad smiled, but his eyes were searching the crowd. Then his gaze landed on me.

He took one step. Then another step, carefully walking toward me on the dock. My mom followed close behind him.

I couldn't help myself. I looked at his legs. I caught a glimpse of shiny metal underneath his tan military pants. I swallowed hard and tried to still my shaking lips.

Here's the truth. My dad was always athletic. He moved gracefully, smoothly. This man walked slowly, tentatively. Anyone could see that each step was a major effort.

I cringed.

Then my father was standing in front of me.

I couldn't move. I couldn't speak. I looked away.

"Jake," he said.

I knew his voice. My gaze inched up from his chest, his shoulders, his neck, and finally into his eyes. They were the same blue. I saw the shape of his face. The lines of his cheekbones.

His straight nose. His brown hair cut high and tight.

I knew this face.

"Dad!" I cried out.

He dropped his cane and I felt his arms around me.

I couldn't hold my tears. I smelled the sweat in his wool military jacket, felt the stubble on his cheek, and best of all . . . his arms around me. All the fears and worries blew away on the sea breeze. No matter what, he was still my dad.

Lucky gave a single bark. Dad released me with a husky laugh and looked down at my dog.

"I'm guessing this furry guy must be Lucky."

It felt so good to hear his voice sound so normal. I wiped at my eyes.

"Yep. Isn't he cute?" I replied, patting Lucky's head.

Dad stuck his hand out in greeting. Lucky sniffed, then licked his fingers and nudged his head underneath Dad's palm. Dad smiled. *Score,* I thought. I wanted them to be friends too.

"My turn!" Honey stepped forward and slipped her arms around her son.

I felt my mother's arm around my shoulders. In that moment, I knew that everything was going to be all right. We were a family. We were together. That was all that mattered.

The party was a big success. Everyone was so happy to see Dad again. A lot of them had known him since he was my age.

Macon and Lovie were a little shy to meet him. After all, his journal had loomed large in our minds all summer long. It was like he was our Obi-Wan Kenobi, guiding us with his words.

"Uh, Dad," I said, waving Macon and Lovie closer. "These are my friends."

"Nice to meet you," Lovie said, offering her hand.

"How do you do, sir," Macon said, clearing his throat.

Dad smiled at them. "You're the Dawn Patrol. I feel like I already know you."

Macon and Lovie smiled.

"You're blessed to find one good friend in life," he said to us. "You found two. It's wise to count your blessings."

"You inspired us to write journals," Lovie said.

"Did I?" Dad looked at me.

I grinned. "Yeah. Honey gave us all journals to write in. Lovie's a real good artist. And Macon is Mr. Google. He collects great facts."

"And you?" he asked.

I shrugged. "I'm pretty good at drawing. But not so good at writing. I wrote you letters instead. I told you what I was doing and seeing." I shrugged again, self-conscious. "It was more fun."

"I disagree with you."

My smile fell.

Dad grinned. "I think you're a very good writer. I have something to show you."

He reached into his bag and pulled out a brown, leather-covered book. He handed it to me.

I carefully took the book and ran my hands across the smooth brown leather. On the front, my name had been painted in red, white, and blue. JAKE POTTER. It looked like my dad's journal.

"You got me a journal?"

"Open it."

I opened the book slowly, with awe. The pages were already filled with handwriting and drawings. Bringing the journal closer, I recognized the workmanship. It was *my* handwriting. *My* drawings.

I looked up at him, puzzled. "These are my letters."

Dad nodded. "I saved them. All of them. I had them bound into a book." He moved his hand to gently squeeze my shoulder. "Jake, your letters gave me hope. Your encouragement, your tales from the island, your infinite faith. Son, you saved my life."

The sun was setting by the time the crowd left. Brilliant orange, purple, and gold spread across the water to shimmer. The end of this perfect homecoming had arrived. Now it was time to go.

My parents boarded the ferry first. Lucky was leashed and pranced by my side. He didn't want to get left behind. It was all over but the goodbyes.

Macon and Lovie walked with me to where the ferry met the dock. They couldn't go any farther.

"I guess this is it," I said, stuffing my hands in my pockets.

After a summer of nonstop talking, no one could find a word to say.

My gaze swept the expanse of the bright green marsh that met the towering wall of trees. I smelled the pungent pluff mud, felt the ocean's breeze on my cheek. It hit me hard that I was leaving Dewees Island. I wouldn't wake up in my loft tomorrow morning, wouldn't do my Dawn Patrol, or take the golf cart out to do my chores and meet my friends. I wouldn't go exploring or show my journal to Honey. I swallowed hard.

"This might sound like a surprise coming from a military kid, but . . . I don't like saying goodbye."

"It's not *really* a goodbye," Macon said. "You're going to live in Charleston. That's totally cool."

"I bet you'll be over here visiting Honey a lot," Lovie said. Then she said coyly, "I'll be visiting my Aunt Sissy, too."

"Y'all are lucky. You get to come back. I gotta head back to Atlanta," Macon said. "But Mom said we'll come back during breaks, if the island house isn't rented. She promised that we'd definitely stay here next summer."

"You better," Lovie said emphatically. "We made a pact to spend next summer together."

"That's right," I added, smiling at my two best friends.

"Hey, guys," Lovie said, spreading out her hands like she was about to make a big announcement. "I, like, know this is last minute, but I came up with the perfect name for us."

We looked at her.

"Our name?" I asked, confused.

"Yes, for *us*. You know, the Three Musketeers, Lewis and Clark, the Water Rats, Dawn Patrol." She made a loop with her finger. "And on and on. You *know*."

Macon and I looked at each other and shrugged.

"What ya got?" Macon asked.

She took a breath for effect. "'The Islanders!'" She looked at us expectantly, her brows raised.

I thought of how this lush green island had opened me up to the mystery of nature. This island—a place I didn't want to go—had become a second home to me. I was leaving feeling stronger than when I'd arrived, unafraid to face my next adventure. And the island was where I met my best friends.

"It's perfect!" I held out my hand. "The Islanders."

Lovie placed her hand over mine. "The Islanders."

Macon slapped his big hand over ours. "The Islanders!"

We threw our united hands up in the air victoriously.

Baaaaamp! The ferry boat sounded its horn and the big engines began to churn. The captain called out, "All aboard!"

Macon gave me a big bear hug. Then he stepped back. "See you, bro."

"Yeah. Soon," I said. Then, feeling tongue-tied, I turned to Lovie.

She was clutching her turtle necklace, which told me she was nervous or upset. "Take good care of the turtle nests for us," I said, feeling awkward.

She looked at me, her cheeks turning pink under her

freckles. She rushed forward to hug me. Then she kissed me. Right on the cheek. Then with a quick smile, she turned heel and rushed away and disappeared in the crowd.

Macon and I looked at each other, our eyes wide.

Then Macon high-fived me and burst into a wide grin. "Next year is going to be the best summer ever!"

RESOURCES

~~~~~~~~~~

For additional information about some of the animals in this book, check out these sites.

For cool facts about loggerhead turtles:
www.natgeokids.com/uk/discover/animals/sea-life/loggerhead-turtle-facts/

To see sea turtles and learn about how injured turtles are cared for:
scaquarium.org/sea-turtle-care-center

To learn more about Dewees Island's habitat and wildlife:
deweesislandblog.com
naturewalkswithjudy.com

ACKNOWLEDGMENTS

It's been a long-held dream of both Angela and me to write a book for middle school children. We love this age of confidence and dreams. Over the years of writing *The Islanders*, we've enjoyed the support of many people and are so grateful. In particular, we send our eternal gratitude to:

Judy Drew Fairchild. Thank you for being our touchstone on Dewees Island. You revealed to us the unique magic of Dewees Island, its natural beauty, the respect of all the inhabitants for habitat, and the resilience and endurance of nature. Thank you, too, for a continuing education on birds, insects, and wildlife on the island. Your amazing photographs and IG series Quick Nature Walk have been a guide for us as we wrote the novel. Claudia Poulnot DeMayo for her support and photographs that continue to inspire us all.

Alicia Reilly. Our other Dewees guide! Thank you for your generous support, your time on decks and docks, sharing insights into family life on a remote island, and for always being there when we needed you. The Dewees Ladies Roundtable. Sincere thanks for welcoming us to your island and sharing your stories and memories.

Paul Spencer at the YMCA Beaufort/Jasper. We appreciate the time you spent helping us to understand the rules of boating, and how to make it fun for children.

Christina Liegl. Thank you for the insights into the life of a C-17 pilot and military family life. Kwame Alexander. Sincere love and thanks to a magnificent spirit and writer who shared with me possibilities. I'm so grateful.

Most importantly, heartfelt thanks to everyone at Aladdin at Simon & Schuster for welcoming us into your publishing family. First, Mara Anastas, we are eternally grateful you saw the promise of the story of three unlikely friends stuck on a remote island for the summer. Your faith in the book was inspiring. Thank you, also, Fiona Simpson, for your great enthusiasm as we came on board, and for the initial edits that guided and shaped the story. A heartfelt thanks to Alyson Heller for your sensitive editing in the important final drafts. We look forward to more! And thanks to Lauren McKenna for making the introductions at Simon & Schuster that made the magic happen.

Angela and I send sincere gratitude to our home team: Kathie Bennett of Magic Time Literary Publicity, Molly Waring of Ballyhoo, and Laura Rossi of Laura Rossi Public Relations. You are the best!

Acknowledgments

Sincere thanks to Faye Bender at the Book Group. You've been a staunch supporter of my goal to write for this age group. Thanks so much for your advice, for sharing books, and so much more.

Finally we send our love to husbands, Markus Kruesi and Jaeson May. You are the wind beneath our wings!

ABOUT THE AUTHORS

MARY ALICE MONROE is the *New York Times* best-selling author of over twenty books, including the Beach House series: *The Beach House*, *Beach House Memories*, *Swimming Lessons*, *Beach House for Rent*, *Beach House Reunion*, and *On Ocean Boulevard*. She is a 2018 inductee into the South Carolina Academy of Authors' Hall of Fame, and her books have received numerous awards, including the 2008 South Carolina Center for the Book Award for Writing, the 2014 South Carolina Award for Literary Excellence, the 2015 Southwest Florida Author of Distinction Award, the RT Lifetime Achievement Award, the International Book Award for Green Fiction, and the 2017 Southern Book Prize for Fiction. Her bestselling novel *The Beach House* is also a Hallmark Hall of Fame movie. An active conservationist, she lives in the low country of South Carolina. *The Islanders* is her first novel for middle-grade readers. Visit her at MaryAliceMonroe.com and at Facebook.com/MaryAliceMonroe.

ANGELA MAY is a former television news journalist and media specialist. She's been working with Mary Alice Monroe for more than a decade as a publicist and assistant. *The Islanders* is their first book together! Angela lives with her family in Mount Pleasant, South Carolina. Connect with her at angelamaybooks.com.